A
Killer
Romance

Also available by Maggie Blackburn

A Killer Romance

A BEACH READS MYSTERY

Maggie Blackburn

CROOKED LANE

NEW YORK

Published in the United States by Crooked Lane Books, an imprint of The Quick Brown Fox & Company LLC.

Crooked Lane Books and its logo are trademarks of The Quick Brown Fox & Company LLC.

Library of Congress Catalog-in-Publication data available upon request.

ISBN (hardcover): 978-1-63910-635-6
ISBN (ebook): 978-1-63910-636-3

Cover illustration by Mary Ann Lasher

Printed in the United States.

www.crookedlanebooks.com

Crooked Lane Books
34 West 27th St., 10th Floor
New York, NY 10001

First Edition: February 2024

10 9 8 7 6 5 4 3 2 1

Chapter One

Summer Merriweather was a nonbeliever—until her mom died. Then strange things happened. If she reflected on it and was honest with herself, strange things had happened right before her mother died. Like the week before she died.

Summer had been in England doing research, and even though it was quite possibly her favorite place on the planet, she was having a lousy time. One unpleasant incident after the other happened: she fell and twisted her ankle, she had food poisoning, and she was having difficulty getting permission to get into the research libraries she needed. Then she had three realistic and terrible dreams about her mom in the three days before she received the call from her cousin Piper.

Now, here she was, in her childhood home, the little pink cottage with turquoise shutters, on the northern tip of St. Brigid, a small island off the coast of North Carolina. And she was running Beach Reads Bookstore, her childhood nemesis, while missing her mom occasionally, but mostly feeling as if she were still there. The sense was so strong that Summer's entire attitude about the afterlife had changed.

Where was her mother Hildy now? A woman with such a strong life essence could not just be flesh and bones. Summer sensed her every day. She'd dash around the corner at the store, floor creaking, and she'd swear Hildy would be standing there, except she wasn't. She'd be watching out over the ocean from the second floor of the bookstore and feel certain she'd heard footsteps or felt breath on her neck and know it was her mom. Only it wasn't. She'd turn and find nothing there, at least nothing she could touch or see. Yet the sensation of closeness with her mom was undeniable. Though she'd exchange all these feelings of closeness for just one more moment with her mom in the flesh.

Hildy had loved to celebrate. She was light and love and fairy dust. Even on holidays such as Valentine's Day. She took it into her bosom and created something from nothing. She'd invited a romance author every year for a "Romance by the Sea" special book celebration. This event had taken hold of the tiny island of St. Brigid, and the town celebrated Valentine's Day with much flourish. The bakeries crafted honey-love cakes, available one day exclusively, and the restaurants carried Valentine's Day–themed specials. The jewelry store always offered a limited charm. And then there was the secret valentine tradition. Each year, residents of the original neighborhood of the island where Summer lived received baskets of goodies on their front porches. Nobody knew who performed such an act. Summer had always suspected it was Hildy. But Hildy was gone, and the tradition continued.

The festivities were good for business during a season of dearth. Most people didn't visit the beach in February. The Valentine's week events brought people in.

But still, of all the made-up Hallmark holidays, Summer's least favorite was Valentine's Day. Even if it was the most popular yearly event on Brigid's Island, certainly at Beach Reads, a romance-themed bookstore, it was pure poppycock.

She had to admit, though, that the first Valentine's Day event she had taken part in as the owner was the best. They'd had Hannah Jacobs come speak. She was Summer's favorite romance author. She'd penned *Nights at Bellamy Harbor*, which was based on the secret romance between Summer's mother and father.

This year, the one town event Summer anticipated was the chocolate fest, offered by the new chocolate shop in town, Gina's Chocolates. Summer could get behind that kind of celebration.

A Killer Romance

She liked the owner of the shop, Gina Giancarlo. A genuine person if ever there was one. Now, there was another new-store owner who sold crystals and CBD products next door. As much as Summer tried, she didn't like Bo Green or his shop. She'd inherited her mom's crystals and thrown away any CBD products she'd had—the science just didn't back up the claims, at least not yet.

"I'd think you'd appreciate the holiday more." Poppy, the assistant manager at Beach Reads, handed her another card to hang on the wall. "Who doesn't want to celebrate love? Aren't there saints and gods and goddesses involved? And didn't your guy William Shakespeare pen the most romantic play, *Romeo and Juliet*?"

"I've tried to explain that to you. It's not a romance. It's a tragedy." With *Romeo and Juliet*, Summer was beating the same drum over and over. Even her half-engaged students at her old university job realized *Romeo and Juliet* was not romantic. At all. But Poppy? She wasn't one to give up. It was as if Summer didn't have that hard-earned PhD in Shakespearean literature.

"I'd call it a romantic tragedy, then." Poppy's elbows went to the counter, and she cradled her chin in her hands. Her large blue eyes, with matching eyeshadow, were full of whimsy.

Summer was too busy with other things to start a full lecture about *Romeo and Juliet*. She checked her phone one more time to examine her list. If it wasn't on her list these days, it didn't get done. Between the online classes she was now teaching and running the bookstore during a pandemic, she had yet to get her bearings. Did she used to remember everything? Didn't she used to get up at five AM with plenty of energy to spare?

When Summer came to Brigid's Island several years ago because her mom had died unexpectedly, she had not been planning to stay and run the bookstore. She'd planned to sell it and get on with her life as a Shakespearean professor in Staunton, Virginia. Yet here she was four years later, still at Beach Reads and teaching online. She had taken a sabbatical and was trying to decide what she wanted to do when the pandemic hit. The university went online, and Summer mistakenly believed it would be easy. She had no idea the toll the online classes would take, for it wasn't just the schools that went online; the bookstore did as well. It had its upside, of course. People across the country could attend the store's online events, and they sold plenty of books. But the computer took away the intimacy of events. It just did.

So, now that it was relatively safe, masks being optional, vaccines available, Beach Reads Bookstore was hosting its first event since the pandemic. Did it make Summer anxious? Yes, yes, it did. She still wore her mask on crowded days in the store, as did Poppy.

The island's population had dwindled with the virus, and nobody was taking any chances now.

She'd have liked to host the event on their deck outside, but February in Brigid's Island was just a little too cold for comfort.

"Think I read about a statue of Romeo and Juliet in Rome," Poppy continued as she straightened cards on the counter.

"It's in Verona, and Romeo and Juliet is a fictional tale," Summer said. There were several origin theories of the play. She, like many scholars, viewed the statues in Verona as nothing more than a quaint tourist trap.

"I wonder what Lana thinks." Poppy walked out of the room.

Lana Livingston, the writer they were hosting for the Valentine's Day event, had written a modern-day *Romeo and Juliet*—but with a happy ending. Not a modern-day *Romeo and Juliet*, then. Summer refrained from adding her two cents and walked to the door, unlocked it, and turned the CLOSED sign to OPEN. They were now open. Come what may.

Chapter Two

Among the many things Summer had found after her mother's death was a secret little red book full of authors' names and addresses. The best thing about this book was that Hildy Merriweather had also scribbled her opinion of every author she'd known and hosted. Not the official opinion. Her business acumen allowed her to invite authors to the bookstore, but not into her home, for example. Hildy had invited few authors to her home, where her then-young, impressionable daughter lived. Lana Livingston was one of the few. Hildy thought highly of her. At first.

The last time they invited her to the store, Hildy made excuses about being busy and not able to host her. In the little red book, she had scribbled, *Lana, no friend of mine.*

Hildy's instincts were dead on. Which gave Summer pause. And it also intrigued her. Though Hildy was sweetness and light, she had been no angel herself, as evidenced by Summer never having known her father and her half brother and half sister's appearance in her life a few years back. Summer's biological father had married someone else and had children with her. They'd grown up on the other side of the island— mostly away at boarding schools.

So Summer was indeed cautiously curious about Lana. She was a *New York Times* bestselling author, which was impressive, but not as impressive as one might think. It didn't mean these writers were better writers than anybody else. Lord, no. It just meant they had sold a certain amount of books at a certain time. And the number wasn't that impressive.

But Lana had a large and loyal fan base. She had written twenty-four books, ten of which were *New York Times* bestsellers. She had a formidable career. So Summer had agreed to host her for the Valentine's Day signing.

She ambled down the aisle, straightening books, and turned a corner. A pale, short woman with white-blond hair and almost black eyes walked toward her. The woman's appearance was arresting. She stopped Summer in her tracks.

"Excuse me." She approached Summer. "I'm looking for the historical romance section. I remembered it was in this area?"

"Ah, yes, we've done a bit of rearranging." Summer had moved the historical romance section to make room for more Shakespeare books, which sold at a better clip than her mom would've predicted. "You'll find them around the corner, to the right."

"Thanks so much," the woman said, and turned, revealing a backpack strapped to her body with books poking out the top. Summer recognized one of them—a guide to poisonous plants. The other was a cake cookbook. The odd pairing of books sent a thought flicking through Summer's mind: Was she planning to bake a cake with poisonous plants?

Summer, you've got an overactive imagination.

The woman went on her merry way as Summer went back to straightening the shelves.

Summer found something soothing about the act of facing books and placing them in alphabetical order. She didn't have to think much. All she had to do was straighten while smelling the close-by coffee. She sometimes found the oddest things people had left behind. Crystals. Bookmarks. Jewelry. Notes. And once or twice, she'd found cookies.

Glads and Marilyn walked into the shop. Both were her mom's best friends and avid members of the Mermaid Pie Book Club—the long-running book club her mom had started years ago.

"Good morning, ladies." Summer stood, finishing up her task.

"Good morning. Are you excited?" Glads said.

Summer supposed Glads was talking about their Valentine's Day event. "I'm not sure. It's the first event since Covid. I'm a little nervous, actually."

"Totally understandable," Marilyn said. "I was anxious when the library first reopened. But we've got to try for normalcy."

"Not me," Glads spoke up. Tufts of her pink hair poked out of her blue knit hat. "Normalcy is not my thing." She laughed as the other two women smiled and shook their heads. "Bo gave me this to give you."

"What is it?" Summer held up the blue-green rock.

"It's citrine. He said it would bring you good luck for the event and many sales." Glads grinned. "You never know."

"Well, I know," Summer said. "The event is going to be great, and it has nothing to do with this little green rock."

White-haired, tattooed Marilyn cleared her throat. "We are here to help set up for tomorrow's event."

"What needs to be done?" Glads asked.

"Everything," Poppy said, walking up to the group. "Follow me."

The three of them left, going upstairs to where the event would be held. The upstairs offered plenty of windows, and people could opt to stand on the balcony and listen to Lana if they so chose. Summer wanted people to be as comfortable as possible.

She walked back into her office, as tests were waiting to be graded. She'd been hoodwinked into helping her university during the pandemic, and somehow she was still helping. She needed to get this group of tests graded before she could pick up Lana.

Her office was a hovel of papers and books. She'd managed to place a poster of William Shakespeare on the wall, along with a calendar featuring Shakespeare quotes. One light hung from the ceiling, and she'd finally purchased a desk light, which helped her see the papers better.

Summer clicked on the computer. And she clicked again. No screen. What the heck? Was it charged? Yes. She'd charged it last night. She plugged it in, just in case. Still no luck. She wanted to scream. The tests were due tomorrow. What could she do?

Maybe she could access the tests through someone else's computer. She dialed Piper, her cousin.

"I'm on my way," Piper said, breathless.

"Wait. Can you bring your laptop? Mine seems to have died, and these tests are due tomorrow."

"Sure. How's everything else going?" she asked.

"Marilyn and Glads are here decorating, and Poppy is being her usual self. And I'm stopping myself from throwing the computer against the wall." What fun that would be.

"You need to stop working for the school. You retired, remember?" she said.

Ah yes, Summer did remember. She'd retired at thirty-seven, two years ago. She had stayed in Brigid's to run the bookstore, write, and get on with her life while living in her childhood home. But when the school called, she hadn't been able to refuse. They were out of options. She'd agreed to help until they could find someone else. But how hard were they searching?

"I think I'm going to tell them I'm out at the end of the semester. That will give them plenty of time to find someone else."

"What do you care? They never treated you right," Piper said.

That was true. But Summer didn't want to think about that now. The way she'd been told to dumb down her class, the way parents complained about her and there was no administrative backup, and worst of all, when those spiders had gotten out of the lab and invaded her classroom . . . instead of supporting her, they'd berated her. Even knowing she had severe arachnophobia.

Piper sighed into the phone. "I'll be there soon. You can grade your tests. The decorating will get done, and we'll pick up Lana. The event will be a smashing success."

Hearing those words from her cousin calmed Summer. They hung up, and the phone buzzed immediately with a text message.

Hi Summer. This is Lana. Just wanted to let you know they delayed my flight three hours.

Summer smacked her head. What else?

That's when she heard the crash.

Chapter Three

S ummer and Poppy started to run upstairs, where the sound had come from, but Glads's loud voice, belying her small stature, stopped them. "We're okay! It's okay! The banner fell! It's okay!"

The banner had fallen? The banner blazed in Summer's mind. White with red hearts and letters: *Welcome to Beach Reads Romance by the Sea Celebration.* She tried to imagine how it could fall and shoved the image out of her brain.

She turned and almost ran into her cousin.

"Piper!"

"What?"

"Don't sneak up on people like that!" Summer said.

"But I didn't. I just got here. Brought my computer for you to use." Piper held it up. Her porcelain skin was red from the cold outside.

"Great!" Summer took the computer and headed for her office. Of all times for her computer to quit on her. She needed to get those test scores entered now.

"I like the posters." Piper followed her into the back. "They're hanging all over town. Someone is making a *Romeo and Juliet* sand sculpture."

Summer placed the laptop on her desk and didn't utter a word.

"Methinks I see steam coming out of your ears, dear cousin," Piper said in a mock Shakespearean voice.

Summer sighed. "It's good for business, I suppose. People are calling Lana's book a modern-day *Romeo and Juliet*, but with a happy ending." She pushed the computer's on button.

"I confess I couldn't read it." Piper sat down, long, lean arms crossed. "I just don't like contemporary romances anymore."

"Not enough vampires or werewolves?" Summer said, half joking, as Piper loved a good vampire romance.

"Maybe," she said, tucking a strand of her long blond hair behind her ear. "Shouldn't we be leaving for the airport soon?"

"Just got word that her flight was postponed."

Piper crossed her arms again. "Wouldn't you just know it?"

"Maybe I can get the tests graded by then, and then I'm a free woman. Um, at least for a day or two?" Summer said.

"Well, tomorrow's the signing, so . . ."

"Oh, please, don't remind me." Summer clicked on the computer and tried to get into her account from there. "Voilà! It worked."

"So you can access your drive?" Piper leaned over and scanned the screen.

"Yes!"

"Okay, I'm going to pick up a few things for Mia and then I'll be back," she said. Mia was her almost-seventeen-year-old daughter. Her birthday was next month. She'd always been a handful but was basically a good kid. These days, romance was in the air for the girl and Piper wasn't happy about it, afraid the relationship might prevent Mia from pursuing an education. She was turning into a beauty—the kind that had grown men turning their heads.

Summer understood Piper's concern. She looked up from the screen. "See you in a couple of hours, then?"

"Yes, see you later." Piper reached for Summer's laptop. "I'll take this to Josh to look at. Don't work too hard!"

"No chance of that," Summer replied. As she glanced over the first test, she realized that statement was a lie. She believed in rich feedback on tests. She settled in while the others were decorating upstairs. A pang of guilt shot through her. It was now her bookshop. She should be tending to the business.

The computer screen flickered. She couldn't keep this up much longer, and she didn't want to.

An hour later, Poppy poked her head in the office. "Hey, boss, do you want to check out the decor upstairs?"

She was at a good stopping point. "Yes." She stood, back aching until she stretched it out.

She walked out into the store, where a few shoppers were browsing. She nodded and smiled at them and kept moving, up the stairs to her mother's pride and joy. The upstairs renovation had happened when Summer was about thirteen, and she'd never forget it. Never forget how much pride her mother took in it. The walls were full of local art. Mermaid art. The floors, like the downstairs floors, had authors' painted signatures on them. But the best thing about the upper level was the floor-to-ceiling windows on the wall facing the beach. And the balcony. Summer had whiled away many afternoons reading on the balcony, the sound of the waves, the scent of the sea air, and the warmth of the sun all part of a contented experience.

As she stepped up the last step into the decorated space, she grinned. It was Valentine's Day at Beach Reads, all right. They'd decorated the table where Lana would sit with a red lace tablecloth, white and pink carnations draping over the side. The banner reading *Romance by the Sea* stood like a beacon behind it.

They'd lined up chairs opposite the podium for the audience. Ribbons and flowers decorated each end chair—red, white, pink, red, white, pink. Summer's crew had put a great deal of time into this. Her heart swelled with gratitude.

"What do you think?" Glads came up behind her.

"I think it's perfect. Thank you for all the hard work," she said.

"Nah, it was fun." Glads shrugged and tucked her fingers into her jeans.

Marilyn peeped up over the stairs. "Piper's here, says you better get going to the airport. Traffic isn't great."

"Oh, yes!" Summer said, and started down the stairs, tripping over her skirt and falling down a few steps. It happened fast—too fast for her to catch herself on the banister as she completely lost her balance—and her feet folded beneath her. One of her ankles twisted and popped. She yowled in pain.

Marilyn and Glads came rushing, and Piper ran up the stairs. "What did you do?"

Summer couldn't speak. She bit her trembling lip, trying not to cry, as the pain rippled around her ankle into her foot. She didn't know what she'd done. She could only watch in horror as her ankle swelled.

Chapter Four

"We need to get you to the ER. That looks bad," Piper said.

"Just get me ice and I'll be fine," Summer managed to say.

"I'll get you ice, to be applied on the way to the ER," Piper said with a finality in her voice that Summer knew not to argue with.

"But we need to pick up Lana." Summer tried to stand. Piper and Glads each wrapped their arms around her. She winced as she stepped anyway. It was as if her pain had taken over her mouth. She couldn't stop wincing if she tried.

"I'll pick her up," Glads said. "Don't worry."

"Okay." Summer hobbled with help down the remaining stairs. She gaped at Poppy, who stood there, appearing dumbfounded. "Can you please get my purse?"

Poppy nodded.

"Please give her my apologies."

They tottered to the front door, pain shrieking up and down Summer's leg. "I should be better by tonight's author dinner." It was a tradition that Hildy had started many years ago with visiting authors: treating them to dinner the night before their event. She aimed to keep it up.

"Don't worry about it." Piper opened the door with her leg. "Someone else can take her out, for god's sake, Summer. Don't be a martyr."

Martyr? Her? Her face heated. She'd have words with Piper later, when her ankle calmed down. But for now, it was all she could do to crawl into Piper's car.

The farther they drove toward Emergicare, the more Summer's stomach roiled. "Can you slow down, please?"

"Why? What's wrong?"

"I feel sick."

Piper rolled down a window and slowed down. "Let's get air."

Summer breathed in and out. Of all the stupid things she'd ever done in her life, this was perhaps the most stupid. How clumsy of her. Her stupid, stupid short legs. Why couldn't she have been blessed with the Merriweather long legs? "How did I do that?" she muttered.

Piper stopped and switched on the turn signal. She shook her head. "You took quite a fall. I missed it, but I heard it."

Summer closed her eyes, breathing in and out, relishing the cold air in her throat and down into her lungs.

"Those ballet lessons your mom made you go to never did take, did they?" Her cousin grinned. Typical Piper. Trying to make Summer laugh when laughing was the furthest thing from her mind.

"Shut up." Summer looked out the window at the shops going by, houses, apartments. Finally, they arrived at an almost-empty Emergicare parking lot.

"Place is packed as usual." Piper being glib again. She parked in the closest spot to the door. "Can we manage, or do I need to get you help?"

"I think we can manage." Summer opened the door, swung her good leg out.

Piper hurried over to her. "Now just hold on. You can't do that yourself."

A woman in sea-green scrubs entered the parking lot with a wheelchair and headed toward them. "Summer Merriweather?"

"Yes."

"Poppy called, said you'd need help." Her eyes went to Summer's ankle. "I'd say help couldn't come here fast enough. You poor thing.

Let's get you seated." Kindness emanated from this woman's eyes. They were deep and caring swimming pools of chocolate brown.

Summer breathed in. A knowing sensation bloomed in her chest: she'd be fine in this capable woman's hands.

That woman was Celeste Gomez. A woman who knew her way around pain and ankles and ice. Summer swore her voice was as soothing as harp music. Everything was okay. Iced up, plenty of ibuprofen . . . until the doctor came in with her x-ray. He clipped it to a lighted panel, flipped on a switch. "It's a beautiful ankle. You didn't break it. You have twisted it, rather severely. Those ligaments don't lie." He pointed to her swollen foot.

"Holy shit," Piper said. "Look at that. That's your foot."

Nothing like seeing your bones, lit up, to make you feel your humanity. Or your age.

"Good news is, it's not broken and it should heal okay, if you follow my instructions. We'll put a boot on you. You should stay off of it completely for a week. After that, I'll check you over, and you should be up and at it with crutches in a week or so."

"A week?"

"Give or take . . . I mean, you will still have the boot on, but if things go well, the swelling goes down, you can go back to work for a few hours every day. Some doctors will tell you two weeks, but the latest research shows it's good to keep moving if you can."

"Wait. What? I can't work?" She must not have heard that correctly.

"I'm afraid not. You'll need to stay off your feet for a few days. Maybe a week. Until the swelling goes down." He pushed his glasses back up on his nose.

"That's unacceptable. I own Beach Reads, and there's an event tomorrow. I have to be there." Summer's voice rose a decibel.

"You don't," Piper said. "I'll take your place. Or Poppy can. We've got you covered."

"I can't even go in on crutches?"

"No. Maybe a wheelchair. We could arrange that for you," the doctor said.

Summer rolled her eyes. Attending a public event in a wheelchair? She mulled it over. Well, other people did it, didn't they? She was no better or worse than anybody else who couldn't walk. "I suppose I could do that."

"But after the event, it would be best for you to rest. Keep your foot elevated. Lay in bed for a few days. Take it easy." He frowned. "A tear like this is nothing to mess with. If it doesn't heal right, you might have problems for the rest of your life."

She recalled her aunt Agatha, Piper's mom, who'd twisted her ankle badly years ago and did indeed still have a problem with it. Summer didn't want that.

"Okay." She resolved to carry out his instructions to the nth degree. But first, she needed to nab a wheelchair.

"Let's get you one of those motorized jobs. You've never had any upper-arm strength." Once again, Piper spoke the truth.

Chapter Five

After tossing and turning and wishing she had a stash of the pot she used to smoke as a teenager close by, Summer found sleep, as fitful as it was. The pain worsened, let up, and cycled through again. The medicine the doc had given her was just a strong ibuprofen and definitely not enough to touch the pain.

Maybe sleeping on the couch wasn't a good idea. Then again, climbing the stairs to her room wasn't going to happen.

She'd been able to forgo wearing her nylon mask for a while now. She'd had arachnophobia so bad that she couldn't sleep unless all of her facial orifices were covered. Her therapist had worked hard with her on that. But she always had it nearby—or in her hand—even as she slept. Like a security blanket.

This wasn't the first time she'd shared the room with Mr. Darcy, the African gray her mother had left behind when she died. The bird didn't exactly snore, but he did make loud breathing sounds sometimes that would wake Summer in the middle of the night.

She awakened with a start. Piper stood over her. "You don't look so good."

"You're no beauty queen yourself." Summer tried to sit up but felt like a car was on top of her body. Pain shot from her foot to her hip. "I think it's time for more pain medicine."

Piper was already prepared with a glass of water and two pills. "I don't know why they won't give you something stronger. It seems inhumane."

Summer downed the pills. "Agreed."

Piper uncovered Darcy's cage.

"Good morning, sunshine," the bird said.

"Good morning, Mr. Darcy," Piper said, then turned her attention back to Summer. "Maybe you should call the doctor today and ask about something stronger."

"You heard what he said. They don't like giving pain medicine out like they used to."

"Yes, but obviously you're not sleeping." Piper gazed around the corner. "Oh, there you are."

Summer turned to see Mia.

"Aunt Summer?" She approached the couch. "If you want to sleep better tonight, you should try a gummy."

"Mia! Honestly!"

"Mom, it's completely legal." The girl's sea-green eyes flicked as she blinked a few times. "If we're lucky, maybe we'll get some in our Valentine's baskets this year."

Silence permeated the room. Pain pulsed through Summer's leg.

Piper and Summer locked eyes. Memories of the two of them as teens experimenting with pot zoomed through Summer's mind—and no doubt Piper's as well. But this was Piper's daughter and awkward.

"Thanks, Mia," Summer said. "I think I'll pass for now." At least as far as she'd tell her niece. But she'd keep that idea in the back of her mind. She wasn't going to manage if she couldn't sleep.

"Maybe they can give you something for sleep?" Piper said.

"I'll call and ask today." Summer didn't need another thing to do today. But sleep was imperative.

"Honestly"—Mia lifted her chin—"would you rather have narcotics or pot?"

Summer pondered it for a minute. "Right now, I'd take anything."

"In the meantime, you have an event today. I think you should just Zoom in." Piper sat in the chair.

"I hadn't thought of that," Summer said. "I have a wheelchair coming today so that I can go."

"But it's upstairs. There's no elevator." Mia spoke up. "I'll stay here with you, and we can make it a party while we wait."

"A party? Does she look like she's up for a party?" Piper said.

"Calm down. I only meant cupcakes and chocolate." Mia rolled her eyes and crossed her graceful arms. "What do you think?"

"Honestly? It sounds better than trying to get around in a wheelchair. I've never used one before, and as your mom pointed out, my upper-body strength is not so good. We weren't able to get a motorized one."

"It's a done deal, then," Piper said. "I think it's a great idea. We can handle the event."

Foreboding moved through Summer. Why did she have such a hard time letting others help her? What could go wrong? Poppy, Piper, and the women from the Mermaid Pie Book Club had experience with these events—even more than Summer. But dread ensued.

She was breaking tradition. Hildy had always entertained the authors out the night before an event. It was silly to think she was disappointing her dead mother . . . but there it was.

Staying home during her bookstore's huge Valentine's event felt like a slap in the face to all those who'd worked so hard to pull it off.

"Summer, it's up to you. But I think it would be best for you to stay here. We're more than happy to fill in for you. We need you to be healthy," Piper said. "I'm sure Hildy would agree."

Would she? She herself had never missed an event. But then again, Hildy had never sprained an ankle or a leg or anything else. What would Hildy do?

Summer looked into Piper's sincere blue eyes. It was more like Hildy to be the one filling in for others who were sick or otherwise incapacitated. That was what Summer herself was like. But to be the person down, the one who needed help, didn't sit well with her.

"Learning to take help isn't easy. But you can do it." Piper grinned.

"Right now, I need to use the bathroom," Summer said, and placed her feet on the floor. Piper and Mia immediately came to either side and helped her step along. Woozy and in pain by the time she made it to the bathroom, Summer knew she had no choice but to stay home. Wheelchair or not, she wasn't in any kind of shape for socializing. She was all about mind over matter—it was the way Hildy had raised her. But her body had a mind of its own, and it was stubborn.

Chapter Six

Cupcakes, chocolates, and hot mint tea at the ready, Mia and Summer settled in front of the screen to watch the live stream of Lana's talk. They both were snuggled in blankets when someone knocked at the door.

Mia glanced at Summer. "I guess that's me going to get the door."

Summer guffawed as her niece unwrapped herself from her fuzzy pink blanket and tramped to the front door.

Summer wondered who it was. Most of the people she knew were at the bookstore.

"Can I see some ID?" Summer heard Mia say. What the heck? Why would she be asking for ID?

Mia poked her head in the room. "Aunt Summer, there's a detective here to see you."

"Me?"

He stepped into the room. "I apologize. I understand you've health issues."

He had a head of wavy auburn hair and deep-brown eyes, giving a startling impression. Summer's heart raced and her face heated. The best-looking man she'd seen in a long time was in her living room, and she was in a rumpled sweatsuit with her leg propped on several pillows.

She managed to point at her ankle. "Twisted."

"I'm Detective Liam Connor. Are you Summer Merriweather?"

She nodded.

"Copper! Copper!" Darcy squawked.

The detective laughed slightly. "Quite a bird."

"Indeed," Summer muttered.

Mia walked around the side of him. "How can we help you?" Her hands went to her hips.

"I really wanted to see Lana. This is the address she gave."

"Oh, she's at the bookstore. It's almost time for her talk," Mia said.

He reached into his coat and pulled out his mobile phone, running his fingers over the screen. "Humph. This is the address she gave. Is she not staying here?"

"No." Summer was beginning to suspect he was up to no good. Why would he think Lana was staying here? Was he a half-crazed fan wanting to track her down? Stranger things had happened.

"Do you know where she's staying?"

Of course she did, but she wasn't going to tell him. Detective? She didn't think so. This couldn't possibly be his jurisdiction, even if he was a detective.

"Not really," she said.

"You're the owner of Beach Reads?"

"Beach Reads! Beach Reads!" Darcy squealed, and flapped his wings.

"Correct."

"And you don't know where she's staying?"

Summer shrugged.

He smiled, revealing two deep dimples on that chiseled face of his. Good looking? Yes. That didn't mean Summer was going to reveal where Lana was staying. Just what was going on here?

"I need that information," he said. "I understand your hesitancy."

"Why do you need it?" Mia said. "What's going on?"

Exactly what Summer wanted to know. But she sized up her maturing niece. Formidable.

His head tilted. "She didn't tell you."

"Tell us what?" Summer asked.

"Well, I can't tell you details, of course, but she is in a legal situation right now where she needs to let us know her whereabouts, especially if she leaves town. And Brigid's Island is pretty far from Pittsburgh. It's not my jurisdiction, but I'm on special assignment. The local authorities know I'm here."

Summer's brain tried to kick in, but her ankle pulsed with pain. If Lana needed to let the police know her whereabouts, that was a big deal. She must be in trouble. Terrible trouble. Summer wasn't sure she liked having a criminal as a guest at Beach Reads. "Is she dangerous? I have a staff and a customer base getting ready to be in a room with her for several hours."

He drew in a breath and shook his head. "I'm sure it will be fine. But I do need to know where she's staying."

"Ask her," Mia said. "Go to the event and ask her."

He cocked an eyebrow. "That's what I'll do, although I hate to cause a scene at the store."

"Come on, Detective, you can be subtle, can't you?" Mia said.

If it weren't for her sloppy bun and bubble-gum-colored fingernails, Summer would have sworn Mia had just turned into a thirty-year-old woman.

He grinned. "How old are you?"

Summer held her breath. Mia was a young woman with agency. This detective did not want a piece of her.

"Does that have any bearing here?" she asked.

"No, I don't think so. I was just wondering what you'd be like ten years from now," he said. "Thank you, ladies. I'm off to Beach Reads."

When the door clicked behind him, Summer pointed at Mia. "That's my girl."

Mia walked around the couch and sat back down on the chair. "Isn't it strange that Lana needed to give the police her whereabouts?"

"It is." Summer winced in pain. "I think it's time for another pain pill."

"Okay. So glad Mom had the time to get the good stuff for you." She left the room to get fresh water and Summer's happy little pills.

Summer picked up her phone and keyed in Lana's name. Just the usual came up: an author website and all of her social media. She kept scrolling, because she had nothing better to do, and her curiosity burned. What had Lana done to elicit police attention? Summer couldn't imagine. The first notion that came to mind was child molesting, because she knew police watched offenders when they moved into another community, but Summer wouldn't believe that was true until she found evidence. But no, wait—with that crime, they also needed to make the local community aware. She kept scrolling.

When Mia walked back into the room, Summer set her phone aside to take the pill.

"What are you doing?" Mia asked, and flopped down on the couch.

"I was researching Lana. Couldn't find anything suspicious—you know, any reason for the police to want to know where she is at all times."

"Did you look her up under her pen name or real name?" Mia asked.

"Oh. I didn't know she was using a pen name."

"Her real name is Elaine Johnson," Mia said, and bit into a chocolate cupcake with fluffy white frosting. "She lives in Aliquippa, Pennsylvania. Near Pittsburgh."

"How do you know all this?"

"Mom told me." She viewed the computer screen. "Looks like they're about to get started."

But Summer couldn't help it. She keyed *Elaine Johnson, Aliquippa, Pa.* into her phone.

"Good afternoon, everybody," Poppy's voice rang out. "Welcome to Romance by the Sea. We hope you'll visit our other retailers who are doing fun stuff throughout the next few days." She held up a heart-shaped card. "Remember to get all the businesses you visited to stamp your card. Turn it in for a chance at the grand-prize vacation for two in Paris."

Murmurs from the crowd.

Summer looked back down at her phone and the string of names on it.

She tapped one. Wrong. Went back, tapped another.

"It's my distinct pleasure to welcome our special guest. A *New York Times* bestseller. A RITA Award–winning author three times over. Critics hail her current book as a romance masterpiece."

Summer scanned the text on her phone. *Local Author Prime Suspect in Murder Case.* That couldn't be true. She increased the text sizes and scrolled down.

It *was* her. Lana was a suspect in a murder case.

She gazed at the computer screen as Lana took the stage.

All of the people nearest and dearest to Summer were surrounding a murder suspect.

Chapter Seven

"What's wrong, Aunt Summer? You just got very pale."

Summer handed her niece the phone.

Mia read over the text as Lana started her spiel. "Thank you so much for taking me to this utterly magical bookstore and wonderful island to celebrate romance during Valentine's week."

"Murder?" Mia's eyes widened.

Summer nodded.

They'd had more than enough murder in their lives—so much so that Summer refused to read anything with murder in it, nor did she watch the police shows on TV. No thank you. Too much violence and hatred existed in the real world. Who needed it in their entertainment?

"There's not much information, other than she might have murdered her husband." Mia pointed to the phone.

"Yep," Summer said. "You'd think that someone would've mentioned that to us while we were planning. Her agent? The publisher?"

Lana wore a red dress with a black jacket that sparkled with sequins. The lighting at the store flattered her. She was small, with short blond hair, huge blue eyes, and a continual expression of bemusement across her face. "*Romeo and Juliet* has always been one of my favorite stories."

Summer groaned, prompting Mia to laugh.

"She doesn't look like a killer," Mia said.

"They come in all shapes and sizes," Summer pointed out.

They turned their attention back to the screen. Summer's pulse raced as she took in the crowd. It wasn't as if she were afraid Lana would freak out and kill everybody, but then again, it happened all the time and you just never knew. And evidently Lana was more than a bit unstable.

Summer's ankle throbbed, and she tried to get comfortable as Lana droned on about *Romeo and Juliet* and how much it had inspired her.

"Inspired by a murder-suicide," Mia said, lifting an eyebrow. "Makes sense, knowing what we know now."

"I'm sure it's more complicated than that."

"Is it?" Mia glanced at her with a challenge in her eyes.

"What I mean is, plenty of people read and watch violence, and they're fine. But when you're already a bit disturbed, it's sort of a powder keg."

"Ah," Mia said.

The camera panned out over the audience. All the usual suspects were there: Summer's half brother and half sister, whom she hadn't known existed until a few years ago. All the women from the Mermaid Pie Book Club. Even Cash was there.

"Well, look there," Mia teased. Summer sank farther into the couch.

Cash was more than an old boyfriend. He was the man she'd left standing at the altar. To say their relationship had been strained after she came back to the island would be an understatement. But they had gradually made their way back to becoming friends.

"Does he read romance?" Mia persisted, her theory being that Summer and Cash were going to get back together. Fat chance.

"Not that I know of, but his daughter does, and she's sitting next to him," Summer said.

"Ach," Mia groaned. "She's so perfect. In school. In life. I mean, look at her."

Summer nodded. "She is lovely. She loves Shakespeare, evidently."

"Shakespeare and romance? Imagine that," Mia said.

"Both can be true." When Summer fell in love with Shakespeare, she'd been a young teen with a mother who owned a romance-themed bookstore. How she'd hated the store and everything it represented in her young mind! The hatred had festered in her as she went on and got her PhD in Shakespearean literature and published a few books.

It had always been easy to demean the romance genre—until her mother died. Summer had necessarily taken over the bookstore, which also meant interacting with the Mermaid Pie Book Club and other romance readers. She had read amazing, well-written romance books, and her mind had gradually changed.

In fact, she had fallen in love with certain writers and certain series.

Now, here she was, leaving behind her academic career—such as it was—and delving deep into a genre she'd always despised. She'd been a fool. And a snob. Taking her teenage rebellion to the extreme.

Lana's voice rang out. "I wanted to write a better version of *Romeo and Juliet*, one with a happy ending."

Summer groaned.

"The ankle or the happy ending?" Mia quipped.

"The ankle feels okay. The medication has kicked in."

"Just as I suspected. It was the happy ending that got you." Mia glanced at Summer over her sparkly painted nails. It was one of the things Piper couldn't understand: Why was she all of a sudden painting her nails?

"It does every time." Summer loved a happy ending, of course, but only when it was called for. And when it was true, this story. Part of *Romeo and Juliet*'s "charm" was the devastating ending. Lana had taken a cheap shot at a classic, and Summer suspected she knew that.

She returned her gaze to the computer. Balloons and streamers filled the screen behind Lana. Red, white, pink. Hearts everywhere. The decorations spoke loudly of Valentine's Day, as did the tower of cupcakes in the background.

Summer reached for a cupcake of her own. "Happy freakin' Valentine's Day." She held it up as if toasting.

Mia grabbed a vanilla cupcake and toasted her back. "Back at you, Aunt Summer." She shoved a bite into her face.

Summer did likewise. As she worked on her cupcake, listening to Lana, she hoped the author left town as quickly as she'd come.

Chapter Eight

G rateful that she didn't have to socialize with Lana and glad she'd be leaving tomorrow, Summer settled in on the couch. The sleeping pill she'd taken was already kicking in, and she dozed off in a cloud of oblivion.

"You aren't looking so good." A male voice awakened her. She opened her eyes. Cash!

"You're no prize either." She pulled the blankets closer around her. What was it with people she liked telling her she didn't look good? It was late. What was he doing here?

"Cash! Hello, Cash!" Darcy said.

Cash laughed. "Hello, Mr. Darcy. Hope you're in a better mood than Summer." He turned back toward her. "I came to check on you. Heard about your fall."

Of all the things and people she didn't need right now, Cash would be pretty close to the top of the list. "I'm still alive."

"Isn't she sweetness and light?" Piper's voice rang out. She must be somewhere in the room. But Summer didn't want to open her eyes again. "Can I get you a cup of coffee?" Piper asked.

"Yeah, sure."

Summer wondered why he'd be having coffee so late at night. She turned over, realizing she needed her pain medicine. And she needed the bathroom.

She opened her eyes again. The room was light. "What time is it?"

Cash smiled. "About seven thirty. Did you have the sleeping pills last night?"

"I did. And I slept." She struggled to sit and finally perched herself on the edge of the couch.

"Good morning! Good morning!" Darcy said.

"Good morning, Darcy." She gazed up at Cash. "Can you help me get to the bathroom?"

He reached for her and lifted her as if she were a feather, not the potato sack she most certainly was.

Piper entered the room with coffee in both hands. "Well, that's one way to do it."

Cash waited for her at the door and carried her back to the couch, where she sat with her leg propped up on the table. Glads entered the room with a tray of breakfast food.

"Where did you come from?" Summer asked.

"Brigid's Island. Born and raised here. Why?" Glads said.

"I had no idea you were here."

"What kind of sleeping pill did they give you?" Cash said, picking up the bottle and reading it.

"The good kind," Summer said. "Better than what I expected."

Summer's cell phone buzzed. Piper picked it up and handed her cousin a fork. Summer stabbed the quiche and brought a bite to her mouth. So fluffy and delicious. The cheese and egg almost melted in her mouth.

"What?" Piper's voice rose.

Cash, Glads, and Summer focused on her. Her voice was laced with urgency, perhaps panic.

"That can't be true! She was fine last night!"

Who? Glads mouthed to Cash and Summer.

"We don't have that information, but I can put you in touch with her agent and publisher. I'm sure they have all that." Piper paused.

The crowd in the room listened to every word.

She must be talking about Lana, Summer thought. Something had happened to Lana.

She went back to her quiche. Had Lana gotten sick? Been in an accident?

Piper set the phone down, her face drained of any color. "Lana is dead."

"What?" Glads squealed.

"What happened?" Cash asked.

Piper shrugged, lip trembling. "She just never woke up this morning. They knocked at her door for breakfast, went in, and found her dead. It's so sad." Her head dropped into her hands.

"She's a youngish woman," Glads said. "How odd."

The room silenced.

Summer's heart ached. The poor woman. She'd died all alone in a strange town, with none of her loved ones anywhere around. That kind of thing always hit Summer hard. She would have preferred to be with her mom when she died. But life and death rarely made sense, or came to a satisfying conclusion like a book or a play.

Summer suddenly remembered the detective. "Last night when Mia was here, a detective stopped by searching for Lana. His card is over there on the table." She pointed. "She told him she was staying here."

"What would a detective want with her?" Glads asked, sniffling.

"She is—er, was—a suspect in a murder case, and they were just keeping track of her." Summer took another bite of the quiche. It soured in her stomach. Lana was dead.

"When were you going to tell us that?" Piper asked, reaching for a tissue on the table and blowing her nose.

"I found out last night when the event was happening. We sent him to the bookstore." She shoved away her plate. It was no use. She couldn't eat right now.

Cash picked up the card. "I'll give him a call."

"Lana was a murder suspect?" Glads said. "That's so strange. I never would have imagined . . ." She stopped short, taking in the group.

"But then again, after the past few years, I guess nothing surprises me anymore."

True enough, the group in this room had come in contact with more murder than most everyday people. Even though one of the murders had happened before Summer was born, it had trickled into the future with far-reaching effects. Summer shivered.

Chapter Nine

"Detective Connor is engaged right now. But he'll stop by later." Cash slipped the phone into his pocket.

"Why don't you call your dad and see if he knows what's going on?" Piper sat up on the chair.

Cash sucked in air and let it out slowly. "Okay. But he's not too happy with me right now."

"Why?" Mia asked.

"Mia!" Piper scolded.

Summer raised her hand. "It's me. Isn't it?" Cash's father, police chief Ben, and Summer didn't have the best relationship. They'd gotten along okay until she'd stood Cash up. And since she'd been back, to say the relationship was strained, if not openly hostile, would be an understatement.

"No. He wants me to fight for full custody of the kids." He paused. "And it's none of his business."

Cash's divorce had been the talk of the island. His wife had left him for the hot firefighter all the women drooled over—even Summer. She'd separated from him and the kids for a while. Finally, they'd reached a shared-custody arrangement. The whole situation had taken a toll on Cash. And his dad, the local sheriff, who was supposed to have retired a few years ago but kept hanging on, didn't approve of his ex-daughter-in-law and her cavorting.

Piper handed him a coffee. "Speaking of it being nobody's business." She glared at her daughter.

"All right. I just asked." Mia spread her fingers and examined her nails.

Summer's head was swimming. Lana was dead the day after her event at Beach Reads—the day after Summer had found out she was a suspect in her husband's murder case. This all made her nervous. Beach Reads Bookstore would again be highlighted in articles about someone's death. And maybe an enterprising reporter would learn about Lana's charges and Beach Reads would once more be mentioned in the same breath as murder.

She needed to find out more about the actual murder case, just in case the cops questioned her and her staff.

Her ankle throbbed with pain. "It's time for my medicine."

"Not quite," Piper said. "You have another thirty minutes,"

"Thirty minutes?" she said, louder than she meant to, prompting the group to laugh.

"Just give her the medicine now." Mia sat on the La-Z-Boy.

"Don't you have school?" Piper said.

"I need to leave in about fifteen minutes."

"Did anybody say how Lana died?" Summer asked quietly. The woman had died after an event at her shop. She'd brought her here.

Glads shook her head. "Nobody knows. It's too early to tell. There will be an autopsy, because it's suspicious." She shrugged. "She just died. When you die in a hotel, or a B and B, or anywhere like that far from your home, they do an autopsy."

"Why do you want to know?" Piper said.

"Just curious." Summer drank her coffee. Maybe the caffeine would help with the pain. She winced as a shot of pain jabbed at her.

Piper seemed nonplussed. "Twenty more minutes, love."

"She's tough," Cash said.

Summer's heart broke for Lana and her family, but another thought occurred to her.

"We better be prepared for questions. We need to call a staff meeting, and we all need to be on the same page." She set her coffee down as the room quieted. "Lana's last engagement was at our store. There will be questions from the police and the media."

"How about this?" Mia said. "There she is, accused of murdering her husband and writing the modern-day *Romeo and Juliet*. Then she turns up dead, like, for no reason, the day after she's speaking about the book. Weird, right?"

Piper's mouth dropped.

There it was, the thing nagging Summer. The whole *Romeo and Juliet* thing. It never had a happy ending. Some stories you could rewrite, but not that one.

"You are one imaginative young lady," Cash said, grinning.

"Not too imaginative," Glads said. "I'd been thinking the same thing. Maybe she killed herself. She was a relatively young woman. In her forties. Young women don't just drop dead, as a rule."

Some writers took publicity too far, but Summer hoped that wasn't the case here. If Lana had killed herself, she'd have no use for the publicity. But Summer had to admit her skin tingled with a strange fear. *Had she killed herself?* Did this have anything to do with the murder case?

"We can get together on Zoom," Glads said. "In the meantime, I'll send a group text alerting everybody and telling them to keep their yaps shut."

"Thank you," Summer said, wondering if it was too late.

Chapter Ten

Later that afternoon, Summer, still lying on the couch and flipping through TV channels, realized it was indeed too late. Mia handed her the local paper. The headline across the top left no doubt.

Author Found Dead after Appearance at Beach Reads

Summer gasped.

"Summer?" Mr. Darcy said. "What's wrong? What's wrong?"

"I'm okay, Darcy."

"Look at the quote from Marilyn." Mia pointed to the paper.

Summer skimmed the copy until she found it. *"She seemed nervous. More nervous than most authors. You know. Just like something was off,"* Summer read out loud.

"Well, it turns out that something was off. She was dying," Mia said.

Summer wanted to throttle someone. Instead, she flung the paper down onto the table. "So much for the Zoom meeting."

Later, Mia and Piper helped Summer dress for a doctor appointment. She hobbled around the house on crutches, practicing, becoming breathless. "I'll never manage this. I just don't have the strength."

"I know that, but you won't have to be on them a lot." Piper opened the door, and Summer made her way through it into the fresh air.

She'd been down only two days, but it was as if she'd forgotten the simple joy of being outdoors. It made her feel so exuberant she wanted to cry. She stood and breathed it in—the air, the sea, the sun.

Mia opened the car door, Piper grabbed the crutches, and Summer clumsily slid into the back seat. How did people do this every day?

* * *

"So, bad news about Lana," the doctor said while examining Summer's ankle. Summer's eyes found Piper's. "Yes, yes, it is." He examined the area around her ankle. "Did anybody notice anything odd about her?"

"Ouch!" Had he just asked her what Summer thought he had? "I wasn't there. I didn't even meet her."

"Sorry," he said. "Your swelling has gone down significantly. That's very good. Now let's get you up and walking a little every day."

"What?" Summer couldn't believe what she was hearing.

"Just a little every day. And your wheelchair has come in. So if you need to get around a lot, I suggest using that. The nurse will be in to reboot you with a more sturdy, permanent boot."

"Okay." Summer watched as he left the room. "Can you believe he asked me that?"

"Nobody ever said all doctors are smart," Mia said.

"But that's not the point," Summer said. "It's rumormongering."

"Get ready for more." Piper leaned back in her chair. "People are lapping this up."

"But why? I mean, I understand curiosity about an author's death, I suppose. But people die every day, even authors."

"It just seems dramatic," Mia said. "To have a huge speaking engagement, then go back to your B and B and die."

Summer mulled that over. She shrugged. "I still don't get it."

The nurse walked in with a new boot. "How are you doing?"

"Not great," Summer said. "I don't know why you can't give me something more for pain."

"We're doing our best," the nurse said. "We have to work within guidelines."

Guidelines? Summer understood. She knew the opiate crisis in this county was skyrocketing. But she also knew she wasn't going to be addicted to drugs—and she was in pain.

"So what happened to Lana?" the nurse said, after putting the boot on Summer.

Summer frowned. "I have no idea."

"What do you mean? She was at your bookstore." The nurse looked incredulous.

"Yes, but I didn't meet her. And she went back to her room and died. Why would I know anything about that?" Summer was trying not to be annoyed. But she hoped her biting tone didn't offend. The woman had been dead less than twenty-four hours, and Summer and her crew had already fielded more questions than warranted. Honestly, how would any of them know how she'd died?

The nurse frowned, her cheeks droopy. "It's too bad. She was a talented writer. I loved her latest—the *Romeo and Juliet* one."

Mia's eyes caught Summer's, and Summer wondered if there might be steam coming out of her ears.

"Do you want to stop at the bookstore?" Mia asked as they got into the car.

Summer imagined herself struggling to get around on the crutches, but she wasn't used to the wheelchair at all.

"Not yet." Her face heated. Here it was, one of the busiest times of the year, and she was completely useless.

When they got to the house, it surprised them to find Marilyn and Glads there with lunch on the table.

Summer smiled. "I should've known."

"Piper let us in. She had to run," Marilyn said, helping Summer with her crutches as she struggled to sit in a kitchen chair. "I guess I owe you an apology. I didn't know this Lana thing would be such a big deal."

"It's okay. It's just the press making a mountain out of a molehill." Summer reached for the quiche. "It smells so good."

"Well, she was a famous author who apparently just keeled over. That's worth an article or two," Glads said. She sat down and sliced a piece of quiche for herself.

"An obituary, maybe. An article? I don't know." Summer, for one, didn't consider dying in and of itself to be newsworthy. But she admitted she wasn't like most people in terms of pop culture. She barely read the paper anymore, and she almost never watched TV news.

"The thing is . . . she was off," Marilyn said. "I know it sounds strange. But her talk wasn't that great. She wasn't really amiable. Like, she barely talked to people when they got their books signed. But still, how sad to die that way. I wouldn't wish it on my worst enemy."

"I just figured she wasn't likable, but maybe she didn't feel well," Glads said. "Let's not forget her murder charge. She was a nuanced character."

"Of all the times for me to miss an event," Summer muttered.

"Right?" Mia said. "Good quiche!"

"Glad you like it, Mia," Glads said. "The event went fine, Summer. And she did fine, even though she wasn't the friendliest person. Sales were great. People are adding too much to her death. As we all know, anybody can die at any time, unfortunately."

It was true—and the pandemic had brought that home to them time and time again.

Chapter Eleven

Just as Summer got situated on the couch with her foot propped up, the doorbell rang.

"Come in," Darcy said. "Come in!"

"I'll get it," Mia said.

Glads and Marilyn were in the kitchen, and Summer's phone rang. Poppy's name flashed on the screen.

"Hello, Poppy," Summer said.

"There's a detective on his way to see you."

And he just walked into the room.

"Thanks, Poppy. How is everything going?"

"Fine," she said. "I've got to go."

"Bye."

Summer gazed up at him, and heat flashed through her. "Detective Liam Connor, how can I help you?

"You remembered my name." A grin spread across his face.

"Of course," she said, hoping she wasn't batting her eyes.

"Can I get you coffee, water?" Mia asked.

"No thank you. Can I sit down?"

Summer nodded.

"I heard about your fall." He took the chair closest to Summer.

"Well, the night we met, I was on my couch with my foot raised," she pointed out.

"You didn't go into detail."

"Why would I?" Summer was confused. "What have you been doing? Why would people tell you about that?" What was this detective up to?

"I've been doing some digging." The detective reached into his coat pocket and retrieved a notebook.

"About me?"

"No. About Lana. Your name came up a few times." He flipped through the pages.

"But I never even met her." Summer shrugged. "I'm not sure what I can add."

"You engaged her, though." His head tilted.

"That's true. And now I wish I hadn't."

He laughed. "Why did you have her and not another author?"

Summer tried to remember the conversation that had brought Lana to Beach Reads. "I believe Poppy, my assistant manager, brought her name up. She figured I'd like her because of the whole *Romeo and Juliet* thing."

"Why's that?" He scribbled something down in his little notepad.

"I'm a Shakespeare professor . . . or I was until recently," Summer answered.

He lifted an eyebrow. "And did you like the book? Like her?"

"Honestly, I couldn't get through it." Summer paused. "But I saw the marketing possibilities, and it's a bestseller."

"Not only a Shakespeare professor but a businesswoman, too."

There was an awkward pause as he looked off into his own distance.

"I'm trying to figure out why she gave your address instead of the address at the B and B." He tapped his pen on the notepad.

"What difference does that make?" Mia interjected.

That was a good question. Summer waited to hear the answer.

"It's just one more thing about her that doesn't add up," he said.

Summer's internal bells and whistles went off. "Is her death suspicious?"

"Of course it is," Mia replied.

"Mia! Please, let the detective talk." Summer flung her arm out as if to say *stop*.

"I'm just attempting to follow procedure." He flashed that smile again. "And because her death was unattended, yes, we have to investigate a little more."

"But you were already here before she died," Summer said.

He nodded. "Did you research her?"

"Of course I did. Do you think that has anything to do with her death?"

"I couldn't say." He shrugged.

"What can you tell us about her murder case?" Mia said.

Glads walked in at that moment. "Murder? I knew it! Someone offed her. Poisoned her, just like in her book! Of course Romeo didn't take it and ruined Merc's evil plan."

"What? No, Glads, that's not what we were talking about. We were talking about the other case, the one where she's the suspect."

The detective turned to her. "Glads, is it?"

Flustered, she nodded.

"What kind of poison did she use in the book?"

"It must be a nightshade," Summer said. "Or maybe monkshood, which is what Romeo used."

"You're right! How did you know that when you didn't finish the book?" Glads said.

"That's what they used in the original play. It just seemed like something she'd do." Summer shrugged.

"I need to make a call," the detective said, and stepped into the kitchen.

Nightshade, Mia mouthed.

Glads face whitened. "Does he think someone killed Lana?"

Summer's heart galloped in her chest at the notion of another murder on their little island. "I supposed he has to check all angles."

"There must be a reason. And I think it has to do with her original murder case," Mia said. "That's what makes the most sense."

"There's not much about it online," Summer said.

"Leave it to me," Mia said. "Mom will be here soon. I'm going to take off."

She grabbed her bag and left. Summer wondered exactly how she was going to find out more about Lana's case. Maybe she had access to internet files that Summer didn't.

The detective walked back into the room.

"Is there anything you can tell us about the murder case she was involved in?" Summer asked.

"It's public knowledge, and she's deceased now, so sure. What do you want to know?"

"Who is the victim?" Summer asked.

"What was the situation?" Glads said.

The detective slid his phone into his pocket. "It was her husband, and he was poisoned."

Chills traveled up and down Summer's spine. Poisoned? Like something out of a book or movie . . . or Shakespearean play?

Chapter Twelve

E ven though Summer had taken a sleeping pill along with her pain medicine, she tossed and turned on the couch that night, trying to sleep. Lana, a woman she'd never even met, plucked at her mind. Had she killed her husband? Summer pulled the blankets closer as she shivered. What had happened to Lana? Why would they think she killed her own husband? Had she been abused and finally fought back? Or did she just snap one day? Or was she wrongly accused? Summer's theory was that women committed more murder than men but were too smart to get caught. This definitely wasn't the case here.

Still, Lana was a writer, and most writers were smarter than your average bear. You'd think if she killed someone, she'd have been smart about it. Unless it was a crime of passion.

The woman definitely had some strange ideas regarding *Romeo and Juliet*.

Summer rolled over on her side and faced the back of her couch, snuggling up to it. Tomorrow she'd venture forth from the couch, as she and Cash had tickets to the St. Brigid Valentine's Chocolate Soiree. They'd promised the town's new chocolatier they'd attend. Summer's half brother and half sister would be there as well. She wanted to support Gina, because every island needed a French-trained chocolatier to boost the mood of residents and tourists alike.

Summer finally drifted off into dreams of chocolate clouds and lakes.

She woke up in a cold sweat with pain jabbing at her. Must be time for more medicine. She uncurled herself from the blankets and sat up. Where was Piper? She must still be asleep. Thank goodness she'd left the meds and water next to the couch. Summer took her allotted amount.

As she took the medicine, Lana's face popped into her mind. The woman was gone, and whatever had happened in the killing of her husband most likely had no bearing on Lana's death. And Summer had other things to think about. Like healing this ankle.

She tried to get up to go to the bathroom. It was tricky business. Where to put her weight as she lifted herself and perched herself on the crutches? She glanced longingly at the stairs. One of these days, she would climb them without a care in the world. That day was not today.

When she exited the bathroom, Piper greeted her with coffee and a bagel on a tray. "Hungry?"

"Not really."

"Well, you should put something in your stomach with the medicine you're taking."

Summer nodded. "Okay."

They made their way to the living room, where Piper helped get Summer situated.

"How are you feeling?"

"I'll feel better once the meds kick in."

Piper smiled. "I bet you will. But you're doing well with the crutches."

Summer didn't think so. It was awkward and painful.

"I'm so sorry we missed Lana. Sounds like she was a character." Piper drank her coffee.

Summer grunted.

"So from what Mia said, she poisoned her husband. I wish we'd known that. We could've pried her about that."

Summer grinned. "Yes. *So, tell us about how you killed your husband. What kind of poison was it?*"

"*And why did you do it?*" Piper said, crossing her arms. "I always feel like when women are pushed to kill, it's long overdue."

"I also think they rarely get caught." Summer had given suicide and murder plenty of consideration even before the strange deaths on their island. You couldn't be a Shakespeare professor without at least a pedestrian knowledge of it. Some claimed they were scholars because of their love of the language and didn't care to dwell on the dark aspects of his work. But Summer was not that kind of scholar. In fact, these days, she wasn't a scholar at all.

Her stomach knotted. It was all she'd ever wanted to do. But it hadn't been working out for her, even before her mom's death and her inherited bookstore. Still, dreams were hard to let go of. Well, everything was—she found quitting difficult.

Mia came bounding into the house. "Good morning!"

"Why aren't you in school?"

"Chill, Mom. I'm on my way. I wanted to stop by with this." She held up a folder full of papers. "A ton of stuff about the murder of Lana's husband. Rocky is so good with the computer." She glanced at her mom. "That's why he's been offered so many scholarships."

Summer noticed Piper's jaw twitch.

Mia handed her the folder. "The evidence is scant. But what they have does indeed point to Lana."

"Interesting." Summer set the folder on her lap. "Reading material for the day. Off you go!"

"Sure. See you later." Mia leaned down and kissed Summer on the cheek and then kissed her mom.

"Tell Rocky thank-you for me," Summer said, and watched Piper's reaction as her daughter left her room. Piper stuck her tongue out at her cousin.

"Very mature," Summer said, and rolled her eyes.

"Rocky! I'm telling you, he's bad news."

"Piper, honestly. The more you fight it, the more she's going to dig her heels in." Summer paused. "And you know that."

Piper melted into the La-Z-Boy. "Yes, I know you're right. But I just can't seem to help myself."

"You need to trust her."

"She's seventeen and all hormones. I know what that's like." Piper frowned.

"You were nineteen and away at college. But I don't think she's destined for the same thing. Do you?"

"God. I hope not," Piper said.

Summer's cousin never talked much about her life. She was still with the man who'd gotten her pregnant. She and Josh seemed happy, though maybe a little bored. And Piper had never been the ambitious sort. So it was news to Summer that she hoped her daughter wasn't going down the same path. Though she supposed it was true that all mothers had hopes of a better life for their daughters. But was Piper's really that bad?

Chapter Thirteen

The day was a haze of pain and medicine. Sleeping and waking. Cash would be prompt, and so Summer tried to get ready. But even taking a shower was a chore.

Piper handed her a dress.

"No, that's not the right one. The red one."

"This is red."

"No, that's maroon," Summer said.

Piper rolled her eyes. "All right." She marched off to the stairs. "What difference does it make? This one is so pretty!"

Pangs of guilt tore at Summer. Piper's life had revolved around hers since she'd fallen. Here she was making a big deal about a dress. "You know what? You're right. It doesn't matter. I'll just wear that one."

"Okay." Piper handed it to her.

Summer slipped it over her head and pulled it down, delighted that it still fit. It had been a few years since she'd worn this.

Of course, the crutches added nothing to it. Maybe she shouldn't go. This was going to be awkward. She eyed the wheelchair folded against the wall, wishing they could get her one with a motor on it, but those were back-ordered.

"Cash could push you around in it," Piper said.

"He'd never let me live it down." Summer's face heated. A man who'd once been crazy enough to want to marry her would certainly help with the wheelchair, but did she want him to?

"Sam will be there too, right?" Piper said.

Summer nodded. Sam Bellamy was Summer's half brother. She still found it hard to believe she had a half brother and half sister.

Piper looked around. "I'll clean up here while you're gone. Glads is going to stay here tonight, so she'll be here when you get back."

Their crew of friends ran like a well-oiled machine when one of them had a need—got sick, had a death in the family, and so on. They organized and supported. Summer's eyes burned. "That's lovely."

"You won't need someone by next week. You're doing good."

A knock at the door. "That must be Cash."

Piper left the room, and Darcy squawked, "I love Cash! I love Cash. He's here!"

"I love you too, Darcy!" Cash walked into the room, carrying a box.

"For me?" Summer asked.

"Yeah, that's what it says." He placed it on the table. "It was on your stoop."

"Thanks." She read over the return address. "It's from the B and B. How odd." She took in Cash, who was dressed in a suit with no tie. He'd always hated ties, but he looked good. Too good. "I'm not going to worry about that now. It can wait. We have chocolate to eat."

"I think you should take the wheelchair." Piper walked toward it. "It's light and can fit into the back of your car."

"I'm no expert, but I helped my mom with one of these for years," Cash interjected. "So we're good to go."

Hearing Cash refer to his mom brought her into Summer's mind's eye. She had been a teacher at the middle school when she was struck down by multiple sclerosis, and she'd suffered for years. She was more a fan of Summer than her husband was.

Summer followed Piper to the car on her crutches. Her armpits were sore, as were muscles she hadn't known she possessed, making it difficult to move freely.

She noticed Cash watching and lifted her chin, smiled, and moved forward.

Isn't this weird? she wanted to say. *Here we are, all these years later, doing things like going to a chocolate soiree as friends, after years of contention.*

* * *

The parking lot of the chocolate shop was almost full. Cash slipped Summer into the wheelchair. "This is going to be fun. Do you have an appetite?"

"Not really." She paused. "But I can always eat chocolate."

He laughed. "I remember."

Summer spotted Tina, the owner of the B and B, walking through the parking lot. "Hey, Tina!"

"Hey, Summer! Look at you. That fall must have been rough. How are you feeling?" she said.

"I'm okay. Listen, I just got a package from you. What is it?"

She frowned. "It's Lana's things."

"What?" Summer's heart skipped a beat or two. "Why send them to me?"

"Your address is her only address on record."

Summer blinked. And blinked again.

"That's weird," Cash said.

Cold traveled through Summer, and she shivered. She didn't know this woman. Why would she have listed her address as Summer's?

Tina shrugged. "I considered it strange. But I talked with the police; they looked it over, found nothing useful, and they said to just go ahead and send it to you."

They all moved through the gravel parking lot together. Summer's wheelchair ride was noisy and bumpy. "Oh, for god's sake," she said.

"That's the first time someone died in my establishment." Tina's voice cracked just a little—enough to make Summer examine her. Dark circles rimmed her eyes, which were duller than normal. Sadness and nervousness played out over her normally jovial face.

"Are you okay?" Summer asked.

She stopped walking. "Thank you for asking. You're the first person who has." She paused. "It was a bit traumatic, walking in and finding her dead."

Summer had questions, but despite her nature, she bit her tongue. "Of course it was traumatic. I'm surprised to see you here."

"Well, I wanted to support our new chocolatier." She moved forward again. "And then there's the chocolate. Everybody knows how good it is for the blues."

"True!" Cash spoke up as he pushed Summer along.

As they came up to the sidewalk, Summer caught her breath. There was no wheelchair ramp. "I don't believe it."

"It's okay. I've got this. Hang on." Cash shifted the weight of the wheelchair all to the back, lifting the front end. He propelled it forward, hooked the front wheels onto the sidewalk, and pushed gently.

"Oh!" Summer's body lurched forward, almost out of the chair, and Tina ran over to secure her.

Cash finished maneuvering the chair.

Now she was on solid ground and wanted to throttle him.

"Told you I had it." He smiled.

Chapter Fourteen

It was an accomplishment just for Summer to be there. She'd never appreciated how difficult it could be to get around in a wheelchair. And in truth, she'd not pondered it much and felt embarrassed about that. She was rethinking the design and layout of Beach Reads to be more accommodating.

They found their seats in the shop. Small tables had been set up, and lit candles sat on each one. Chocolate-brown tablecloths rimmed in gold edging draped the tables. The edging caught the light of the flames, giving a little spark and glow to the evening. Pink doilies sat in front of each seat on the table.

Gina, the chocolatier, was a charming, brown-eyed woman who emanated care and warmth. Every chocolatier Summer had ever known was a warm and happy person. Who wouldn't be in that profession? She spoke with a slight Brooklyn accent about the joys and history of chocolate, then a bit about her education as a chocolatier.

Summer tried to focus on Gina's presentation, but she had to admit, the pain in her ankle was distracting her.

Her half brother, Sam, sat next to her, drinking in everything Gina was saying. Maybe Summer would pump him for information later.

Summer's glance drifted out the window. Yes, the sea was still there, though she'd not seen it in several days. How she missed it—walking along the beach, drinking in the sea air. She gazed back at the table, then at Gina.

Summer tried to will away the pain in her ankle. *Go to your happy place*, Hildy would always say when Summer had any kind of pain. *Breathe in, breathe out, and go to your happy place.* Summer closed her eyes and pictured Stratford-upon-Avon, the village she always longed to be at. She breathed in and out and found her chin dropped onto her chest.

"Now for the tasting!" Gina said. Was she being extra loud, or had Summer fallen asleep and jolted awake?

Her mouth watered as the server brought plates of chocolates over.

She turned her head to see Mia's reaction. The chocolates were crafted with such a meticulous hand, they were little works of art. Gold leaf on one. The hint of red sparkles. Swirls and dips. Flower-shaped chocolates. It was astonishing.

Summer's half sister Fatima's eyes lit up. She'd had chocolate all over the world and considered herself a chocolate connoisseur.

But when Summer turned her head, she spotted the detective at the table behind them. Odd. What was he doing here? Why wouldn't he go back to Pittsburgh where he'd come from?

There could be only one reason: he suspected Lana had been murdered and was investigating that possibility. He'd come to the chocolate soiree because he was watching someone. Summer took in the crowd. All the usual suspects . . . Nobody here was a murderer, and she could tell him that.

She reached for the darkest chocolate. Fatima slapped her hand. "You should start with the lightest and work your way up. Or down, however you want to figure it."

Sam lifted his plate. "She knows what she's talking about."

Summer grabbed the milk chocolate with the red sparkles. Popped it into her mouth and allowed it to sit there and melt. The flavors erupted in a smooth connection of delight.

"Wow." Cash finished his first chocolate and appeared to be in a swoon over it. "This is the first time I've had chocolate like this."

"We've ruined you," Fatima said. "You'll never be able to get dime-store candy bars again."

Summer felt eyes on her. Was she being paranoid, or was the detective watching her? She tried to casually glance his way.

Indeed, he was watching her. She quickly looked away.

Fatima leaned in. "That man has the hots for you."

"What man?" Cash said.

"He does not," Summer said. "He's a detective investigating Lana's death."

"So? He likes you. I'm sure of it." Fatima spoke with confidence and a twinkle in her eye.

"Once again, she does know what she's talking about," Sam said, grinning. "I've seen it a lot."

Summer popped the next chocolate in her mouth, feeling her face heat.

Cash cleared his throat. "That might be considered unprofessional of him."

"Not if she isn't a suspect." Fatima smiled a wider, lipsticked smile. She was persistent.

"Maybe she is a suspect," Sam quipped.

"Don't be ridiculous; I was home with my sprained ankle. I didn't even get a chance to meet her, let alone kill her. Though given half a chance, I'd give her a piece of my mind about her *Romeo and Juliet–*themed book."

"What do you mean?" Cash asked.

"*Romeo and Juliet* with a happy ending?"

Sam, a Shakespeare freak too, guffawed. "Then it's not *Romeo and Juliet.*"

Cash laughed. "You two are peas in a pod."

They had not been raised together. In fact, neither of them had known about the other's existence. Summer had never known who her father was; Hildy had kept her secret to the grave. As had her father. After they had passed, Sam had found letters that brought him to Summer.

Summer's half brother and half sister added so much to her life, and sometimes she still pinched herself. Suddenly having siblings after growing up as an only child was magical. It was another thing that Hildy might have had a hand in, even after she died.

Summer stopped herself, as she always did when she had those ruminations, and stepped back, telling herself she was being ridiculous.

She took a deep breath.

Ridiculous but true.

Chapter Fifteen

On the way out of the shop, the detective stopped Summer. "Good to see you."

Summer nodded. "Thanks. I believed you'd be back home by now."

"No. I'm working with the local authorities, lending them a hand. I asked for a rush on the preliminary tox reports. Hopefully, I'll get them soon, and then I can go home." His eyes moved from Summer to Cash, who was behind her wheelchair.

"Well, safe journey, Detective," Cash said. He wheeled Summer away, out into the fresh air. "And don't let the door hit you."

Summer laughed. "Okay, I guess you don't like the detective."

"I work with a lot of them, and most of them I like, but this guy? Something's not right about him." Cash the lawyer was rearing his head.

"What exactly do you mean?"

"Just call it a gut instinct." They stopped at the end of the side-walk. "This will be harder. Can you stand up? I'll place the chair on the ground and then get you."

Summer nodded and forced herself to stand, with Cash's help. He lifted the chair as if it were nothing. "Well, at least the detective will be gone in a few days."

He lifted her into his arms, cradling her, and for a moment her memory zoomed back to when they'd dated. When they'd been madly in love. Did that kind of thing ever go away?

He placed her in her chair. "He won't be gone if there was foul play."

"What are the chances of that?"

"Your guess is as good as mine. It's all very strange. A woman her age doesn't just die."

He was right. But then again, sometimes people that young did die. Sometimes they had a hidden disease. Or took medicines that didn't react well together. Maybe that was the case with Lana.

But knowing that Lana was a murder suspect added a layer to the whole event. They thought she'd killed her husband. Summer needed to study the details of the case. "Hey, Cash, can you find out more about her?"

"Maybe. And I might do that if the detective stays."

She pulled her seat belt into place. Detective Liam was a good-looking man, but Cash was right: something was off about him. Cash was just as good looking, even if he was older. He'd aged so well. His blue eyes seemed bluer, and there was a dash of gray in his sandy hair. "Let's hope that doesn't happen, Cash."

If it did happen, that would mean someone had killed Lana. Someone would have to have poisoned her. It would've had to be someone at the B and B, Summer reckoned. Which seemed unlikely. Most of Tina's staff were family, and why would any of them off Lana?

Summer shuddered. The world was becoming crazier by the minute—people opening fire on schoolchildren and clubs full of people. She supposed it was within the realm of possibility that someone who worked at the B and B had poisoned Lana. But who? Tina's daughter, Jessie, took turns cooking breakfast with Tina and her granddaughters. Didn't she have a niece or daughter involved in the police? Summer couldn't quite remember.

"What are you thinking so intently about?" Cash said.

"I'm thinking if she were poisoned, it would have to be at the B and B. I'm trying to remember everybody who works there."

He stopped the car at a stop sign. "That's not necessarily true." He continued to drive. "There are slow-acting poisons and drugs."

Summer cogitated. Right before the B and B, the bookstore would've taken Lana out to eat. She was unsure where Poppy decided to take her. But if the detective was methodical, he'd already know where. And before the restaurant, she'd been at . . . Beach Reads.

"Shoot," she said.

"Yep. This could get messy." He flipped on the radio. "Let's hope it doesn't."

Chapter Sixteen

After a fitful night of trying to get comfortable, Darcy waking her up with his weird bird snores, and notions of Lana being poisoned, Summer finally gave up and turned on the TV, keeping it at a low volume so as not to wake Piper sleeping upstairs.

The blue light of the TV flickered through the room. Summer spotted the pain medication. Should she? It wasn't quite time yet. But she could certainly use it, and maybe it would help her sleep.

She reached for the bottle and downed a pill. She leaned back on the pillow, watched reruns of *Downton Abbey*, and eventually drifted off.

A loud knocking awakened her.

Piper ran down the stairs, disheveled. "I'm coming!" she yelled.

Summer's heart thundered in her chest. What a way to wake up. Brutal.

"Detective Connor, how can I help you?" Piper's voice rang out.

Summer wanted to cover her head with the quilt. Why was he popping over so early in the morning?

He walked into the room. "Sorry to awaken you."

"Honestly!" Summer said. No matter how hot or nice he was, this was beyond the pale.

"I've just gotten the preliminary toxicology results, and I thought you wanted to know immediately." He rocked back and forth on his feet.

"And?" Summer lifted herself up to more of a seated position.

"She was poisoned, all right." He'd donned a serious expression.

The air seemed to leave the room. A few beats later, Piper cleared her throat. "I'll make a pot of coffee. Please have a seat, Detective."

He sat down. Summer was at a loss for words, which didn't happen often. Lana had been poisoned? Beach Reads had brought her here to meet her death. Summer wanted to cry.

But this had nothing to do with the bookstore. She recognized that. Did the detective?

"I've just been to the B and B and gotten a list of employees. I'll need a list of employees from your store."

"You may have a list. But it won't get you anywhere. The women who work at Beach Reads are not killers, and I seriously doubt anybody who works at the B and B is a killer."

"You'd be surprised, unfortunately." He took a cup of hot coffee from Piper, who asked if he wanted anything in it. "No, thanks."

Summer appreciated the truth of that statement. She had experienced it deep in her bones. A woman she considered a friend had murdered her own mother. Another murder had been committed years ago, setting the wheels in motion for her mother's life of loneliness.

"Could it be a revenge killing?" Piper handed Summer her coffee.

"Revenge for what?" Summer asked.

"Killing her husband." There was a long silence. "Or at least by someone who presumes she killed him."

"That's certainly one trail we'll follow." The detective sipped his coffee.

"Did she kill her husband?" Summer asked him.

"Everyone is presumed innocent until proven guilty. But my instincts say yes." He rested his coffee on his knee.

Chills ran through Summer. She shivered. Was it his words or the matter-of-fact way he delivered them?

"Do you know the case well?" Piper sat on the edge of the couch.

"I've been working on it from day one."

"What can you tell us about it?"

His phone rang, interrupting Piper's line of questioning, which Summer was in awe of. She was having a hard time forming a complete sentence in her head. The pain medicine made her foggy.

"Sorry. I have to take this." He stood and walked into the hallway.

"This is all so mind-boggling," Summer said.

"Agreed. Did you read about the case?" Piper asked.

"A bit," Summer said. "Did you read the article Mia printed about possible mob connections?"

"No. What?" If Piper were a dog, her ears would have risen.

"Her husband's family had ties with crime families." Summer took a sip of water.

"Oh lord."

"Yes."

"Then maybe she was killed by one of them. It would make sense that it wasn't someone from here."

"Well, Brigid's Island is certainly changing. It seems like new developments are being built every day, and new people are moving in all the time."

It was true that St. Brigid was growing—though not as much as some people wanted to see. And for most of the locals, any growth at this point was too much.

Summer's half brother and half sister had grown up on the other side of the island, and their father had bought a great deal of property to keep developers away. But gradually, even that property was being sold off. Sam and Fatima didn't spend as much time there as they used to, both preferring their place in London. Summer couldn't imagine living like that.

Wait, maybe she could. But imagining was one thing; living it was another.

Chapter Seventeen

Moving her body was good. Even though Summer was hobbling around with crutches, it felt better than lying on the couch. She wasn't exactly comfortable with the crutches up under her armpits, but the rest of her body sighed in gratitude as she moved.

"Not bad, Aunt Summer. You should take a break." Mia helped her to the couch to sit.

"I think I can go to work tomorrow."

"Just as long as you give yourself breaks," Mia said. "I'm not sure you can do that if you're helping customers."

"Maybe I'll stick to the back of the house." Summer let out a groan as she sank into the couch cushions.

Her phone buzzed. The screen said it was Marilyn. "Hello?"

"You'll never believe it!" Marilyn was breathing so hard it was difficult to make out the words.

"Are you okay?"

"Yes! It's Glads. They've arrested Glads for the murder of Lana!" She gasped for air.

"What?" Summer's voice went up several octaves, prompting Mia to mouth *What?*

"You heard me. She's at the police station with that detective." Marilyn breathed into the phone.

"They arrested her?" Summer's brain was having a hard time keeping up with this download of information.

"I called Cash. But he doesn't do criminal law," Marilyn went on.

"He can still help. He went to the station anyway, right?"

"Yes. How could they think she killed Lana? It's crazy!"

"Lana was poisoned." Summer's brain attempted to make connections. "Did they find poison at Beach Reads?"

Mia's eyes widened, and her mouth dropped.

"I don't know. I don't know what's going on. I just know Glads didn't poison anybody." Marilyn's voice trembled.

Summer pictured the tiny pink-haired Glads sitting in jail. No, she'd not fit in there at all. Not with the convicted murderers and drug dealers and who knew who else.

"I don't understand why. Detective Connor was speaking as if he was being methodical about this investigation." Summer's ankle screamed in pain. She sucked in air.

Mia grabbed the phone. "Listen, this is Mia. Both of you need to calm down. Glads is no killer. I'm sure they don't have any proof. There must be a mix-up. Cash will sort it out. She'll be home by nightfall. In the meantime, Summer needs to rest. If you hear anything, let us know, and we will do the same."

Summer heard Marilyn say "Okay," and that was that.

"That is some scary stuff." Mia set the phone down. "But you're in pain. Let's get more meds for you."

Summer nodded, once again in awe of Mia and the way she'd handled the situation. She leaned back into the couch and lay down, propping her foot up on the pillow that was already there.

How odd. Glads, of all people. Why? What could have led the detective to her? It was pure craziness. Glads was one of her mom's best friends. She'd been around Summer's whole life, one of the original members of the Mermaid Pie Book Club. A do-gooder. She was light filled and awesome. Summer hoped this experience wasn't too much for her.

Summer didn't know how old Glads was. She was one of those women who never seemed to change. So spritely, even though she'd had pink hair for years—it didn't have an aging effect on her. Well, at least not to Summer.

Mia entered the room with a glass of water. "So weird. Glads. There must be a horrible mistake."

Summer nodded and then downed her pain meds. "It's ridiculous and wrong. I'm sure they will realize that soon enough."

Mia sat down and sighed. "Could she have killed her by mistake?"

"What do you mean?"

"Like giving her one of her herbal concoctions?"

Summer winced again, but not from pain. "I hadn't considered that. I hope not." Glads was an amateur herbalist. She grew her own herbs and made tea from them. Summer loved her peppermint tea—there was nothing like fresh peppermint. "As far as I know, she doesn't grow any of the poison herbs, just ones you can use."

"Speaking of herbs, do you want some tea?"

"Sounds great." Summer hoped it might relax her a bit. *Glads, what must you be experiencing? What is happening to you at that police station?* Summer wanted to cry at the thought of Glads in jail.

She picked up her phone and noted the tremor in her hand. She texted Cash. *Please touch base about Glads ASAP.*

No response, not even the three little dots. He must be busy. He might not even have his phone on if he was taking care of business. She trusted that he'd get back to her.

A wave of warmth traveled through her. She trusted him. How . . . odd. She'd not trusted anybody other than family in years.

She heard the front door open and assumed it was Piper. Instead, it was Piper's mother, Agatha, just back from her Caribbean cruise. Tanned and every hair of her silver page boy in place. She took one gander at the house and Summer and gasped. "What on earth has happened?"

"Calm down, Gram," Mia said, entering the room with two cups of peppermint tea. "Everything is under control."

A Killer Romance

Agatha grabbed her chest. "Mind your tone. It doesn't look like anything is under control, Mia." Her eyes darted to Summer's leg—and to the pills scattered across the table, which was full of magazines and dirty cups and glasses. "What happened to you?"

"Sit down, Aunt Agatha. I'll fill you in." Summer took the steaming peppermint tea and breathed it in.

Aunt Agatha was back.

Chapter Eighteen

After Summer and Mia had duly informed Agatha of all the happenings during her absence, Summer's phone buzzed, alerting her to a text message.

She's out on bail. I'm on my way to your place.

Her place? Why?

Okay. See you soon.

"Glads is out on bail." Words Summer had never imagined saying left her mouth.

"This is the most ridiculous thing I've ever heard." Aunt Agatha crossed her arms, and her bracelets jangled. She was tan and crisp in a light-blue oxford shirt, which made her blue eyes pop. "Glads? No way."

"Cash is on his way over to fill us in."

Aunt Agatha's right eyebrow lifted, the way it always did when she was amused. "Cash? Is he still hanging around?"

"Sure. We've become good friends." Summer perceived where this was going, and she didn't like it. Not one bit. She changed the subject. "How was your trip?"

"Fantastic. The weather was perfect. I met a lot of interesting people and had a great time exploring the Caribbean. I fell in love with St. John." Winsomeness played across her face. "It was like a fairy tale. And the food? My god."

"Oh my god!" Darcy squawked. "Oh my god, Agatha! I love you, Agatha!"

Summer laughed. Those were words Darcy had probably heard Hildy say over and over again.

"I love you too, Mr. Darcy."

He paced back and forth in his cage.

"Mia, can you let him out? He probably needs some exercise."

"Sure." Mia opened the cage, and he popped onto Agatha's lap and purred. Along with meowing like a cat, it was a trick Hildy had taught him, and she'd laugh and laugh about it.

Agatha stroked him for a few moments. "What a pretty boy."

The doorbell rang.

"I'll let him in," Mia said.

Darcy popped down off Agatha's lap and followed Mia, waddling behind her.

Agatha's face grew serious. "It must be devastating for Glads. I'm going to check on her." She stood and grabbed her bag. "I'll be back. I'll stay with you tonight to give Piper and Mia a break, okay?"

"Sure."

She leaned in and kissed Summer's cheek. "You're going to be fine."

Summer didn't realize how much she'd needed to hear that. Agatha was the next best thing to her mom.

"Please tell Glads I love her." Summer's voice cracked. Poor Glads.

Agatha nodded and exited the room just as Cash, Darcy, and Mia entered. They exchanged pleasantries.

Cash and Mia sat down. Cash leaned his elbows on his knees. "She's not doing well with this."

Summer didn't like the tone in his voice.

"We're going to need to get her help," he said.

"That's what you are."

He shook his head. "No, I mean, like a counselor or someone. She's taken this hard and needs someone to talk to."

"Of course she has. They've accused her of murder." Summer understood. It would be a nightmare to be accused of a murder you didn't commit.

"I mean she scared me. She was despondent. I called Marilyn, and she's meeting her at her place."

"Gram is on the way over as well," Mia said.

"Good." He sat up. "The evidence against her is troubling." He sighed. "During the questioning, Glads admitted she brought Lana the tea. They found traces of the poison in that cup—even after it had been washed. So it was a hefty dose."

"Poison? At Beach Reads?"

He nodded. "And Glads gave it to her."

"There must be something we're missing." Summer tried not to sound hysterical, but that was how she was feeling.

"I hope so. That's why I'm here. I'd like to go through Lana's things. I don't know what that will tell me. But I need to start somewhere."

"Is the detective helpful?" Summer asked.

"Connor? He's trying to prove she's guilty. So I'd say he's not helpful." Circles rimmed Cash's eyes, and little lines kissed the corners, more pronounced from the stress of the situation.

"Have at it. I don't understand why it was sent here to begin with. That seems odd."

He reached for Lana's box, which had been sitting on the floor next to the coffee table, opened it, and started spreading stuff on the floor. Darcy oversaw the proceedings. There were some clothes, toiletries, a few books, a box of chocolates, crackers, and mints.

"That's it?" Mia said.

"I'll get someone to examine these." He held up the toiletries. "It is the only thing I see that could have poison in it. The chocolate box is empty." He threw it off to the side.

"Paper can be laced with it," Summer said. "Let's see that book and the journal." He brought them to her. "It doesn't look like the book has even been opened." She set it aside. "Mia, can you please get my gloves that are in the bottom kitchen drawer?" Rubber gloves weren't something she ever had owned before the pandemic, but she was glad she had them now. She slipped them on and opened one book.

Summer drew in the air. The scent of the book was exactly as it should be. She detected no unexpected smell. "I think this book is fine."

"You can't always smell poison," Mia said.

"No. But I know the smell of ink and paper, and if anything was off, I'd probably notice it."

"I have a kit that will show traces of poison. I'll grab it from the office and bring it here."

"Why not just take the stuff with you?" Mia asked.

"What? Keep it in his office? We may never see it again," Summer said. "All of the things would disappear into the bowels of the Neverland that is Cash's office."

He cocked an eyebrow. "A little dramatic. Don't you think so?"

"Not really," Summer quipped.

"I still don't understand why the stuff is here," Mia said.

"It was definitely a mistake," Cash said. "But it's one I hope to take advantage of."

"But nothing looks out of place," Mia said.

"That in itself says a lot." Cash stood, hands on hips. "She wasn't expecting to die."

A chill traveled through Summer. "No indeed."

"I'll take the toiletries with me and leave you with the books and clothes." He smiled. "Take your time smelling those other books."

Chapter Nineteen

Summer tossed and turned that night—well, as much as she could, given that she was still sleeping on the couch. It wasn't just the pain in her ankle; it was Glads. Summer knew the woman wasn't capable of murder, so she had to wonder who'd poisoned Lana. Was it a personal vendetta, or would there soon be a spate of murders on Brigid's Islands? If a person could kill once, Summer was sure they could kill again.

She needed to see Glads and talk to her about the circumstances that had led to her arrest. Maybe she'd see her tomorrow at Beach Reads, her first day back at work since she'd sprained her ankle.

* * *

When Summer and Piper entered Beach Reads, Summer observed a group of women near the register. She blinked and moved forward on her crutches. It was the whole Mermaid Pie Book Club. Had she forgotten about a meeting?

But when Marilyn turned and greeted her, Summer concluded by the bereft look on her face that this was not a meeting.

"We're worried about Glads," she said.

"What's going on?"

"She's taking this really hard. Being accused of murder is like an assault on her." Marilyn lifted a cup to her mouth, revealing the daisy tattoos on her wrist. *I want to cover my body in wildflowers,* she had often said when asked about her many tattoos.

"It kind of is," Piper said. "I can see that."

"But she didn't do it," Marilyn said. "We all know that. She knows it. We're just meeting to figure out how to best support her."

Summer took in the bookstore. There weren't many customers milling about this morning. Still, she considered it best to move the meeting somewhere less public.

"Why don't you all go into the back, and I'll help you," she said, moving forward on her crutches, Piper at her heels. The group followed her to the rear of the shop. They gathered around as Piper pulled a chair over for her. "Thank you." It felt good to sit and give her armpits and muscles a rest.

"It seems like there's been a huge misunderstanding. She'd never poison anybody," Marilyn said.

Summer stretched out her leg. "Yes, I know that, but Lana was poisoned."

"Does anybody know how this happened?" Piper asked. "Like, why did the police think it was her?"

"She brought Lana her tea. Lana asked for tea. Glads took it to her. That was the cup that was laced with poison," Marilyn said.

"How did the cup get laced with poison?" Piper asked.

"It would stand to reason that the person who brought it to her did it. But we know Glads would never do such a thing. So who did? And who made sure she had that cup?" Summer asked.

"I'd like to know answers to those questions as well," Marilyn said. "But I think the police will find out. What I'm worried about is her mental health."

"We need to set up a schedule to make sure she's never alone," one of the members said.

"Certainly." But Summer's mind was racing. Who'd put poison in Lana's cup? She knew it wasn't Glads. But someone had engineered this—and engineered it well. She shivered.

"Summer is not going to be on that schedule," Piper said. "She's got her own problems right now."

"But—"

"No *buts*," Marilyn said. "She's right. You need to focus on healing."

Summer looked at the group and shrugged. They had this. For sure. But Glads was so special to her and her mom. She wanted to help. She'd call Glads later on. At least she could do that.

"Okay then, you ladies make your schedule and let me know if there's anything I can do to help." Summer stood, grabbed her crutches, and found her way to her office. She plunked down in her chair and turned on the laptop.

"I'm going to take off," Piper said. "If you need me, text or call, and I'll be right over."

Summer took in her cousin, a woman she'd known her whole life. What would she do without her? "Thank you, Piper."

Piper nodded. "You owe me." She grinned.

"I do indeed," Summer said.

Piper left, and Summer's office went silence. The desk light and the computer lit the room. She glanced over her list of things she needed to do and reasoned that she'd tackle the orders first, then write the blog post, then maybe try to walk through the store.

It was hard to get Glads off her mind. But she clung to hope because Cash was on her case and she was innocent. The system would work for her. It had to. Cash had said the poison had all the markers of thallium, though it would be a week or so before they knew for sure. Glads wouldn't even know what thallium was, let alone how to use it to kill someone. Summer wasn't that familiar with it either. She keyed the word into her computer.

Thallium: the poisoner's poison. Thallium is an ingredient in rat poison and insecticide, but it's also a crucial part of green-colored fireworks, imitation jewelry and electronic components. Because thallium, a heavy metal, is colorless, tasteless and odorless, it's been a historical go-to for poisoning. From classically trained chemists to regular people buying rat poison at the corner market, thallium has been logged in too many murder case files to count.

Large doses of thallium cause vomiting, abdominal pain and diarrhea, as well as damage to nerve endings that make affected people feel like they are walking across a bed of burning coal. It causes loss of control to the bowel and bladder, and in the end, a heartbeat so irregular that it brings death. Even small doses, especially over an extended period of time, can be extremely damaging and result in death.

But as far as Summer was aware, Lana hadn't been ill. She dialed Tina. "Hi, Tina, how are you doing?"

"I don't know, Summer. This is all so strange. The police were here this morning in her room again."

"That is weird. They arrested Glads."

"I heard. How ridiculous. How can I help you?"

"Well, I've been reading about this poison. It can make you violently ill. Was Lana sick?"

"Not that I know of. And there was no sign of sickness in her room. No medicine or anything. Maybe they have the poison wrong."

"It's my understanding that it can be given in smaller doses over a long period of time, and you wouldn't know it," Summer said. "I'm betting that's what happened."

"What do you mean?" Tina said.

"I mean someone may have been poisoning her for a while, and the dose she took at Beach Reads was the final dose in a long line of them."

"If we find the person who administered it . . ."

"It would have to be someone she knows, right? Someone close to her, close enough to give her tea and cupcakes laced with it."

"Cupcakes?"

"Anything. Cupcakes were just the first thing I considered. It's tasteless, evidently."

The computer fell into sleep mode, prompting Summer to end the conversation. She needed to finish ordering. "Thanks, Tina, for chatting with me."

"Anytime. And hey, keep me posted, okay?"

"Will do."

Summer focused on making the orders and paying invoices, and then she turned her attention to her blog post. As she mulled it over, she concluded that she'd write something about Lana: how sorry everyone at the bookstore had been to learn of her death, what a beacon to the romance writing community she'd been, and how badly they all felt for her family. All true.

She wouldn't mention that Lana had been murdered in this very bookstore. No indeed.

Chapter Twenty

When Summer was finished writing the blog post, she needed to get up and walk around a bit. She eyed her crutches. She hated them. Her arm was sore, and she was developing bruises on the pads of her hands.

But it was the only way for her to walk through the store and check things out. It was part of her habit as owner and manager to see that everything was in order. To show her face and be approachable to book buyers.

And she loved talking about books—even the romances. After all the years of despising the genre, she'd warmed up to it. After all, she needed to know when the next Marina Adair or Susanna Kearsley would arrive, both of them writers she now anticipated reading.

She hobbled out of her office and glanced at Poppy, who was at the register with a customer. She swung herself toward the stacks and made her way to the aisle. Poppy, of course, had not been able to do much straightening of the books, as she was too busy running the store on her own.

Summer blinked, taking in the mess, and then picked up a book and placed it in the right spot. The simple act of straightening books always soothed her. It brought back memories of helping her mom, begrudgingly liking it, and not allowing her mom to know it. Silly girl.

"Excuse me."

Summer turned toward the voice.

"I'm looking for a book for a friend of mine. She likes sweet romances. I can't seem to find that section."

"The sweet romances are upstairs," Summer said. She despised that term, but she supposed it was better than clean romances. What kind of a world did they live in where things had to be labeled because they didn't have sex in them?

"Thank you." The woman turned and walked away with a slight limp. Summer hoped the stairs wouldn't be too much for her.

After straightening the books in this aisle, Summer eyed the over-stuffed chair. *Yes, please.* She sat beneath Anne Rice's autograph on the wall. One row of books down. Scanning for discomfort in her ankle, she thought she could manage one more row. Maybe.

From this vantage point, most of what Summer could see was books.

"They say she was murdered," a voice said.

Summer whipped her head around. Where had that come from?

"I don't believe that," another voice said. "I'm sure she killed herself."

Yes, the conversation was getting closer, and coming from the vampire romance section. Summer's heart raced. Were they talking about Lana? Was the gossip already spreading?

"Why would you think that?" the first voice asked.

"It's all in her book. She had a romantic notion about suicide. Maybe you could even say suicide ideation runs through the book."

Summer's brain clicked into gear. Could Lana have committed suicide? Could she have poisoned herself? Maybe she'd placed the poison in her own cup.

"Well, that's a flimsy theory at best. She was a successful author with plenty to live for."

"We don't know that," the other voice said. "Perhaps since her husband died, she didn't want to go on."

"Okay, I'll give you that."

They were right around the corner.

"But to do it after her signing here? That doesn't fit."

"Unless there's something we don't know about this place."

Summer's heart lurched.

"There was another murder committed here, remember?"

Summer stood, grabbed her crutches, and hobbled into her office. She didn't want to hear anymore. The next thing she knew, her store would become known as the "murder bookstore." She couldn't have that. It was so antithetical to what her mom had built. She needed to get on top of this public relations problem before it escalated.

She hated to think about it like that. After all, someone's life had been taken.

She drew in a breath and released it. She needed to consider her next steps.

Chapter
Twenty-One

Summer dropped onto her couch. It was quite possible that she'd never been so tired in her life. Getting around on crutches was exhausting. She just wanted to melt into the couch. She lay there and drifted off until she heard the front door open and shut. She reluctantly opened her eyes.

"Summer!" Aunt Agatha's voice rang out.

"In here," she managed to say.

Aunt Agatha strolled into the room with a bag—something good, no doubt. And it smelled divine. "I brought you lasagna. Are you awake?"

"I am now."

"You need something in your stomach before you sleep, especially with all the medicine you're taking. I'll bring you a plate." She scurried off to the kitchen, leaving Summer and Mr. Darcy alone in the quiet room.

Summer flicked on the TV and turned the channels, one after the other. She couldn't find anything to watch, so she settled on the news.

That was a bad idea. Her chest tightened, and she shut off the TV.

"All these channels and nothing to watch," Summer muttered.

"What?" Agatha had returned. "Oh yes, your mom and I used to talk about that all the time." She set the plate of lasagna on the table next to Summer. Smells of garlic, cheese, and tomato wafted toward her. Mouthwatering.

Summer drew the plate to her lap, feeling its warmth on her thighs.

"I'm worried about Glads." Aunt Agatha poked at her lasagna.

"Me too. What's the latest?" Summer brought a bite to her mouth and shoved it in, savoring the homemade dish. "So good!"

"Thank you." Agatha swallowed a bit. "Glads has always been a strong woman, but she's also sensitive. She's taking this very hard. Like, personally."

Summer understood. Glads was a do-gooder, always volunteering and happy to lend a hand with any project. "It must be difficult. I keep thinking if she didn't do it, then who did?"

"Me too. The cup must have already had poison in it. Glads wouldn't have known. Who put the poison in the cup?"

"I know! We taped the event. Maybe we could spot something on the video?" Summer's brain fog was dissipating, but her ankle hurt, so she'd need to take more medicine. She wanted to not feel the pain, but she also wanted to have a clear head. She decided to just keep eating the lasagna.

"Where can we get that?" Aunt Agatha's blue eyes had lit up. "It seems like that's our ticket to getting Glads released."

"It should be online now," Summer said. "Can you bring me the laptop out of my bag? Josh still has mine."

Agatha set down her lasagna and went to fetch the laptop.

Summer wondered why she hadn't considered this before. Well, maybe it was the painkillers and the pain. How did one think when one was in pain? When was it going to stop hurting so much?

Aunt Agatha handed her the computer. She logged in, went to the Beach Reads page, and found Events. Click. There were all the events—except the last one.

She picked up her phone and rang Poppy, who didn't pick up. "Hi, Poppy, it's Summer. I'm looking for the clip of the—"

"Hello? Summer?"

"Yes, Poppy. How's it going?"

"Mia's helping out tonight. What a relief."

"Good to know. I've been trying to find the reel of the event on the web page."

"It's not up yet. I've not had a chance to get it up. I'm sorry. It's been fairly busy, as you know."

Summer realized that Poppy was doing the work of at least two people, and she appreciated that. "I'm sorry. I don't mean to push. But Agatha and I were just sitting here wondering if we might see something or someone that could help Glads out."

Silence. Summer could almost see the wheels moving in Poppy's brain. "Oh, I see. Well, I'll get it up tonight. How does that sound?"

"Good. Ping me when you're finished, okay?"

"Sure, boss. How are you feeling?"

"Frankly, I got home and crawled on the couch and fell asleep. The crutches are brutal."

"I bet. Will you be in tomorrow?"

"I hope so."

"Good. I just feel better when you're here."

"Thanks, Poppy. I appreciate all of your hard work."

They clicked off, and Agatha stood, pacing between the La-Z-Boy and the stairs.

"Not ready, huh?" she asked Summer.

"No. Poor Poppy. My accident has left her frazzled. I was there today, but I'm not sure how much help I was. She'll have the event live sometime tonight."

Agatha picked up her plate. "Do you want another piece?"

"Do I? Yes, I do!"

"All is well, then. When a Merriweather doesn't want a second piece of lasagna, then I start to worry."

Chapter
Twenty-Two

After Summer finished eating, she checked the website again. "Nothing."

"Well, as you said, Poppy is busy. I'm sure it will be up tomorrow. It's not as if we can do anything about it tonight anyway." Agatha stood up and collected the dirty dishes. "You look tired, Summer. Are you ready to sleep?"

"I don't know. I'm tired but wired."

"Maybe read a book." Agatha's voice trailed off as she went into the kitchen.

The familiar sounds of water running and dishes clanking soothed Summer. She glanced around for something to read, and her eyes landed on one of Lana's books. It looked a bit different from the other books. It had a different shape. Maybe it was a journal? Was that Lana's journal? It had never been put back in with the rest of her things.

Summer picked it up. Should she? The woman was dead, murdered at Beach Reads. Maybe Summer should respect her privacy and not read the journal. She set it down on the table.

Then she picked it back up. There could be something in these pages that would lead to finding out who'd actually killed Lana. Of course she should read it.

She cracked it open and read the first page.

I want the world to know how we are loved.

I especially want women to know there are good men out there, men who are worth whatever heartbreak may come.

Losing you did more than break my heart, it shattered everything I thought I knew about myself. Everybody told me I needed to pick up the pieces and move on without you. How could I? At some point I realized I didn't have to. You were still here. I could feel you when I would lie down at night. I swear the bed creaked on your side. I could smell you when I was in the shower. I know you are still with me.

I had to find a way to be okay with our new relationship.

Summer blinked as tears welled up. This was crazy. But it was a journal, so why would Lana lie? These were her exact, unfiltered thoughts. And Summer could relate. She hadn't experienced anything as drastic as what Lana had written, but she often felt her mom near her. It was a knowing. Sometimes it was prompted by a smell, or a sound.

"What's that?" Aunt Agatha set a cup of herbal tea on the table. "This will help you sleep."

"This is Lana's journal," Summer said, setting it aside.

Aunt Agatha's mouth dropped.

"I know what you're thinking. But I decided that it might hold some clues as to who offed her."

"And?" One of Agatha's silver eyebrows shot up.

"So far, nothing, but I'm going to keep reading. Just in case." A heaviness crept into Summer's chest. This might be difficult reading.

"Find out anything at all?" Agatha blew on her own cup of tea before she brought it to her lips.

"Just that she loved her husband. I have a feeling this is a journal about her grief. I don't know if I'll find anything else out about her. But it's worth a shot to try to help Glads."

"It's a mystery to me why it was sent here."

"Cash thinks it was an error."

"That's a big mistake to make." She took another sip.

"Well, thank goodness for it. Because I have some reading material," Summer said, and picked up her tea. Passion flower and chamomile, both of them herbs she was familiar with from her mother teaching her about them. They usually worked.

Pain shot through Summer's ankle. She winced. "It might be time for more medicine."

"I've got you." Agatha gave her the pills. She downed them and closed her eyes. It would only be fifteen minutes or so, and then she'd feel the pain's slow dissipating.

Her phone buzzed. It was Poppy.

"You're not going to believe it."

"Try me."

"I can't find the video. It's like . . . I don't know . . . it completely vanished."

"What? How can that be?" Summer's voiced rose. "How?" Their one hope of getting Glads's murder charge dropped easily!

Agatha sat straighter, then leaned in.

"I don't know. I'm going to call the company who filmed it in the morning. I'm hoping they kept a copy. There's absolutely nothing on the file they sent me."

"Well, okay. Let's hope they do have a copy," Summer said. *Please, please, please have a copy.*

"I'm sorry. Thai is the first time this has ever happened."

"I know. And I know this isn't your fault. I'm sure the company has a copy. Let's touch base tomorrow."

Summer locked eyes with her aunt. "The file had nothing in it."

"So I gathered. Was there just one file?"

"One file sent to Poppy. The company who filmed may have a copy. It's worth a shot."

"I'm sure they have a copy." Agatha sat back in her chair. "I'm hoping that between that and the journal, we'll come up with a way to help Glads. She's a mess."

"Cash is helping her, so whatever we find, we'll need to loop him in."

"He's not a criminal attorney, and that worries me."

"He can do it. I have every confidence in him."

Agatha chuckled. "Well, I have never heard you say that before."

"I don't think I ever really knew him before. We're such good friends now." It was true. Maybe they weren't meant to be together romantically. Maybe they were meant to be just friends. And that was fine with Summer. She could always use a good friend.

"Be careful, Summer. I don't think he could take another heartache."

Summer's head almost spun around. "I'm not interested in him. I've told you that."

"Does he know that?"

Summer shrugged. "I believe he does. We don't talk about it. Why would we? That all happened so long ago."

"That doesn't mean the feelings weren't real—especially on his part."

Summer's chest burned. "I don't want to rehash this with you. I've felt horrible about it for years. Cash and I are in a great place right now. We've put the past behind us."

"Whatever you say."

Summer set the journal down and sank into the couch. She hoped she and Cash were on the same page. She absolutely didn't want to hurt that man again. Ever. She cherished their friendship. Should they talk about it? Maybe. But that might just ruin everything.

Chapter
Twenty-Three

Summer, fully medicated and a little sleepy, picked the journal back up. Reading anything always helped calm her mind. She had so much to think about, along with her sprained ankle. Aunt Agatha was sleeping upstairs.

She opened the journal.

No young couple talks about death as freely and openly as they should. Who wants to talk about death when you have all those love hormones to deal with? We did talk about it from time to time. I remember back when we were still dating . . . I remember sitting at a coffee shop with you—was it Cleo's? Yes, yes, I think it was . . . Anyway, I remember it as if it happened today. Your chiseled face across the table, the light in your green eyes, and you said you hoped you went first because you couldn't live without me.

Summer's heart burst. Wow. Intense.

I remember laughing. It made me so nervous to think of either of us dying then. I didn't want to think of living without you either.

    Yet here I am. You are on the other side of the death question. Now we both know more about it.

    I think some of my friends think I may kill myself to be with you.

But they don't know that would be the last thing you'd want for me. I am here for a reason. Even though we no longer touch in the flesh, I know you are here too.

Summer's eyes were burning. Time to put the journal down and get some shut-eye. She needed her rest. She planned to go in to the bookstore again tomorrow and hoped that each day would get a little easier with her ankle.

*   *   *

After breakfast with Aunt Agatha, Summer made her way in to Beach Reads. She was a little late and was surprised that no customers were in the store.

Poppy's lifted her chin at her from behind the cash register. "Good morning, boss."

Summer stopped. "Good morning. Wow. It's quiet. Maybe we can get some real work done today."

Poppy's eyebrows rose. "You haven't seen, then."

"Seen what?"

She slid the local paper across the counter. *"Local Woman Questioned for Murder at Beach Read Books."*

Summer's heartbeat sounded in her ear. A thunderous pounding took over her rib cage. She wondered if her faced glowed as red as it felt.

"Summer? You don't look so good."

"Who did this?"

"A reporter," Poppy said, as if stating the obvious. "Nobody talked to her, but she pieced everything together through the court records and other news outlets."

Summer needed to do something about the reputation of the bookstore. That's why nobody was in this morning; she'd bet her life on it. Nobody wanted to go to a bookstore where a murder had happened. "Have we found the taped event yet?"

"No. I left a message again this morning."

Summer needed to call in a PR consultant. She was acquainted with one back in Staunton but was unsure if there was one on the island. She'd call Macy, the woman she knew in Staunton, first.

Summer snatched up the newspaper and hobbled into her office.

Poppy followed. "I thought I would get some of these books unpacked while it's still slow."

"That would be great, Poppy," Summer tried to sound normal, but she didn't feel normal at all. The bookstore was built on love. She'd not have it come crashing down because of one unfortunate incident.

"What are you going to do?" Poppy said.

"I'm calling a woman I know to ask how it's best to handle this." Summer wanted to hide under the desk and not deal with any of it. But the reputation of the bookstore was paramount.

"That's a good idea. I wonder if we should issue a statement or something."

"Who knows? It may be best to just do nothing."

"Well, I hope you get some answers."

"Me too."

Poppy left the room, and Summer could hear her moving and opening boxes.

She dug her phone out of her bag and found Macy in her contacts. She dialed her.

"This is Macy," the voice said.

"Hi, Macy. Summer Merriweather. How are you?"

"I'm great. Where've you been? Someone said you retired."

"Yes, I'm now running my family bookstore on Brigid's Island."

"That's not a bad gig. I heard an island and I heard a bookstore, and my ears pinged."

Summer laughed. It was a lovely store on a beautiful island. She had much to be grateful for. "Yes, it's a great place, but something unfortunate has occurred, and I wonder if I could hire you to tell me what to do about it."

"Tell me what's going on. I'll give you an hour for free, and then we can chat about whether or not you need to hire me."

"Well, that sounds like a good deal."

"It is. So, what's going on?"

Summer reported the whole situation to her.

Silence on the other end of the phone.

"Are you there?"

"Yes, I am. I'm just thinking."

"Okay, think away."

"Did you tell your employees not to talk to the press?"

"Yes. One has, but her bit was fairly harmless."

"That's good. You should keep it that way. I'd suggest laying low for a while. Just going about your business. I think this will blow over. These things always do."

"What about issuing a statement of some kind? I've already written a blog post."

"That's enough. I don't think you need more than that. It will further add to the news cycle, and I think you just want it to go away as quickly as possible."

Summer had been torn between giving a statement and keeping quiet. Now she had reason to keep quiet. "Okay. That makes sense."

"Now, if something happens, like another angle to the story comes up, call me."

"Can you give me an example of what you mean?"

"For example, the reporter digs up dirt on the suspect and prints a profile of her."

"Geesh. I hope that doesn't happen."

"Right," Macy clipped. "I've got to run, Summer. Good talking with you."

Could anybody find any dirt on Glads? It dawned on Summer that Glads had always been in her life—a friend of her mom's since she was a little girl. But there was little she knew about her. One thing she did know was that Glads was no killer.

Chapter
Twenty-Four

The only people who came into the bookstore were those on the Valentine's Hop. Customers were given a paper heart they could get stamped by all the local businesses. Once their heart was filled with stamps, their name went in a big barrel for a drawing for a grand-prize vacation in Paris. All the local businesses had chipped in—including Beach Reads.

They didn't stay long. They came in, didn't even glance at a book, and got their cards stamped. This was the first day of the hop. The Valentine's week of activities and events would be over soon. Valentine's Day was in two days, and Summer was ready for it all to be over. She didn't care for the holiday, and all this tourist stuff in the midst of a murder investigation made her even more nervous.

Two young women came in, and Poppy was on her break, so Summer stamped their hearts.

"Is this the murder bookstore?" one asked.

Summer rubbed her palms on her pants, leaving a hint of sweat on them. She was speechless.

"Get your cards stamped and move long. You'll get no gossip from her!" Poppy came out of the back, and the two young women did as she suggested.

"That was amazing," Summer said, embarrassed by her own lack of action.

"I've more experience with the public," Poppy pointed out.

Indeed. And the public was different from the classroom. At the university, the professor was expected to be in charge, and a certain amount of respect existed. Most of the time. Since Summer had been back at Beach Reads, she had noticed that most of the public were lovely. But for some, the minute you got behind a counter or had an employee tag on, they treated you as less-than.

Summer recognized that these folks were probably unhappy in their own lives and were projecting their unhappiness onto the clerks. But it was no excuse to mistreat people.

Aunt Agatha entered the bookstore. "Hello. I didn't expect to see you behind the register. How's your ankle?"

"Not bad. Poppy's on a break."

"It's over," Poppy announced. 'I think you should go in the back."

Agatha lifted a bag. "Lunch!"

Summer hadn't realized how hungry she was. "Yes, please."

"You like hummus, right?"

"Yes, I do." Summer grabbed her crutches and followed Agatha into her office.

After they got situated, each with a hummus and bread, between the stacks of paper on Summer's desk, Agatha pulled a newspaper out of her bag. "I suppose you've seen this."

Summer nodded.

"Did you read it?"

"No. I didn't have to."

"Well, good. No worries, then. What's the plan?"

"I spoke with a friend of mine who's in PR. She suggested keeping our head down and doing what we do best. Not to issue a statement or anything."

Agatha looked pleased. She dipped her bread in the hummus. "Sounds like good advice."

"Indeed."

"I was with Glads this morning." She took a bite of her hummus-covered bread.

"How is she?"

Agatha finished chewing her bread and swallowed. "She's not handling this well."

"What do you mean?"

"I mean she's not herself at all. She's been grumpy and mean."

Glads? That was hard to imagine. "What?"

"I know. It doesn't make any sense at all."

"She's been around forever. But I don't know much about her. Do you?"

"She's a private person," Agatha said. "Come to think of it, I don't even know what she did for a living."

"Did?"

"She's retired now—or at least I think she is."

Summer chewed her hummus and bread and swallowed. "She must be. She volunteers here so much, and she also volunteers at the library."

"Well, Marilyn got her into that."

Marilyn was the town librarian. She was also a member of the Mermaid Pie Book Club—and a good friend of Glads's.

"How's Marilyn doing?"

"I don't know. I've not seen her. The library keeps cutting staff, and she's in up to her neck."

"So she's not been around Glads?"

"I think she's been in and out, but as I said, she's been working a lot."

Summer was sure not seeing Marilyn was part of Glads's problem. Those two were always together. "It's a traumatic thing to be accused of murder. She probably feels like she's living in a nightmare."

"I get that, but it doesn't take much more energy to be polite with people trying to help you."

Summer shook her head. "Once again, I'm unsure of what to say, because that's not the Glads I know."

Poppy stuck her head in the doorway. "Someone here to see you. A reporter."

"Please tell them I have no comment. And don't talk to them after that. I mean it, Poppy. Say nothing to them. Except 'No comment.'"

A reporter to see her? The audacity! One article out about Lana's death as a potential murder at the bookstore, and now the reporters were swarming?

God! As if she didn't have enough on her plate.

She crossed her fingers that he'd listen and go out the same door he'd come in.

Chapter
Twenty-Five

"How are you doing?" Agatha asked, after she helped Summer to the couch.

Summer let out a huge breath. "It hurts."

"I'll go and get the medicine. You only have two pills left. Are they going to give you more?"

"I'll call the doc and find out." She'd assumed she could go to the bookstore on a daily basis. But the way her ankle was hurting, she wasn't sure she'd done the right thing. She'd have to stay home tomorrow.

Aunt Agatha brought in a glass of water and the pills. "It's a shame the video company hasn't returned Poppy's calls."

Summer downed her pill. "I'm beginning to think there is no video."

"I hear you, but why? The company has a good gig doing your events. Why would they want to screw that up?"

Summer realized her aunt was right. Maybe she should send someone in person to their offices. "There must have been a problem or a misunderstanding. Poppy said they just sent an empty file. Which is weird."

"I agree." Agatha sighed. "I'm tired. I think my travels are finally catching up to me. I'll reheat the lasagna, then I'm afraid it's bedtime for me."

She stood and walked into the kitchen.

Summer picked up Lena's journal and read further:

*Do you remember the summer we met? I remember it so clearly,
I can almost taste the pierogis I was eating that day. I was sitting
at a table at the food festival and had my mouth full when you
approached me. "Excuse me," you said. (You being the ever-polite
person you are.) "May I sit next to you?"*

*When I looked up at you, it was weird, right? We've talked
about this before, but there was an instant of knowingness the minute our eyes met.*

Oh, brother. Summer had heard of such things, and she'd read
about these moments in romances, of course, but nothing similar had
ever happened to her. She'd always assumed it was all the stuff of story.
But here Lana was writing about it in her journal, not trying to prove it
to anybody. Summer sighed out loud.

"Bored?" Aunt Agatha brought in the lasagna.

"No, not at all. They were just very much in love."

"Who?"

"Lana and her husband."

"I wonder what went wrong."

"What do you mean?"

"Well, she's a suspect in his murder, so something must have
happened."

"He was poisoned . . . she was poisoned . . . Maybe the same person
did it."

Aunt Agatha swallowed the bite of lasagna she had in her mouth.
"It does seem odd they both went the same way."

"I haven't heard from Cash. Have you?" Summer asked.

"No."

Summer picked up her phone and dialed him.

"Hello, Summer."

"Hello, Cash. I just wanted to touch base about Glads's case."

"I can't tell you much about it. I'm her lawyer, remember?"

"Okay. I just want to know if she's going to be okay. Like, is there a lot of evidence against her? Can you tell me that?"

"No solid evidence. That's why they let her go. But they are working hard to get more evidence. That PI guy? He's a piece of work."

"Really? How so?"

"I can't get into details, but he's gunning for a conviction. It's like he's on a mission—whether or not the person is guilty."

"I suppose he has his reasons. He's been working on Lana's case for a while. He probably just wants some satisfying conclusions."

Cash breathed into the phone. "Don't we all?"

* * *

Summer watched Agatha pick up the dishes. A wave of weariness came over her. She sank back into the pillows, wishing she were upstairs in her bed.

Agatha came back into the room. "I don't mean to scare you, but there's someone on the front porch."

Summer sat up. "What? Just sitting out there?"

Agatha nodded.

Summer often had problems with tourists taking a seat on her private porch. But it wasn't tourist season.

"Shall I open the door and find out?" her aunt asked.

"Hand me my crutches. We'll go together." Summer didn't think there was much danger, but she wanted to go with Agatha just in case.

Summer hated these awkward situations where people didn't realize someone actually lived here. The pink house with the blue shutters that needed a few repairs—okay, a lot of repairs—couldn't possibly be occupied?

They made their way to the front door and opened it. The little person sitting on the stoop stood up and turned to face them.

"Glads?"

"I'm sorry. I just couldn't think of anywhere else to go," she said meekly.

"Come in out of the cold," Agatha said. "Let's get you warmed up with some tea."

"No thanks, Agatha. I just wondered if you had an extra bed, Summer?" She lowered her head, not meeting Summer's gaze.

"Sure. I'm still on the couch. What's the problem with your bed? What's going on?" Summer said.

Glads took a deep breath and released it. "I just need some peace and quiet. Everybody cares about me, and I get it. They are always there in my place. But it's too much. I need space and time to think this all through."

Summer's heart went out to her. Poor Glads, suffocated by well-meaning friends.

"You can stay here. No problem."

Chapter
Twenty-Six

With Glads and Aunt Agatha asleep upstairs, a quiet fell over the house, and Mr. Darcy and Summer drifted into slumber too.

Summer was awakened the next morning by a phone call. "Summer. We can't find Glads," a panicked voice said.

Summer's half-asleep brain was brutally kicked into gear. "Calm down. She's here."

"Why?" Marilyn said.

"There were just too many people around for her comfort. You know how she is."

Marilyn sighed into the phone. "Well, thank god she's okay."

"She's fine."

"Okay, I better let the others know. We were getting ready to launch a search for her."

Typical. This group of women meant business. When they cared about you, you were aware of it.

"Have a good day, Marilyn."

"Thanks, Summer. You too."

* * *

An hour later Glads, Summer, and Aunt Agatha sat at the kitchen table eating the rest of the lasagna for breakfast.

"You make the best lasagna," Glads said.

Summer was not a morning person, but she was trying to be cordial and supportive of Glads. Small talk was not her forte. Just sitting here stuffing her face was almost more than she could bear.

"Thanks," Aunt Agatha said.

Glads did not appear to be well. Her bearing was off. She hunched over the table, staring into space, and her eyes were rimmed in dark circles. Summer's heart went out to her. What would it be like to be accused of killing someone when you hadn't done it? Especially after one of your best friends had been murdered?

"How are you doing, Glads?" Summer said.

Glads reached up and tucked a strand of hair behind her ear. "I'm afraid I'm guilty."

"What?" Aunt Agatha and Summer said together.

"I mean, I gave her the poison. There's no getting around that." Her voice trembled.

"Yes, but you didn't know it was poison." Summer slid her plate away from her face and reached for the hot cup of coffee.

"That's true." Glads sat up a bit. "But it's hard to prove, right?"

"You've got a great lawyer working with you," Aunt Agatha said.

She nodded. "Cash is awesome."

"Where did the poison come from?" Summer asked,

"I've been thinking about that. I think it came from Lana. She gave me the tea, you see. She handed me a tea bag and asked me to make her a cup of tea."

Summer's heart sped up. How could they prove that? It was almost as if someone had set Glads up. She didn't believe for one minute that Lana had killed herself intentionally, not after reading parts of her journal.

"That's also hard to prove," Aunt Agatha said. "But we will."

"What about the cup?"

"It was her cup. I mean, it was her second cup of tea, so I just reused it."

"Was it a cup from the store?'

Glads nodded. "Yep."

That was the part that boggled Summer's mind. A cup from the store. So if the poison had been in the actual cup and not the tea, someone had to have placed it there in the store. And how would they know that was the cup Lana would use? It made no sense. "I'm sure we can puzzle this out. It would really help if we had the video of the event. Poppy is having a hard time getting another copy. The first one never came through."

Summer caught a glimmer of hope in Glads's eyes. "Fingers crossed she actually gets it. It would help in a lot of ways. I'd love to see it."

"Wouldn't we all?" Agatha stood and gathered the dirty plates.

Mr. Darcy waddled into the room and turned around in an awkward bird dance. "Cock-a-doodle-doo!"

The three women laughed, and the room broke into another mood. Not joyous, but less strained.

"Are you going in today?" Aunt Agatha asked Summer.

"I don't think I will. It's just so exhausting with the crutches. Is Mia available to help at the bookstore? Today is Saturday, right?"

"I believe she's already planning on it. But she and her boyfriend are going out to a Valentine's dinner tonight, and Piper isn't too thrilled about that."

"Oh boy," Glads said.

"What are you going to do today?" Agatha asked Glads.

She shrugged. "I don't know. I've been told to stay away from Beach Reads until this all blows over."

"Stay here with me," Summer said. "We can hang out all day."

For the first time since Glads had come into the house, she cracked a smile. "Okay."

* * *

The doorbell rang, and Darcy vaulted toward the door, as he usually did when he was out of his cage.

Agatha moved toward the door and shooed him away. She opened the door. "Good morning, Detective. Please come in. Can I get you some coffee?"

"That would be great, thanks." The detective followed her into the kitchen. He smiled at Summer and nodded, then glimpsed Glads. The smile vanished. "What is she doing here?"

"She is sitting right there and can speak for herself," Summer said. It was a phrase she'd used often in academic settings in regard to herself.

Glads shrugged. "I'm visiting my friends."

"Friends?"

"I've known Glads my whole life, Detective."

"Well, it might not be a good thing to have her here while she's being investigated." His patronizing tone annoyed Summer.

"That's absurd," Agatha said. "She's a dear friend. And we all know she didn't kill Lana."

His eyebrows lifted. "Do we?"

"I'm going to ask you to leave," Summer said. "If you are going to make accusations against Glads, you won't be doing it standing in my kitchen."

He reddened, stiffened, and cleared his throat. "Fine. I'll go."

Chapter
Twenty-Seven

"I didn't mean to bring you any trouble," Glads said.

"You are not the trouble," Agatha said. "That detective was out of line."

"You're free to go where you want and talk with who you want, including me," Summer said.

Summer's phone buzzed. Poppy's name came up. "Hello?"

"Check the site now. Your video is live."

"Thanks, Poppy." Summer told Poppy she wouldn't be in to work. It had worked out well, anyway—she could stay home and review the video.

"Mia's coming in, so that shouldn't be a problem."

"Thanks for everything, Poppy."

"No worries, boss."

They hung up. "Can you bring me that laptop?" Summer asked Agatha. "The video of the event is live on the website. Hopefully, we can spot something that will help you out."

Agatha brought the laptop in and set it on the table. Summer turned it on and clicked until she found the right page.

Glads and Agatha scooted their chairs over to see the video.

The video started in the minutes before the event and showed the crowd on film. Summer's eyes scanned over every person standing, sitting, trying to find a seat. She spotted the regulars. And her half brother and half sister. But no menacing figures appeared. Except maybe Bo, the crystal and CBD seller, who looked a little dirty and rumpled. Stoned, but not really menacing. He always appeared stoned. He couldn't be that stoned all the time, could he?

What did a poisoner look like?

The camera panned to Lana holding a cup of tea. "That's her first cup," Glads said.

Then the camera pulled away for another crowd scene. A young woman had slipped in. Summer recognized her but wasn't sure from where. The woman turned, and for a brief moment, Summer spotted her backpack.

She stopped the video.

"What is it?" Glads asked.

"That young woman right there." Summer's heart thudded against her ribs.

She reversed the video.

"Yes? What about her?" Agatha said.

"She was in the store the day before the event. Do either of you know her?" Summer pointed at the screen.

"No, I've never seen her before," Agatha responded.

"I remember seeing her that day. She's kind of unusual looking," Glads said.

"I saw her with a book about poisonous plants," Summer said.

The women went silent.

"I think you should call Cash," Agatha said.

"I just texted him. He'll be right over," Glads said. "This is good news."

"Okay, let's watch the rest and see what happens." Summer clicked, and the film moved forward.

The young woman sat down, and the camera went back to panning the crowd. A hush came over the room as Poppy took the stage.

The camera zoomed in on Lana. Glads was next to her. Lana handed Glads the cup, and Glads moved off-camera.

"There. I was right. She gave me the cup."

"Okay, let's scroll back and see if we can see someone talking with her or, I don't know, standing near her before this." Agatha's bony finger pointed to the screen.

Summer did so.

"There! Stop!"

Lana was gazing up and talking with someone. But the person was just offscreen. There was a brief, grainy shadow over her. Her cup was in her hand. Then she set it on the table. A shadow moved across it. Summer blinked. The shadow's hand appeared to move toward the cup.

"I don't know. It looks like that might be our killer," Agatha said.

"I can't say for sure." Chills moved through Summer. Could they save Glads with a shadow?

"It's not enough," Glads said.

"In order to convict you of murder, the evidence has to be so solid that nobody has a doubt against your guilt. This will definitely plant some seeds of doubt," Summer said.

"I think we need to find out who that young woman is too." Agatha said. "But how?"

Summer mulled over what records she might have of that day. "I know! Here's what I can do."

The doorbell rang.

"Come in!" she yelled.

Cash entered the room.

"We've got good news!" Glads said. "Have a seat."

He pulled up a chair, and they showed him the video.

"Interesting. This is good. Very good for your case," he said.

"Summer? What were you saying before he came in?" Glads said.

"I'm going to examine sales records for that day. It may not give me exactly what I need, but it's a start. I'll go through and eliminate all the people I know, plus those who've been at events before. That should give us a list of people not known by the system. I hope that list will give us the name of our killer."

Cash's eyebrows went up. "That'd be some great detective work." He paused. "I can take your list and run it through the system for anybody with a criminal record."

Glads's face crumpled, and she let out a sob. "Is it too much to hope for?" She leaned on the table.

Cash's hand covered hers. "It's going to be all right. I mean, look at your legal team. You can't lose."

For the second time that day, Glads cracked a smile. "I think I'll celebrate with a second cup of coffee."

Chapter Twenty-Eight

Summer sat at the kitchen table with her leg propped up on another chair. At least she was sitting, not lying on the couch. She had begun the tedious work of checking the sales on the day of the Romance by the Sea event.

Glads was in the living room with her nose in a book and Mr. Darcy on her lap.

Summer rubbed her eyes. The screen was taking its toll on them. After deleting 57 sales to familiar people or longtime customers, she still had 134 names. She was searching for a woman. She deleted the men's names and still had 98 women to study. But she sent the list of all the names, both men and women, to Cash.

She yawned. Her medicine was catching up with her. Maybe she should take a nap.

No. She studied the female names on her list. None of them looked familiar to her at all. What should she do next?

She could key each one into Google to see if she could find the young woman she was searching for. That might take a couple of days. But maybe Cash's running of the names through the system would land something faster.

She decided to break it down into groups of ten. She'd search for ten names now, then take a nap.

She keyed in the first name. Ann Yardley's name led her to a Facebook page. Nope, that wasn't her person. Next was Jen Pippins. Nope, not her either.

It struck Summer how odd it was to just be able to research anybody on social media. Powerful. And scary.

She continued with her search, and the first ten led her nowhere. None of them even resembled the young woman she was looking for. She yawned, lifted her leg from the chair, and made her way to the couch—without crutches. How about that?

Mr. Darcy and Glads were snoozing in the La-Z-Boy. Summer lay down, wondering when she'd be healed enough to sleep in her own bed. She didn't love having a sprained ankle or having to sleep on the couch, but she did love afternoons like this. It felt like a snow day. The need to stay home allowed her to work on what she wanted, when she wanted. Time seemed to stretch before her—not like during the grind of the workweek, where time slipped by so quickly that it was kind of scary, really.

Time. What an odd thing.

She drifted off thinking about time, names on a screen, and how cute Mr. Darcy looked cuddled up next to Glads. She dreamed about the woman with the white-blond hair and almost-black eyes. In her dream, the woman was on the beach in a white gauzy dress, sun and surf behind her. The water glistened, and gentle waves came in. She walked along the beach barefoot, the water kissing her toes as she walked along.

"What do you know about poison?" Summer asked her in the dream.

The woman just laughed and twirled about, the sun's rays playing around her body. Summer grabbed her. "I hate to stop you from twirling, but my friend Glads is in trouble."

"Let me go!" The woman screamed—a shrill, high-pitched scream. Summer sat up.

What was that?

It had stopped.

Glads and Darcy were gone from their seats. How long had she been sleeping?

"Did the teakettle wake you? I'm sorry. I tried to get to it quickly." Glads held a cup of tea in her hands. "Want some?"

"Sure." Summer lay back down and considered her dream. That young woman was unusual looking. She remembered her vividly. She never forgot a face. She also remembered how awkwardly the young woman appeared to move. It was as if she was uncomfortable in her own skin. Odd.

Glads left and soon reentered the room with Summer's cup of tea. "Should you be taking another pill?"

"I think in another hour. I'm feeling pretty good and might not take it."

"I would. You need to stay on top of the pain." Glads sat down in the Lazy Boy. "I had a great nap. I dreamed about your mom. She was telling me that everything was going to be all right. And she handed me a cookie." Glads laughed.

Summer laughed a little too. "Such stuff that dreams are made of. If she were here, I'm sure she'd be baking up such great cookies right now."

Glads became serious. "But she is here. Can't you feel it? I mean, granted, she won't be baking cookies, but I feel her strongly here and at the store."

Summer didn't know what to say. She had tried hard to not feel her mom the way Glads suggested. But she couldn't deny that every word Glads said was true.

*　*　*

Twenty names into her search, Summer was starting to worry that this might be a waste of her time. She had to set aside the laptop.

Glads shut her book. "Well, that was a good one." She appeared as satisfied as a cat with a full belly. She curled up in the chair. She might start purring any minute.

"I wish I could say the same thing." Summer slid the laptop farther away from her. "This is tedious work. I'd never make a detective."

"Some people love it."

"I don't get it."

The room fell silent for a few minutes, then Glads let off a huge sigh. "What should I read next?"

"There's plenty of books around here." Summer gestured all over the room.

"Oh! This looks interesting." Glads stood up and walked toward Lana's stuff. There was a stack of books along the wall. Cash had arranged them neatly and left the clothes in a pile in the box.

"Those are books that Lana had. All of that stuff is Lana's."

Glads stopped in her tracks.

"You may as well take them. I don't think the police even know they're here. For some reason, all of Lana's stuff was sent here."

Glads lifted one book. She turned it over to read the back, and the front cover opened, sending something flying out of the book. Glads gasped. "What is that?"

"What is what?" Summer twisted herself around so she could see. Glads picked up a sizable bag filled with white powder.

Summer's head spun. Drugs! Lana had been carrying drugs.

"Glads, put that down. We'll need to call the police." Summer's mind raced. The police? Was that the right thing to do? "No. Maybe we should call Cash first."

Glads placed the bag back into the book. "What have I gotten myself into?"

"Nothing, Glads. You were just looking for a book."

"My prints are all over this stuff. If Connor finds them, he'll twist things round."

Would he? Summer was beginning to be annoyed by this detective. She had assumed annoying detectives were the stuff of fiction. Evidently not.

She reached for her phone and pressed Cash's number. No answer. She left a message. "Cash, please come over as soon as you can."

Aunt Agatha walked through the door with bags of groceries. "Hello."

Summer said a stiff hello, and Glads nodded.

"What on earth is going on here?"

"We found drugs in Lana's books."

"Found what in where?" Agatha dropped the bags.

"In here," Glads said, still holding the book as if it were a bomb.

"Well, for goodness' sake, put it down, Glads!" Agatha moved forward and took the book out of her hand. She set it with the others. "What about the rest?"

"We don't know. We've called Cash. I didn't know whether to call him or the police."

"Good move. He'll know what to do." She took Glads by the elbow. "You need to sit down."

But before Agatha could get her to a chair, Glads wobbled to the floor and passed out. Summer stood and hobbled quickly to the kitchen to get an ice pack and some water, pain shooting in circles around her ankle. This was not good. But she pressed on.

When she entered the living room, Glads was stretched out on the floor with Agatha cradling her head and shoulders.

Summer set the ice pack down next to her and handed Agatha the water. Glads drank from the cup and reached over for the ice pack. Summer pressed it to Glads's head and patted her with her other hand. "Glads?"

Glads groaned.

The doorbell rang.

"Come in," Summer yelled. None of them could quite get to the door.

In walked Cash again. "What the heck is going on here?"

"Glads passed out." Agatha still held her.

"I see that, but is this why you called? Should I get an ambulance?" he asked.

"No. She'll be fine. She had a fright." Summer paused. "And that's why we called you."

"Let's sit you up," Agatha said to Glads. She propped her up and tried to give her more water. Glads wasn't having it.

"What's going on?" Cash said.

Summer, still standing, hobbled over to the couch, and Cash followed her. "Should you be on that foot?"

Summer shot him a glare. "No." She sat down. "Glads was seeking something to read and started going through Lana's books over there, and a bag of white powder dropped onto the floor. We assume it's drugs. Cocaine?"

Cash's blue eyes widened. "What?"

She nodded. "And Glads touched it because it came out of the book she was reading. So she's frightened it will be another thing that detective will use against her."

Cash's hand's went to his forehead. "Okay. We need to call the police. It's unfortunate, because then we'll have to explain why all the stuff is here."

"It was sent here. It's not like we stole it."

"You're right. It's just that this whole thing is so strange. So much of it doesn't make sense." He started pacing. "But if there are drugs involved, that could answer a lot of questions." He paused. "Unfortunately, those answers are not good."

"What do you mean?"

"I mean she was accused of poisoning her husband, but he died by an overdose of morphine."

Summer's heart plummeted. "What does morphine look like in powder form?"

"I don't even know." He lurched back. "How would I know? I've never taken any kind of drug."

"Well, that's BS, and you know it."

"What? We smoked pot a few times. That was it. And now it's legal."

"If you two lovebirds are finished, what's the next step?" Agatha said as she helped Glads to the Lazy Boy.

Summer's face heated, and Cash's turned red. He crossed his arms.

"We're calling the police," Cash finally said. "I have no idea what else to do. I'm glad you called me, though."

"He's going to use this against me, isn't he?" Glads said in a weak voice.

"He'll try, but we have witnesses, correct?" Just like that, Cash's flustered red face turned into something else. Summer understood him well. She wondered if anybody else noticed the tiny beads of sweat on his temple.

Chapter Twenty-Nine

C hief Ben Singer was not happy to be here. He'd tried to retire twice over the past few years and hadn't been able to manage it. He'd taken some time off to deal with his cancer, but that was as far as it had gotten. He'd never been a fan of Summer's, but he adored her mom, Hildy, and he'd gotten nicer to Summer over the past few years. Age softened those hard edges in people sometimes, and Summer held no pretense that the man actually liked her. But she understood his hard edges had long since gone.

"Well, I've never seen anything like this before," he said.

"Me either," Cash replied.

Ben eyed Glads. "How are you holding up?"

She looked away and shrugged.

The two of them had known each other their whole lives. Ben, the person, not the police officer, was concerned about her. Such was the double-edged sword, sometimes, of small-town-on-a-small-island life.

"Okay, so forensics is coming in and bagging up everything. I'll make a note that you all have handled everything." Ben gazed at his son, Cash, and shook his head. "Why did you leave the stuff here?"

"This is where it was sent." Cash lifted his chin the way he'd done for as long as Summer had known him. It happened when he thought he might be in trouble, like he was girding his loins, letting the world know with that chin that he'd done nothing wrong. If you thought so, you would be in for a battle.

His focus went to Summer, who had stood up on her crutches to watch over everything. "Why was it sent here?"

"I have no idea. I talked with Tina, and she said those were her instructions."

"Tina? Owner of the B and B?" he asked, as if there were more than one Tina on the island.

"Yes," Summer replied.

He nodded. His eyes moved from Summer to Glads to Cash, then to Agatha. "Anything else you need to tell me?"

Agatha crossed her arms and rolled her eyes, indifferent to Ben and his questions.

Cash shifted his weight, and Summer sweated profusely. She'd done nothing wrong, wasn't hiding any evidence, and certainly hadn't hurt anybody—so why did he make her feel as if she had?

From the looks of things, Cash might be feeling the same way.

"I don't think so," Cash said. "We've just trying to do the right thing. By the book."

"If it was by the book, son, you'd have turned this all over to the authorities when it was sent here."

Cash gave a little shrug. "I think the police studied all this when it was at the B and B and sent it over. I didn't know there were drugs in those books. I just figured it was a bunch of books. Come on, Dad."

"All right. Here comes the forensics team. I want you all to cooperate. It's what's best for Glads. Do you understand?"

"Of course we do, Ben," Agatha snapped at him.

Ben walked away from the group to welcome the forensic team from Raleigh.

Summer swung her way over to the couch. Cash, Glads, and Agatha followed. Her borrowed laptop was on the coffee table. her list next to it. Names had been crossed off with red ink. Summer loved her red pens.

"What's all this?" Cash asked.

"This is my way of finding a needle in a haystack, though I fear my attempt is futile."

"You sent me the names, and we're running them through the system. I considered that the end of it."

"No. I spotted someone the day before Lana's death who had a book on poisons. She was also at the event. I surmised she might be the shadow in our video. I mean, she had a book about poisons sticking out of her backpack. I've been going through the list and checking social media to try to find her, but nothing so far."

He leaned in. "Let's keep your work on the down-low. I appreciate your help. But Dad and his ilk would not."

"So, like, you have a secret assistant?" Glads whispered with glee.

Cash's eyes caught Summer's, and he flushed. "Indeed."

"That sounds like a fun game," Agatha said drolly. "But Summer, you've got an ankle to heal, and it's almost time for your pain medication. How are you feeling?"

"Okay. Do you think I need to take it ? It's not hurting that bad, really."

"Take it anyway, so it won't hurt you in the middle of the night."

"I'm going to head out," Cash said. "Are you okay, Glads?"

"I'll be fine," she said. "I'm worried, but anybody would be, right?"

"Right. Catch you all later." Cash turned and left the room.

Glads sighed. "There goes one of the good guys."

"One of the best," Summer said.

"Not bad looking, either," Agatha said. "Now, what can we eat? How about I order pizza?"

Summer nodded and continued thinking about Cash being good looking and one of the good guys. Not for the first time, she wondered if she'd make a mistake by standing him up at the altar. It was a cruel thing to do. She hated that she'd done it. But she had been so young and foolish. She'd had odd ideas about the world, about her life and the way she wanted to live. She didn't think her career would be enhanced by being married. She wanted to be a professor and a writer. Love was a distraction. It often kept women from living up to their true potential. She wouldn't have that.

But now that she was getting older, maybe she was softening too. She'd been observing that people and relationships were more important than anything—even a career in academics. Perhaps especially a career in academics.

Back then, she'd had no idea how hard it would be to be taken seriously as a woman. It was still true in academia, even now. And she understood it wasn't just women. She'd witnessed the way others were marginalized as well.

But she'd had no plan to give up teaching and writing until her mom's death. Being back home, among people who loved and (mostly) respected her, had been a shock to her system. She'd begun to peel back layers of herself that had been so tightly woven before.

She'd had the wrong idea as a young feminist. You didn't have to give up relationships to be taken seriously in this world. She now realized that if that was expected, it wouldn't be worth it.

Still, things were what they were now. She was thirty-nine years old, and she had planned on being in Staunton her whole life. Now she was home, in the thick of it, and finding herself loving Beach Reads and everything it stood for—which was exactly what Hildy had wanted. Peace. Love. Stardust.

Chapter Thirty

After everyone had settled into their collective bedroom and couch spaces, Summer shifted some of her things around on the table. She chastised herself for not getting further on her search for the woman. Oh well, tomorrow was another day.

She spotted the journal. Uh-oh. That probably should have been added to the pile Ben took with him. She'd call tomorrow and let him know.

In the meantime, why not read it?

I'll always remember your proposal. It wasn't anything grand or fancy. It was like us: real, charming, and heartfelt. I'll never forget the look on my dad's face when you asked for my hand, nor will I forget the music that was playing in the background.

Oh! He'd asked her father for his acceptance. Some would find that a sweet gesture, but Summer cringed. Women had their own minds and didn't need their father's blessing. It hearkened back to the day when women were basically owned by their fathers, then their husbands. Summer turned the page.

My father didn't hesitate. He loved you almost as much as I did. Of course, you two were so alike. Your compassion, especially toward animals, your love of the opera, your humility. The way you both enjoyed single-malt after dinner. To me, it all spoke of another time—one I longed for. Times I have tried to recreate in my writing. When respect was popular. Compassion was admired, not made fun of, like it is today.

Summer blinked. She'd made all sorts of assumptions about Lana. It turned out that many of them just weren't true. How often in her life had she done that? Too often. Too, too often.

When my father died, you grieved as much as I did. And we spoke openly and honestly about life and death and the things we wanted. And what we did not want. Neither of us wanted to burden the other.

Summer's heart almost stopped. But then the narrative changed.

We rarely fought, you and me. There was the conversation about suicide and such, where you made me swear to never hurt myself, no matter what. Then there was the conversation about your children. I insisted they treat you well. You allowed them to run all over you. You gave them everything and they gave you nothing. I wanted to love them. But their actions prohibited it. After that fight, I vowed not to bring them up again. And I haven't. It almost killed me to keep my mouth shut (very difficult for me, as you know).

Summer smiled. She knew that feeling. She rarely refrained from voicing her opinion, but when she did, it hurt. Almost as bad as really biting her tongue.

And then there was the conversation about Hildy.

Summer gasped. Out loud. *Hildy?* Her mother? She then remembered the note in her mother's little red book: *Lana is no friend of mine.*

I still think you had a thing for her. To this day, she's not invited me back to Beach Reads. She claims she was hurt by my accusations. But really, would she or you have admitted to any of it? I doubt it. I know you'd do anything to spare my feelings. But Hildy? She collected men as if they were toy soldiers. Or some other kind of trinket.

Summer groaned. That wasn't quite true, but she could see how someone might think it was. Hildy had probably never loved anyone the way she loved Omar, the father Summer had never met.

Some people could bounce back from heartbreak and move on. Hildy, however, had been deeply affected by what had happened in her youth with Omar. This was all new to Summer. She hadn't known their story until recent years, after her mother's and Omar's deaths. He'd gone on to marry and have the family that was expected of him. And Hildy had raised their daughter on the other side of the island.

Hildy had a bevy of admirers throughout her life. But she'd never fallen in love again—not that Summer perceived, anyway. It hurt Summer to think about it. Her mother had never loved again. She'd been alone in her life until the day she died.

A sharp pang tore through Summer's chest, moved through her throat, and escaped as a sob. Was she doing that in her own life? Why had she never had a successful romantic relationship? What was she running from? Was she carrying the curse of her parents' failed relationship?

"Summer? Are you okay?" Aunt Agatha was coming down the stairs.

Summer reached for a tissue and blew her nose. "I was just thinking of Mom and Omar." She'd not tell her aunt that she was making connections to her own life. It was too raw.

"Oh." Summer's parents' love for each other was a sore point with Agatha, who'd never known about the relationship her sister had that had resulted in Summer. "What brought that up?"

"Lana's journals sort of did." Summer closed it. "Turns out that Lana accused her husband of having a thing for Mom."

"Oh, he did."

"What?"

"Yes, but that was years before he met Lana. They dated for a few months, I remember." Agatha sat down on the couch at Summer's feet. "And I remember that for some reason your mom didn't invite her back. I wondered if she was aware of their dating history and made some accusations."

Summer nodded. "Evidently."

"As you know, your mom kept her love life sort of secretive. Part of the reason was you. She was protective of you and didn't want to confuse you. She'd never bring around a man, because she didn't want you to get attached. She never had any intention of ever marrying, I suppose." Her voice drifted off.

"She didn't tell you about my father because she was protective of you as well," Summer said. It was true. Her parents' relationship had carried deep, dark secrets, and Hildy had figured that the fewer people who were aware, the better.

Agatha nodded, tears forming. Soon she stood and went off to bed. "Good night."

"Good night, Aunt Agatha."

Summer continued to read the journal until she fell asleep. She drifted off into dreams of a young Hildy and Omar walking along a beach with the sun setting in the background, streams of crimson and blue jetting across the sky. Sand beneath bare feet and waves rushing in their ears. Him embracing her in a dance with the sea, sunset, and salty air.

Chapter
Thirty-One

Summer awakened with a feeling of contentment, even though her ankle was throbbing. "Good morning, Summer!" Darcy squawked.

"I'm sorry I slept in a bit. You need medicine, I'm sure." Agatha stood by the couch. Summer blinked, hazy from her dream and sleep.

"I was dreaming so deeply about Mom." She took the pill and water from Agatha and downed her medicine.

"I think I've dreamed of her every night since she died," Agatha said. "Grief is odd, isn't it?"

Summer nodded. She caught a whiff of something sweet. "What do I smell?"

"Glads baked blueberry muffins."

"Smells divine." Summer struggled to sit up. Agatha handed her the crutches. "I'm going to need some of those muffins. And I know you're going to make me work for them."

Agatha grinned. "You got to keep working at it, Summer. Keep moving."

Summer grabbed the crutches and hefted her way up. She had never been graceful, not like the long, lean Piper. She was shorter, rounder, and had never been able to dance well. She imagined a taller, lithe woman would have no problem with these crutches.

She gasped when she entered the kitchen. Glads had made more muffins than a dozen of them could eat for breakfast. There were muffins on the counter, muffins on the table, muffins on top of the refrigerator and on the stove. "Glads, what's going on with the muffins?"

"Have some. They are pretty good. I found some frozen blueberries, and I figured I should use them all."

She was nearly covered in flour, and her eyes were bright and excited. She set a cup of steaming coffee in front of Summer and a plate of muffins on the table, butter and jam at hand.

"Some people drink when they're stressed," she finally said. "I bake. It helps me to think."

Agatha giggled. "You are a dear. We love you so much, Glads. But my goodness, you are a messy baker!"

Glads laughed too. "That I am. But I also love to clean after I bake. I know it's not a cool thing to admit. Most people don't like to clean."

"Mom loved doing dishes," Summer said. "She said it was meditative for her."

"It also helped her get away from crazy family situations." Agatha sat at the table. "She'd be the one who cleaned up and did the dishes, and she realized nobody else would help."

"Not you?" Glads asked.

"Good god, no," she replied. "I despise cleaning. Always have. You know God doesn't give you cleaning genes just because you're a woman."

"Amen!" Summer cracked open a still-warm muffin and spread butter on each side. Bit into one half. The blueberry flavor popped in her mouth—Glads hadn't been stingy with the berries—and the light dough had an interesting texture and flavor, almost tangy, like cheese. She swallowed a bit. "Glads, what do you put into the dough? These something else in it . . ."

"You've got great taste buds. I used a little cream cheese. It just adds a bit of something to it."

"Hmmm. Yes!"

"To Glads's muffins!" Agatha held up her coffee in a toast.

"Indeed!" Summer met her toast with gusto.

*　*　*

Later, as Glads cleaned the kitchen, Summer sat at the table, finishing off the coffee of the morning, and plunged into the research of finding the young woman with the white hair and black eyes. Lord, this was tedious, but she was able to find enough details on some of these people to make it interesting from time to time.

One person listed taxidermy as a hobby. Really? Ewww.

Another person was a champion ballroom dancer.

One woman was a preacher at a local church. Interesting. Summer had gone to church when she lived in Staunton, but she hadn't done so since her mom died and she'd returned to the island. Maybe, when her ankle healed, she'd check out this preacher and her church. After all, she'd been to Beach Reads and had purchased nearly seventy-five dollars' worth of books.

But none of these people were the woman Summer was seeking. Gah!

Her doorbell rang, and Agatha headed for the door.

"Oh," she squealed. "Roses!"

"Roses?" It struck Summer that today was Valentine's Day and she had completely forgotten.

"Oh my lord! They are gorgeous!"

Well, someone must have purchased some flowers for her aunt. How sweet. Summer's heart burst with joy for her, and at the same time she wondered if she'd ever have romance in her life again.

"Summer! Would you look at these?" Agatha said as she moved into the room. She placed the box of roses down on the table. Summer counted a dozen yellow roses. Yellow?

"Why would he get you yellow roses? Shouldn't they be red?"

"They aren't for me," said Agatha. "They're for you."

"Me?" Who on earth would send her flowers? "Who sent them? Give me that card!"

She opened the envelope to handwriting she didn't recognize. "'Dear Summer, I want to bury the hatchet and get to know you. Please give me a chance. Liam.' *Liam?*"

"The detective?" Aunt Agatha and Glads both squealed.

Summer flushed with embarrassment and anger rolled into one. "How inappropriate. Of all the people I'd like to get to know, what makes him think it would be him? Absolutely not."

"I have to say, he's thoroughly unlikable," Glads said quietly.

"Maybe so," Aunt Agatha said. "But he's hot."

"Aunt Agatha!"

"I may be old, but I'm not dead."

"Throw them away," Summer said.

"I certainly will not. They are gorgeous. Why shouldn't we enjoy them?" Glads agreed. "And if I were you, I'd pretend you never got them."

"Okay. Do whatever you want with them."

Agatha dug around in the cupboard until she found a suitable vase. "This ought to do it."

She arranged the roses in a pretty display. Summer had to admit they were beautiful. "The audacity."

"Well, at least they aren't red, because that would be even more presumptuous," Glads said.

"Indeed," Aunt Agatha said.

The doorbell rang again.

"It's like Grand Central Station here today," Agatha said, as Glads went to answer the door.

Summer heard muttering and then spotted Glads ushering Cash in. He was dressed in jeans and a soft blue cable-knit sweat that nearly matched his eyes.

"Would you like a muffin?" Summer asked. "We have fifty-two thousand muffins."

"What?" Confusion played on his face.

Summer nodded in Glads's direction. "She bakes when she's stressed."

He lifted an eyebrow. "Sure! I love blueberry muffins."

"Have a seat," Summer said. "I'm in the middle of my research and haven't found the girl with the white hair and black eyes yet."

He set a package on the table. It was a white box with a red ribbon.

"What's that?" Summer asked, half looking at her computer screen, where she had Lacy Andrew's Facebook profile pulled up. Lacy was a budding romance writer who lived in Savannah. Wow, she'd come a long way to be at the Romance by the Sea book event.

"It's for you." Cash pushed it toward her.

"Hmm?"

He reached over and shut the laptop. "I said, it's for you." There was an edge in his voice. "You and the damn computer."

"I'm trying to help." She paused, then looked at him and the package. "You brought it for me? I don't understand."

"What's so hard to understand, Summer? The man brought you a gift on Valentine's Day," Agatha snapped. She and Glads stood behind him.

"Right?" he said, and grinned up at them. "Now maybe you two should find something else to do."

Summer's face heated. *No*, she wanted to say, *please stay*. What was going on here? Her heart thudded against her rib cage.

Both women scurried away, but not without Aunt Agatha giving her the glance that said *I told you so.*

"Open it, please," he said in a light tone, as if it were nothing to buy the woman who'd stood him up at the altar years ago a gift on Valentine's Day. (Valentines' Day, of all days!)

"Sure," she said, matching his tone.

It took her a moment to unwrap it. She lifted the lid and unfolded the red tissue. It was a book. Not just any book. A Shakespeare folio of *Romeo and Juliet*. This must have cost him a slight fortune. Tears sprang unwillingly to her eyes. "How lovely, Cash. I don't know . . . I mean, thank you."

"No. Thank you."

"For what? I don't understand."

"Your friendship. I don't know how I could have gotten through the past few years without you."

"Oh, Cash—"

"I mean it. And we're both grown up now. When we were kids—I loved you. But now I see that you were right to go away."

"What do you mean?" She could hardly breathe.

"I never would've worked out then. I wasn't ready for you, for the responsibility of marriage—or any kind of relationship, really. I just need you to know that, even though for years I harbored resentment for you, I don't think I'd ever stopped loving you. But I've finally found peace. Peace in our friendship."

Summer's heart bloomed in little fireworks. She nodded. "I feel the same way. I cherish our friendship. I was so young and foolish. I've thought about you and us over the years."

His eyebrows hitched. "I guess I'm surprised to hear that." He grinned. "But I'm also flattered."

She smiled and reached for his hand. Warmth spread from his hand to hers.

"Let's put it all behind us," he said. "Could we start again?"

"I'm confused. We have started again, as friends. Right?"

"I mean more than that. I'd like to . . . you know . . . date you. In fact, I'd kind of like to kiss you right now."

"Right n—"

His mouth was on hers in a split second. She wanted to pull away, but her lips would not let her.

Chapter Thirty-Two

After the kiss, Summer's mouth couldn't find words. Her mouth hung open in an effort to find them. *Close your mouth, Summer. You must look like an idiot sitting here with your mouth hanging open.*

"Will you think about it?" Cash finally said.

She nodded. Yes, yes, she could at least nod.

"Where did the flowers come from?" he asked, as if he'd just spotted them.

Summer licked her lips and took a drink of water. "The flowers came from the detective."

"What? Are you—?"

"Calm down. No. I'm not. I considered it highly inappropriate and wanted to throw them away, but Glads and Aunt Agatha insisted on us enjoying them. They are pretty."

His jaw twitched. "You're right. It is highly inappropriate." He stood. "What made him think you'd even be interested?"

"I don't really know. In fact, the last time he was here, I asked him to leave." She shrugged.

Cash whipped his head to face her. "Why?"

"He was standing in my kitchen, accusing Glads."

"I don't like that guy," he said, after a beat. "There's something about him . . ."

"I know what you mean." There they were, talking as if they hadn't just kissed. As if he hadn't just turned Summer's world upside down. She watched as he studied the flowers and then looked back at her. "You should go out with him."

"What?" Summer snapped.

"Calm down. I mean, you could do a little undercover operation."

"Do you mean a keep-your-enemies-close kind of thing?"

"Yes. I don't like the idea of you going out with someone else, but it's a ruse. Maybe you could find out something about him or the case that might help Glads. I have an appointment tomorrow to show the video to the courts. I'm hoping that will be enough to get her off. But it couldn't hurt to have more information in our back pocket."

Summer's thoughts tumbled into one another. Could she do it? "I really don't want to spend more time with him than necessary."

"One date should do it."

"Okay. What kind of information do we want?"

"Anything."

"That's helpful."

"I mean it. You often don't know what you don't know until you need to know it."

Summer grinned. "Say that three times."

Glads walked in with a coffee cup. "Is there any more coffee?"

"A bit," Summer said.

She pointed at the flowers. "Summer has an admirer."

Cash's eyes went to Summer's. "Yes, yes she does."

After Cash left, Summer tried to get back to work on her list of people who'd made purchases at Beach Reads the day of Romance by the Sea, but focusing was difficult. Maybe she needed a nap. Maybe she needed another kiss. Given that the kisser was gone, she decided to hobble over to the couch and lie down.

She lay on the couch and ruminated about going out with Liam. It almost made her skin crawl. At first, she'd kind of liked him. And he was handsome. But then she'd found out how hard he'd been on Glads, followed by the incident with him in the kitchen.

She'd get as much information as she could from him and then drop him. After all, he didn't even live in the area. He was from Pennsylvania. Where exactly did he say? She'd forgotten.

Anyway, it wasn't like they could even have much of a relationship. Which made the whole thing ever odder. Perhaps he was seeking information from her as well. That made more sense.

If he wanted information, she'd give it to him. Oh yes, yes she would.

She lay on her side facing the coffee table, and her eyes landed on the journal. She'd forgotten to give it to Cash so he could take it to the police. Perhaps she could do it tomorrow. After all, today was Sunday. Not much was happening in the courts on a Sunday afternoon.

She reached for it and read from where she'd left off.

Of course, we didn't know then that you were probably sick by that point. That is the one thing that bothers me sometimes. If we'd found the cancer sooner, maybe you would have had a chance. But I'm working on letting it go. It tears me up. I'm trying to rewrite the story. Our story. I want a happy ending. I want a happy ending for you.

The man whose body brought so much joy to mine. The man who was so full of love and light and opinions and laughter and love of food and wine. This man who woke up next to me for almost 15 years.

This man now lies empty, kept alive by a tube. I don't know many things about life, it turns out. But I do know this man is not the same man. He left the body weeks ago. The man I knew wouldn't want this. I pray for mercy.
MERCY.

Summer's eyes blurred. She lay the book on her chest and drifted off to sleep.

"So?" Agatha stood over her.

Summer blinked awake.

"What's going on?"

"What do you mean?"

"With Cash."

"I can't really think about that right now," Summer said. "I agreed to go on a date with Liam."

"What?"

"You know, as a spy."

"Spy? That sounds dangerous."

Was it? They were going to be in public, Summer supposed. How dangerous could it be? He was a detective, and probably the only danger was that she'd spill the beans about something—who knew what. "I don't think so."

She just needed to get this over with, so she called him.

"Summer! It's so good to hear from you."

Butterfly tingles in her stomach. "Hi, Liam. I'm just calling to thank you for the flowers. They're beautiful."

"You're very welcome. That color reminds me of you. You were wearing a shirt that exact color when I first laid eyes on you."

Shirt? Oh, it was her pajama shirt, with yellow flowers all over it. She'd been on the couch—the first day of her twisted ankle. She didn't tell him that, though.

"I've been curious about you since then."

What, a week ago? Summer bit her tongue—which she didn't do often. *Think of Glads. Think of Glads.* "Really?"

"Yes. I know it's slightly inappropriate, since I'm investigating a murder case and your friend is the suspect, but I couldn't help it."

Oh boy.

"Are you available tonight?"

Might as well get this over with.

"Yes, but I do have a hurt ankle. So it will have to be an early dinner, you understand."

"Absolutely. See you at five thirty?"

"That sounds great," Summer said, and they hung up.

Could he really be that interested in her? Or was he playing some silly game? It must be the latter. Summer hadn't been looking her best since spraining her ankle. She hadn't ever been one for wearing a lot of makeup, but what little she wore certainly helped—and she hadn't had it on in days. It was all she could do to put on clothes and brush her hair.

"Are you really going out with him?" Glads walked into the kitchen.

"I'm spying on him. Don't worry; I have no interest in him. It was Cash's idea."

"Cash? Why? Is he not confident in my case?"

"Yes, he's pretty sure the video of the event will be enough to drop the charges. But we all just want to be sure. So I'm going to try to see if there's anything else we don't know about that they've twisted against you."

Glads's face softened. "Okay. I guess it won't be too bad for you."

"What do you mean?"

"He's not bad to look at." She grinned.

"No, indeed," Agatha said as she walked into the kitchen and sat down. "But how are you going to question him without him knowing? I mean, he is a detective."

"That's a good point." Glads sat down.

"I'm not going to be blatant about it."

"Well, good luck, and be careful."

* * *

Here she was, going out to dinner on Valentine's night. *The things I do for you, Cash. Going out with a man I don't like on a day I don't like.*

Wait. It wasn't really for Cash. It was for Glads, wrongly accused of murder. Yes, Summer could do this, and do it well, even with a hurt ankle.

They sat down to dinner at Ambrosia, a new Mediterranean restaurant. The place was packed with other couples who were eating early on Valentine's Day,

Some folks took a second glance at her. Was it the crutches? Or the fact that she was on a date? Or that she was with the detective everybody was talking about, according to Aunt Agatha?

She tried not to think about the pain in her ankle.

"How's the ankle?"

"Not good. But better."

"How did you do it?"

"I fell down the steps at Beach Reads. I'm not the most graceful, even though my mom made me take ballet. It didn't take."

He laughed. "Funny, my mom made me take ballet too."

"You?"

"And I loved it. I danced for years. In fact, dance was my first major in college."

Summer's mouth dropped.

He laughed again. "That is a typical reaction."

A ballet-dancing detective? She'd heard about athletes taking ballet, how much it helped them. But she had a hard time imagining it—and certainly had a hard time thinking of Liam leaping across the floor with pointed toes.

"Well, there's more to you than meets the eye, evidently," she said. "What other surprises do you have?"

"Ah, sorry. I think that's it. I still love ballet—watching it, not doing it. It's just such a beautiful form of storytelling. There's nothing like going to the ballet. Have you been?"

"Yes, once. Years ago. Cash and I went to a ballet in Raleigh."

"Cash? As in Cash Singer?"

"We dated many years ago." Shoot. She'd just told him something he could use against them. "Now we're friends, of course. That was over a long time ago."

As the word rolled off her lips—words she'd said many times to people over the past few years—she felt the lie in them. She hoped Liam didn't see it.

Chapter Thirty-Three

Summer ordered ravioli stuffed with pumpkin and Liam ordered lasagna. She never had been good at small talk, but she was capable enough to do it.

"So, where did you go to school? In Pennsylvania?"

"Yes, I went to Pitt." He sliced a piece of lasagna.

"Great school," Summer said. "What made you decide to become a detective?"

"I lost my brother when I was twenty. He was murdered."

Summer stopped chewing.

"It was devastating, of course. The police on his case were amazing. They were my heroes. I wanted to be like them." He fiddled with the food on his plate. "Even though they found his killer, grief is a funny thing, and it didn't really help with that."

"No." Summer understood exactly what he was talking about.

"On the one hand, it did give us some measure of resolution."

"Yes, I hear you." She paused. She didn't like to talk about her mom's death. But maybe opening up to him would allow him to trust her. "My mom . . ."

"I know. I remember reading about it."

The server came by and topped off their wine.

"So, do you specialize in murder?"

"Mostly, yes. I've investigated other violent crimes as well. I have a knack for it."

Did he? Summer made a mental note to research him. She mulled it over. He was on a personal mission for justice, that was clear. But had he jumped the gun before, like he was doing now with Glads? People on a mission were often tunnel visioned.

"So, do you think Lena killed her husband?" Summer took a drink of her wine. Fruity and light.

"I know she did. I know how she did it too. But there were complications in that case." He made a gesture with his hand. "I don't really want to talk about all that tonight."

Of course he didn't. But it was good to know about Lena. Summer hoped the journal would provide more clues to her husband's death. She seemed very much in love with him. But there was a fine line between love and hate.

"I don't think I'd make a good detective." Summer set her glass down. "I mean, so much of the work is tedious."

"True." He grinned. "But I have underlings that help with most of the tedious things. I used to do all of that. But no more."

Summer contemplated the list she was still going through to find the white-haired women with the black eyes—probably a task he'd reserve for his "underlings."

"There was a woman in the bookstore the day before the event. She wore a backpack, and in that backpack was a book about poison."

"And?"

"She also was at the event."

"And?"

"Have you seen the tape of the event? We turned it over to the police along with the drugs."

"Yes, I've seen it. Of course."

"The woman had white hair and big dark eyes. Do you remember seeing her?"

"I'd have to go back and look. But just because she had a book on poison doesn't mean she's our killer," he said with a condescending tone.

Summer held her tongue. "But it's worth considering."

"I don't know about that. I think we have our perp." His face reddened a bit.

"Glads is no killer."

He laughed. "If I had a dime for every time someone said that to me."

Summer gazed into her ravioli. "You saw the tape, and I think it's pretty clear someone else dropped something into her drink."

"Touché," he said, and lifted his glass. "A shadow means nothing. The world is full of them. Glads brought her the drink. Case closed."

He was making no sense at all and contradicting himself. Summer refrained from rolling her eyes. Bottom line: he believed Glads was the killer. It would have been sad if it weren't so maddening and dangerous for Glads. Summer held on to the shadow, but she wouldn't let him know. She wasn't a lawyer, but she understood that juries would convict a killer only if they had no doubt. She knew Cash and Glads were banking on that. Liam must know something else about the case—or Glads—that he wasn't revealing. What could it be?

She shrugged. "I hope you're wrong. I can't imagine Glads harming anybody. She's so kind."

"How well do you know her?"

"I've known her my whole life, and what's more, so did my mom. They were close. Glads had no reason to kill Lana. Where's your motive, Detective?"

His face reddened. "That's the one thing that trips me up. I have no idea why she did it."

Summer smiled.

"But I know she did it, and I'm never wrong."

Summer excused herself from the table. She couldn't take any more of his cockiness.

She went into the ladies' room and splashed a little water on her face, patted it off with a paper towel. What an arrogant ass.

She dialed Cash.

"Summer! Aren't you supposed to be on a date?"

"I'm in the restroom. He's just unpleasant."

"Have you learned anything?"

"He doesn't think the shadow across the film means anything."

"Well, he's wrong."

"He's cocksure of himself. He asked me how well I know Glads. Is there something we don't know about her?"

Cash didn't answer. Which told Summer everything she needed to know.

"Okay, well, whatever it is, I know it's not murder."

"Okay, you need to get back out there and charm him. Don't make him angry."

"Not sure I can do that."

"I'm sure you can."

Cash had faith in her. Was she screwing this up by allowing her true feelings about Glads to spill out? She took a deep breath, straightened her back. She'd go back in and charm Liam, all right.

Chapter Thirty-Four

When she returned to the table, he was smiling at her. "You are so pretty."

Summer's face heated. "Thank you."

"I just wanted to say, let's not talk about work anymore. The case. I just wanted a chance to get to know you. Everything I've heard about you fascinates me. Shakespearean scholar. Bookstore owner. Very interesting."

Nobody had ever considered her being a Shakespeare scholar interesting. At least not that she had sensed and not by any "regular people"—aka nonacademics.

"Oh, that's fine with me." She tried to sound flippant, as if that hadn't just hit her in the guts. Was he really interested in her Shakespeare work? Maybe he was. After all, he had been a ballet dancer and was more cultured than what she had first gleaned.

His phone buzzed. He pulled it out of his jacket and examined at it. He grimaced. "Excuse me, I have to take this." He stood and walked into the lobby area.

Could it be something happening with the case? Summer hoped it was someone telling him to back off of Glads.

Summer finished eating—why should she wait until he came back? She was still hungry, and it looked like he had gobbled down all his food while she was in the bathroom talking to Cash.

By the time he returned, she was finished.

"Dessert?" he asked.

"Certainly," she said.

They ordered dessert.

"Tell me about your passion for Shakespeare."

She filled him in on how she'd fallen in love with Shakespeare's words and ideas. How it had set her apart from most kids and many people even in college.

"It's fascinating to me how some people pick just one thing to focus on," he said. "My interests are too scattered."

She had other interests, all right. But she wasn't about to tell him about them. "What are your interests?"

"Well, I already mentioned ballet, the theater, and reading. I also love to run, meditate."

"Meditate?" He had to be the most interesting policeman she'd ever met. Not at all what she had expected.

"The job can get stressful. Meditation helps. And so does medication—which reminds me. Time to take my meds." He pulled out a pill bottle and searched for two different pills.

"Is it too personal for me to ask?"

"High blood pressure."

"But you're so young."

"Yeah. It's hereditary."

She couldn't keep her eyes from glancing at the finished chocolate cake.

"Diet doesn't really help. I know that's what they say. But when you inherit it, it doesn't matter what you do."

Summer didn't think that was true, but she was going to find out. "Both pills are for your high blood pressure?"

"Yes, for different aspects of it." He sat up and motioned for the server. "Can I get the check, please?"

Had she offended him?

"I hate to call this night over, but I have to tell you, I'm beat. Usually my medicine makes me even more tired. I know you need to get home as well."

"Yes, I do." Her ankle was holding up, surprisingly enough. But she did have to take her own meds and go to bed.

When Liam dropped Summer off at her house, she thanked him and exited the car. As she walked closer to the door, she spotted a basket full of Valentine's goodies. The mysterious Valentine's gifter was still at it. She lifted the basket and peeked inside. Honey cakes from the bakery, chocolates from the new store, a pink crystal from Bo's store, and candy hearts with a Valentine with no signature. Some things never changed.

* * *

Later, when Summer was tucked into her couch bed, she dialed Cash.

"Hi, Summer. How did it go?"

"Well, he was a perfect gentleman and kind of an interesting guy." She filled Cash in on the details. "There was one odd thing. He has high blood pressure and pulled out two pills and took them at the table. When I asked about them, he seemed . . . I don't know, impatient. Then he asked for the check."

"How old do you think he is?"

"Maybe forty. Maybe. He says it's hereditary."

"Medical records are private. I can't get in. But there may be something listed on his work records. If he had such high blood pressure, his bosses would have to be alerted to it."

"Of course, this has nothing to do with the case."

"No. But I'm beginning to think our detective has some issues. Maybe exposing him will get him to back off Glads."

"He's definitely not going to stop. He said that shadow meant nothing at all."

"He would say that. But I've seen cases dropped for less than that."

Summer's heart cracked open with hope, just a bit. "Oh, there was one more thing. He's fairly certain there's something I don't know about Glads's past. What could that be?"

Cash paused. "If you want to know more, you should ask her. It's not my story to tell."

"Okay." Summer respected that. Evidently there was something in Glads's history that both Cash and Liam were aware of. But did she really want to know? Would it change her mind? She didn't think it would. Not only was Glads her friend, but she'd been one of her mom's best friends since they were young. Hildy was definitely a better judge of character than Summer. Summer had always known her mom wouldn't let harm come to herself or her child due to trusting the wrong people.

If only Summer had that skill. She'd wished for it many times. Now, more than ever, Liam seemed like a nice, hardworking detective. What she couldn't resolve was how he could be so adamant in his disregard for Glads.

Chapter
Thirty-Five

The next morning, Mr. Darcy awakened the whole house with a "Cock-a-doodle-do!"

Summer tried to turn over and go back to sleep.

"Wake up, lazy bum," the bird said.

"Darcy, you are a lazy bum!" Aunt Agatha came down the stairs. "What has gotten into you?"

Summer gaped at him as he twisted his head around.

"Summer is a lazy bum."

Summer laughed. "I've been on the couch too long. Mom hated it when I laid here for too long and would jokingly call me that." She paused. "Okay, Mr. Darcy, I'll try the steps today."

A disheveled Glads came down the stairs. "Is there a rooster somewhere? I swear I heard a rooster."

"It's Darcy," Agatha said, and tramped into the kitchen.

Summer heard her rummaging around—probably to make a pot of coffee. Glads sat down in the La-Z-Boy. She, evidently, wasn't a morning person.

"How was your date?"

"Uneventful."

"You found out nothing?"

"I don't think I found anything else that could help your case. I'm sorry." Summer sat up. "He did say that I didn't really know you."

Glads looked as if she'd been slapped.

A shot of embarrassment tore into Summer. "Glads, you're my friend and I love you. Mom loved you. If there's something you're hiding, it's okay. I don't need to know. I'm not really working on your case. I'm just trying to help."

Agatha brought a coffeepot and three cups in and set them all on the coffee table. "Why is it so quiet in here?"

"Um. Because it's six o'clock in the morning?" Summer said. "God, that coffee smells good."

"Good morning!" Darcy squawked. "Food! Food!"

"I'll feed you in a minute." Agatha poured the coffee. "That bird!"

"Darcy loves Agatha!" Darcy said.

"Oh, you're such a Romeo," she replied.

"No. I'm a Mr. Darcy."

Agatha and Glads laughed. Summer joined in. Romeo and Mr. Darcy all in one morning. The thought of it delighted her.

"Do you think you can climb the stairs today?" Agatha asked. "I'll help you."

"I can try. I feel pretty good. I can't believe it's only been a week since my fall. It seems that a lot has happened since then." Summer sipped at the hot brew.

She mulled over the past week. She'd fallen and been laid out on the couch, gone to the chocolate fest, where she'd glimpsed almost everybody she knew (including Liam), gone to Beach Reads and worn herself out, and gone on a date with Liam last night. A strange Valentine's week. And the two most important things that happened were that Glads was a suspect in Lana's murder case and Cash had announced that he wanted to try again. Summer was caught in a whirlwind of activity and emotion. She'd had no time to sort through any of it.

"I think I'm going to try to go to Beach Reads today," Summer said.

"Why? Everything is under control there. Piper and Mia are helping, and Marilyn is popping in when she can," Agatha said. "Don't bother."

Glads sighed. Summer realized she'd rather be at the bookstore. But she was in hiding, and it didn't suit her.

"But—"

"Really, no reason for you to go." Agatha stiffened.

The room bristled. "What's going on?" Summer asked.

"We didn't want to tell you. We want you to focus on your healing. Please let's not talk about this right now," Agatha said.

"What's going on? It's my bookstore. I need to know." Summer's heartbeat kicked up in speed.

"It's just been quiet," Glads said.

"That's not unusual this time of year."

"Someone painted graffiti on the door."

"What? What did it say?'

Agatha took a deep breath. *Murder Bookstore.*

Summer gasped. "I don't understand. Nobody has talked to the press. Have they?"

"No, but there was a write-up about the connections to several murders the bookstore has," Agatha said. "I'm sorry, but there it is."

She was talking about her mom's death, of course. And about the connections with the cold case on Mermaid Point.

"Great. Absolutely fantastic."

"You should sue that reporter," Glads said.

"It's all true. What kind of a case would I have?" Summer asked.

"My advice is to stay home, let the others deal with it. You need to heal that ankle."

Summer understood the logic in that. Of course, she wasn't going to listen to it. Not one word.

"I think I should go in just to save face. I won't stay long. But people need to know how ridiculous that is. One way to do that is to show up and do your best while everybody is watching." Summer crossed her arms.

Agatha frowned. "I figured you wouldn't listen to reason. That's why I didn't want to tell you about it. I'll make breakfast. At least you'll have a full belly to face the day."

"I'll help," Glads said.

"No thanks," Agatha said. "We still have enough blueberry muffins to feed an army."

"I can whip up some biscuits. Or maybe cornbread?"

"Okay, let's see what you do with biscuits," Agatha acquiesced.

Summer sat on the couch, considering whether she should call her PR friend again. She might just give her the same advice. Still, it probably was worth another call. Yes, she'd call her later today.

Chapter
Thirty-Six

Summer missed her walks along the beach every morning on her way to the store. Instead, she had to catch a ride with Agatha and then hobble along on the boardwalk, past what used to be the arcade, now Gina's Chocolates and Bo's Place. She stopped and took in the view. With few people dotting the sand, it was exquisite. The waves were serene, glistening in the sun, giving off gentle sparks.

She drew in the sea air, which had always been good for her. It was the air of home, where she finally stood, in almost every sense of the word. Her pink cottage with the turquoise shutters wasn't much, but it was home. Where she'd grown up. Where she longed to place her head after working all day.

As she opened the door to the bookstore, she experienced another sense of home. The mermaid over the door gazed down on her, and she noticed a ping of comfort. The scent of patchouli met her nose, but as she walked farther into the store, the bittersweet aroma of coffee greeted her. There were no customers anywhere. It was worse than she'd imagined.

"What are you doing here, Aunt Summer?" Mia popped out of the back.

"I wanted to see how things were going." She paused, taking in the empty rows of bookcases brimming with books. "I wanted to save face. To show that we have nothing to be ashamed of. We are not the murder bookstore."

Piper came from somewhere behind Summer. "Well, do you have a plan? I don't know if this is going to blow over."

"No, I don't." Summer shifted her weight a bit onto her bad foot, ever so slightly.

"Maybe we should have a sale?" Piper suggested. "Another event? Where sales go to a really good charity."

"That's a good idea. I'm going to call my PR friend and see what she says. But let's consider that. Our clients are so loyal that I'm inclined to think this won't matter so much." Summer placed her crutches against the counter, leaned on her other foot, and propped herself against the counter as well.

"How's the ankle?" Piper asked.

"Getting better," Summer said. But right now it was killing her.

"How's Glads?" Piper asked.

"It's hard to say." Summer wanted to ask her if she knew anything about Glads's past but decided to wait until Mia wasn't around. Mia was no longer a child, but she certainly wasn't an adult—no matter what Mia herself believed. "She's doing a lot of baking. There's a box of muffins on my car seat." She threw Mia the car keys. "I couldn't manage the crutches and the muffins."

"Got it," Mia said, and rushed toward the door.

"What's really going on?" Piper leaned in.

"I don't know. But Liam—"

"Liam?" One blond eyebrow shot up.

"Yes. Well, we have some catching up to do.'

"I'll say." She crossed her arms.

"He said Glads has something in her past."

"Glads?"

She nodded. "And Cash told me so as well. Of course, he couldn't go into details."

"No."

"But I asked her about it this morning, and she clammed up. She also seemed hurt that I would ask, so I dropped it."

"I see." Piper examined her fingernails. "I'd have done the same. No matter what she did in her past, we all know she didn't kill Lana."

Piper's eyes didn't quite meet Summer's.

"Do you know something about this?" It was a hunch.

"No really. Just rumors."

"Rumors?"

"Yes. I've never had the courage to ask. You know, she's so kind and tender."

Summer considered that. Yes, she was, but there was a kick-ass side to her. "What did you hear?"

"She was in prison for several years."

Summer couldn't imagine that. "Where did you hear that?"

"You know, I can't remember. I wish I could. It might have been a rumor at school."

"Why don't I remember that?"

"Because your nose was always in a book?" Piper smiled.

That was true. Summer's passion for reading had taken her out of most activities of the general school population. She'd never regretted that. Piper, however, had been a cheerleader and prom queen, with her lithe figure and fresh girl-next-door looks. Summer was short, rounder, with dark hair and eyes, which she now realized came from her father's family. There might have been a time when she'd wished for height and blond hair and blue eyes like her cousin, but now she appreciated her difference from Piper. Her long, straight nose came directly from her father. It wasn't too large; it was just the right size. Her mom had always told her she was beautiful—as had Cash—but Hildy had also insisted that she was more than her beauty. She had more important qualities. And that nugget of wisdom was what had gotten Summer through the awkward years. She'd developed those other parts, and loved herself all the more.

Chapter
Thirty-Seven

M ia brought in the muffins, and the four of them gathered near the coffee station as Poppy poured coffee for Summer, then herself.

"I want you all to know that we will get through this," Summer said. "Our customers are loyal. This is generally a slow time of year. So let's keep that in mind."

"That's true." Poppy bit into a muffin.

"But this slow?" Mia gestured to the store space. Not one person was inside. It was a Monday, the day after Valentine's Day. Maybe that was it. Maybe the Romance by the Sea days had done them in.

Summer sighed. "I'm going to speak with a friend of mine who handles PR. In fact, I spoke with her once, and she said these things usually blow over. She also said a couple of other things. One, that it's important that none of us speak to the press. And two, it's important that we carry on like normal."

"Why?" Mia said. "Maybe we should just close down a few days and give the staff a break."

"Because, Mia, people are watching. That would be totally suspicious, like admitting that Glads killed Lana." Piper stirred sugar in her coffee.

A bell clanged, alerting them to someone entering the store. *A customer!* Poppy mouthed.

But when Summer turned around, she noticed Marilyn standing there with a basket full of chocolate. "Desperate times call for chocolate."

"I can't argue with that," Piper said.

"Gina sent it. She's concerned about everything. I told her I'm sure it's going to be fine, but she insisted." She shrugged, revealing a Virginia bluebell on her collarbone. "Who am I to argue?"

"We should send her something back." Summer glanced around at the books. "What does she like to read?"

"I have no idea," Marilyn said.

"Well, how about some culinary romances?" Mia asked, walking toward that section.

"Fabulous!" Poppy said. "I'll get a gift box, and you go and pick out some books."

Mia beamed. The assignment was right up her alley.

A lightbulb flicked on in Summer's brain. "What other local businesses can we thank with some books?"

"The B and B, for sure," Poppy said, grinning. "Tina loves Regency romances!"

"How about the flower shop? The flowers for the event were spectacular," Piper said. "Sounds like we have a plan. Let's make up some gift baskets." Summer didn't think it would solve their problems. It was a good-faith gesture, in any case. They always thanked local businesses, but this time it would be a bit more personal. It felt good and right. And it was perfect timing.

"Let's put an envelope of Fatima's tea in each basket." Fatima, Summer's sister, had started a company selling her handcrafted tea, and Beach Reads was one of the few places in the States that carried it. It was mostly sold internationally.

The group was soon happily sorting and packaging. It kept their minds off the lack of customers. And that was a good thing.

Summer needed to sit down, and she found her way to the chair behind the register.

"Oh! It feels good to sit."

"Are you okay?" Poppy rushed to her.

"Oh, I'm fine. Standing for a long time isn't in the picture for me these days." Summer winced as pain circled her ankle and shot up through her leg.

"I'll get you an ice pack." Poppy hurried off to the back.

"Thank you." Summer tried to maintain a little composure.

"After that, I suggest you let me take you home," Piper said.

"I'm not going to argue with you. What do you think of that?"

"I think you're in more pain than you're letting on. That's what I think," Piper said.

Poppy brought an ice pack, and Mia found a box to prop Summer's foot on.

Ice was good. Summer had never realized how good it was before this fall. It was a healing balm. Yes, so good.

The door to Beach Reads opened again, and to Summer's surprise, it was Fatima. "Hello!"

"Hello, sister." She came around the counter and hugged her and pecked her on the cheek. "I bought more teas. I was going to ask how your ankle is, but I can see. Not so good, hey?"

"It comes and goes, frankly. It's only been a week. Thanks for the tea. We've included some of it in some thank-you packages we're assembling."

"Oh! That's grand!" Her dark eyes widened. She lowered her voice. "And what are we going to do about the reputation of the bookstore?"

"I hope it all blows over. But in the meantime, we're going to do our best to remain a good business. We have such a loyal customer base. I'm certain we'll be fine." It was her new mantra. The loyal customer base.

"Maybe it's time to release a statement?" Fatima said.

"That's one of the things we're doing with these baskets," Piper said. "A little more subtle, but we hope it counts."

"And what about Glads?" Fatima asked. "How can I help her?"

"By leaving her alone," Marilyn said as she came closer. "She doesn't want to be bothered."

"She's dealing with it by baking." Mia lifted the box of muffins. "Want one?"

Chapter
Thirty-Eight

Piper drove Summer home. "So, Mom said something is going on with you and Cash, and then I heard the name Liam cross your lips. What's going on?"

Summer drew in a breath. "Something is going on between me and Cash. And he asked me to go on a date with Liam to see if I could get any information pertaining to the case."

Piper turned into Summer's driveway. The neighbor's cat was sitting on their porch, peeking in the window. Mr. Darcy was probably peeking back at her.

"Did you?" She turned off the ignition.

"Not really. Nothing useful. I just figure he's trying to do his job. Unfortunately, he truly thinks Glads killed Lana." She unbuckled her seat belt.

"That's too bad. But I don't think they have enough proof. The video clearly shows someone else there."

"He says shadows don't mean anything." Summer opened her door. Piper got out and withdrew the crutches from the back seat. She came around and helped Summer to her feet.

Summer made her way to the front door. The cat didn't pay any attention to her. She was too busy peeping in the window.

"What about Cash? What's going on?" Piper asked. "I can't believe the cat and the bird." She shook her head.

"Yeah, cute. I know." Summer took a breath. "Cash wants to start dating."

Piper's face fell. "Oh no."

"What?"

"What did you say?"

"I said I'd need to think about it." Summer slipped the key in the door and opened it.

"You aren't going to agree to that, are you?"

Summer kept walking toward the kitchen. "Something smells good."

"Summer! Look at me!" Piper said, stepping in front of her. "You are not going to date that man. First, there's the obvious. You two have a past—a past wherein you stood him up at the altar. Second, he's fresh off a difficult divorce."

"He's been divorced for three years," Summer pointed out. "And I grant you, we do have a past. And, well, it's a lot to think about."

"Hello." Glads walked into the kitchen. "Agatha left vegetable soup for us, but she had to go home. I'm your nurse tonight."

Summer and Piper looked away from each other. What was Piper so concerned about? Summer wondered.

"Thanks, Glads," Summer said. A wave of weariness moved through her. "I need to lie down."

Glads and Piper helped her to the couch. She sank into the blankets and pillows and closed her eyes as Piper and Glads chatted about the bookstore.

She drifted off and was awakened by Piper shaking her gently. "Time for your medicine."

Summer sat up and downed her meds. "I can't believe how exhausted I am."

"Your body has been through a lot. It's healing. It takes energy to heal. Plus, you've been playing spy." Piper rolled her eyes. "Cash ought to know better."

"Don't blame Cash. I agreed to do it," Summer said, and lay back down.

"The soup is delicious," Piper said. "Should I get you a bowl?"

But Summer was too tired to answer. She turned over and placed her face against the back of the couch.

* * *

She woke up at five AM, still dressed, teeth unbrushed, with Darcy curled up on her stomach. What had happened? She struggled to get up without waking Darcy. She scooped him up and placed him back in his cage.

A soft snoring sound came from the La-Z-Boy. Piper was splayed on the chair with a quilt thrown over her. Odd. Summer had assumed Piper was heading home after she dropped her off. She grabbed her crutches and made her way to the bathroom.

What to do when everybody in the house was asleep and you didn't want to wake anybody? It would be noisy to make coffee, especially on crutches. She went back to the couch. She eyed her laptop. She had more work to do, but it might wake up Piper if she were to pull it out. She spotted Lana's journal and picked it up. Now, where had she left off?

Mercy is all that I wanted. It's all that I prayed for. Mary Laura thought I was evil when I said I prayed for God to take you. We had words. I won't lie.

Who was Mary Laura?

But it's not the first time, as you know. You've even said yourself how difficult she can be. So much like her mother. If only she had more of your personality.

Aha. Must be a daughter from another marriage?

In any case, I feel if you love someone, you can't stand to see that person suffer and do what you must to help them be comfortable.

Summer's skin prickled.

I love you more than my own life. Seeing you suffer is horrible. Yet I ask myself, is there any hope? And sometimes I say yes, yes there is hope. You hear about miraculous recoveries, don t you? When I think about helping you to move on, that little sliver of hope stops me.

Stinging tears sprang to Summer's eyes.

I live on a tiny edge of hope. Every night when I curl next to you, I hope and pray it won't be the last. And yet I also hope and pray that God will relieve you of your suffering. It is pure madness. An edge that might finally take my sanity.

To say Lana's situation had been difficult was most certainly an understatement. Yet Summer recognized that many people had to grapple with these situations and decisions every day. She herself had been spared that. Though her mother's death had left her unresolved in many ways, she thanked the universe that Hildy hadn't lingered and suffered.

Chapter
Thirty-Nine

"I don't know what happened to me last night," Piper said at the breakfast table.

"Nor I." Summer buttered a blueberry muffin.

Glads shrugged. "Sounds like you had a tiring day. Happens to me a lot."

"It was tiring," Summer said. "It was a bit stressful."

"I can see you being tired, but me? Like, I didn't even feel I could drive home."

"Get your iron checked," Glads said.

"I will."

Summer drank her coffee and took a bite of her buttery muffin as the doorbell rang.

"I'll get it." Glads got up from the table.

They heard her squeal when she opened the door. "Oh! They are beautiful!"

Summer and Piper glanced at each other. Glads brought in a box of a dozen red roses.

"Jesus," Summer said. "Who are they from?"

"The card says, *Thank you for the beautiful Valentine's Day. More, please? Fondly, Liam.*"

Summer's mouth dropped open, and Piper laughed hard.

"He's a little pushy," Glads said.

"Indeed," Summer replied. "I'm just going to tell him I'm not interested."

"I'll say." Glads dropped the box. "What happened Valentine's night?"

"Nothing. In fact, he had to leave a bit early, which suited me fine. As you know."

"He's up to no good," Piper said. "Even if I didn't know the situation, I'd say that. Just to be clear. This is overkill. The yellow roses are still blooming in the living room. And he sent you a second dozen. Red? It's more than audacious. It's suspicious."

"I don't know whether to be offended or not." Summer cracked open the laptop.

"Don't be. Any man would be lucky to have you. What are you eating?"

"I'm still examining sales records. I ran across a name this morning that was quite unusual, and I figured I'd check to see if it could be on this list before I continue with this tedious job."

"What if the guilty party didn't buy anything?" Glads asked.

"It's a process of elimination. We look at all the people we know about being there first."

"What will you do next? If the list doesn't give you what you're seeking?" Paper said.

"Then I start calling some of the attendees to see if they observed anything suspicious that day."

"Police are doing that, aren't they?" Glads said.

"I don't know what they're doing. They have the drugs, which makes me feel better. But I've no idea what they're doing with any of it. This happened in my store. And it's happening to you. I feel like I bear some responsibility to figure this out for you, Glads."

Glads's face reddened. "Thank you."

Summer scrolled through the list and blinked hard. For there it was—Mary Laura Roberts. "I found the woman I'm looking for." Her voice quivered with excitement.

"Who is she?"

"Mary Laura Roberts. She was Lana's stepdaughter. Lana and she had words about the death of her husband."

"Motive?" Piper said.

"I don't know. But family . . . I read in Lana's journal that she was struggling with his pending death, and I think she wanted . . . mercy. And his daughter wouldn't have it."

"Oh! That makes a kind of sense. She may think that Lana killed him."

"How awful!" Glads said, bringing her hand to her chest—and spilling water all over herself. "Oh! I'm such a klutz!"

"No worries, Glads, we've all been there," Piper said, standing to get towels and help Glads clean up.

Summer swallowed. "From what I read, I don't think Lena killed him. She loved him and seemed to be struggling with that decision."

She went to Facebook and keyed in the name *Mary Laura Roberts*. Click. Staring back at her was the woman with the white hair and black eyes. She gasped.

"Now what?" Piper said, coming around to the other side of the table.

"That's the young woman I told you about." Summer pointed to the screen.

"I remember her," Glads said. "She was very striking."

Summer nodded. "The day before when she was in the shop, I noticed a book on poison in her backpack."

"We need to call Cash."

"And Ben."

"Immediately."

Though Summer had half a mind to call her or visit the woman herself, she'd learned so many lessons about sleuthing that she knew the best thing was to hand all of this over to the authorities. Which was exactly what she'd do.

She dialed Cash first.

Chapter Forty

"This is pretty good detective work," Cash said.

Ben grunted. He wouldn't admit it. And that was okay with Summer. She'd long ago gotten over caring about Ben Singer's opinion of her. "It's something to go on," he said. "But it's flimsy. You were searching for a woman because she had a book on poison in her bag?"

"And Lana Livingston was poisoned the next day," Summer said. "Then I discovered she's her stepdaughter."

"Come on, Dad." Cash rolled his eyes.

"Okay then, we need to find her and question her."

"She lives near Pittsburgh," Cash said. "Can you call the authorities there?"

"I can."

"But she was here just a few days ago. Could she still be here?" Summer asked.

"It's possible," Ben said. "Lana's body hasn't been released. She could be here dealing with all those details." He paused a few beats. "I'll check around. I'll get some guys from the local hotels and B and Bs. If she's here, we'll find her."

"Great!" Glads piped up. "There's hope!"

Summer thought so. She considered it too coincidental that this out-of-town young woman had been carrying a book on poison and

160

was in Beach Reads for a reading by her stepmother—a stepmother she didn't even like, according to Lana's journal.

Summer shivered as she considered the possibility of Lana's stepdaughter killing her. She'd always heard that people were most often murdered by someone in their lives. And family members were often suspects until proven otherwise. So she knew this theory of her was not too far out in left field.

Ben made a few calls. "I'm heading out," he said.

"Oh, wait! Ben? I wanted to ask you about the drugs," Summer said.

"What do you want to know?" He stopped and hooked his thumbs on his belt loop.

"What kind of drugs was it?"

He laughed. "You mean you don't really know? It's cocaine. Thousands of dollars' worth of stuff."

Summer's mouth dropped open.

"You're going to catch flies, hon." He smiled and kept going.

"Thousands of dollars' worth of cocaine was in my house." Summer's hands went to her chest. *Heart, are you still beating?*

"What the hell was she doing with all those drugs here?" Piper asked. "I mean, why St. Brigid? She certainly wasn't going to use it herself, was she?"

"No. It was definitely brought here to be sold. That was a huge amount. I've never seen anything like it in my life," Cash said.

A few beats passed in silence. But Summer's brain was racing a mile a second. She understood there was a burgeoning drug problem on Brigid's Island, but why would a highly successful author involve herself in such shenanigans?

"This is scary," Piper finally said. "Was she bringing those drugs to sell here?"

"If she was, they never got delivered. The cops have all of it," Cash said. "We do have a drug problem on the island, unfortunately. It's everywhere."

That wasn't what was currently scaring Summer, and she wondered if Piper was picking up on the same idea. "What happens when the buyer comes around searching for his drugs?"

"Exactly!" Piper said. "What then?"

"I'm going to say that he or she probably already knows that Lana is dead. It was in all the papers and on the news. They are probably gone, hiding somewhere," Cash said.

"Unless they paid in advance?" Glads piped up. "Then they're going to want their drugs, right?"

"I don't know how any of this works," Piper said. "Do people buy drugs that way?"

Nobody answered. Nobody knew. Wrong crowd.

"We are a bunch of super-straitlaced losers," Summer said.

"Speak for yourself," Cash said, smiling.

"So. Anybody want coffee? Tea?" Glads stood and went to the stove.

"It's too late for coffee," Summer said. "I'll have some mint tea." God, she was becoming like Hildy!

"I need to run," Cash said, and stood, turning to go. He spotted the red roses. "More roses?"

"He was smitten," Glads said.

"Not really." Summer tried to downplay it. "He was just thanking me for the date. I've no intention of going out with him again."

"Yes, it's probably not a good idea. With this new evidence, the case may get a little tricky. I guess it's best to stay clear of the detective," Cash said. "I'll ping you later."

She nodded. The roses were lovely, but they weren't worth the hassle she'd gone through. She'd had enough of spying for one lifetime. She hadn't found out anything relevant, and her ankle was not happy with her. And she'd gotten behind on her reading of the journal and her research.

So not worth it.

Chapter
Forty-One

Summer settled on the couch to read the journal, which was turning out to be a fount of information. How else would she have known about Mary Laura? About Lana's struggle with her husband's end of life? Who knew what else she might be able to find?

"I hate to interrupt your reading," Piper said, "but I'm a little worried that these drug people might come looking for their drugs. What if they come here?"

"What would they do? The drugs are with the police." Summer tried to go back to reading.

"They might not know that."

Summer closed the journal. "If they came looking for them, they'd go to the B and B."

"And Beach Reads," Piper said.

"It's a long shot. Like Cash said, they're probably long gone because Lana died."

"I'm going to head over to the B and B to talk with Tina. I'm worried. Do you want to come?"

"Why don't you just call her?" Summer asked.

"I like to look at a person when I ask if a drug lord came to visit," Piper said.

Summer reluctantly put the journal down. "Okay." She glanced at her ankle. "But you're driving."

Piper rolled her eyes. "Do you want to go, Glads?"

"No, thank you. I'm thinking about doing some baking. Just haven't made up my mind what I'm going to bake. Do you have chocolate syrup?"

"I believe so."

"I might make brownies." She walked into the kitchen.

For a brief moment, Summer worried about what condition she'd find the kitchen in when she came back home. But then the idea of warm brownies quelled any care she had.

"Come on. I'll help you to the car." Piper reached for Summer.

"I think I can manage," Summer said, and grabbed her crutches.

* * *

"What are you going to do about Cash?" Piper asked as soon as they pulled out of Summer's driveway.

"I don't know."

"Come on, Summer. How do you feel about him?"

That was a good question. She needed time to sort her feelings. There was a fine line sometimes between love and best friendship. If you were lucky, you could have both—like Lana and her husband.

"I know I love him as a friend."

"And?"

"I'm still attracted to him."

"Summer, you have no idea what he went through all those years ago. It was awful for him. You're my best friend, my cousin, and I love you. But I don't want to see Cash hurt again. Please be careful." Piper stopped at a stop sign.

"Of course I will be. I don't want to hurt him." Summer hesitated. "You know, I never meant to hurt him before. It didn't take him long to get married after that, so I figured I made the right decision."

"I thought so too. But she turned out to be a cheater, and the whole island knows that she left him for another man. So that's two women that left him, you know?"

"I hear you." Summer didn't want to talk about this anymore. She was glad they were pulling up to the B and B. Cash said he wanted to try again; Summer was thinking about it. End of story.

* * *

The B and B was a large Victorian house, decked out in slate blue, with cranberry-red shutters and gingerbread trim. During the summer, the garden was resplendent with roses of all shades.

As Piper walked and Summer hobbled with her crutches along the flagstone sidewalk, the front door opened. "Why, hello, you two! Come on in!"

Summer and Piper followed Tina to the kitchen, where a plate of cookies sat on the table. "Sit down and have one," she said. "They're molasses cookies. The recipe was handed down through my family. They're still warm!"

Summer reached for one and bit into it. Her taste buds popped and pinged in her mouth. Spicy. Sweet.

"Delicious!" Piper said.

"Tea? It goes well with those cookies." Tina brought some cups to the table, then a teapot, and filled the cups. "Now, what's up? You two rarely pay me a visit, especially together."

Summer cleared her throat. "We found out that Lana had a lot of drugs in her things."

"What? How did you find out?"

"The drugs were in the books she had in her bag," Piper said.

"We gave them to the police, of course." Summer blew on her tea, then took a sip. Tina was right—the molasses cookie and the tea were a great pair.

"We were wondering if anybody has come by looking for her things," Piper added.

Tina squinted as if she was trying to force herself to remember. "I think so. Yes. And I told them that you have her things."

Summer's heart dropped to the floor.

Piper shot her an *I told you so* look.

"Who was it?" Summer asked.

"There've been a few people. A young woman . . . with an unusual name . . . Mary Laura."

"That's Lana's stepdaughter. She lives in Pittsburgh. When did she stop by?"

"Hmmm. Maybe a day after Lana died. I'm surprised she didn't come and see you."

"Maybe she had to leave," Piper said.

"She did mention something about needing to get back home. She didn't say where that was."

"Okay. Who else?"

"The detective. You know, Liam Connor."

"He asked for her things. When was this?" Piper asked.

"I believe it was also the day after she died. There was so much going on for those few days, so many people in and out. But I think that's right."

"You told him the same thing? That the stuff was at my place?"

"I'm sure I did."

"Of course, he'd already been there by that point. He came to my place while Lana's event was going on."

"Whatever for?" Tina asked.

"She'd told him she was staying at my place, and he needed to keep track of her," Summer asked.

"This situation is so strange," Tina said.

"Indeed."

"Is that all you can remember?" Piper asked.

"Like I said, there were a lot of people in and out of here, but those are the two that I remember asking about Lana's things. It didn't strike me as odd, because of course her stepdaughter would want to collect Lana's things. And the detective, well, he was just doing his job."

He sure was. Summer wished she could remember whether or not Lana's things were there the last time he visited. Her head was such a blur from all the medicine she'd been taking. But she had an inkling he'd seen the boxes—even if he didn't mention it.

Chapter Forty-Two

"That detective is not what I would imagine a detective to be," Piper said when they got into the car.

"They come in all shapes and sizes, evidently," Summer replied. "Do you mind swinging by Beach Reads? I just want to check on things there."

"I can do that. Back to the detective."

"What do you think's going on? Do you think he's not really a detective?" Summer asked.

"I'm sure Cash would know if he wasn't. But there's something strange about him. The way he's coming on so strongly with you is, well, unprofessional."

Summer agreed. "It made me feel icky."

"Icky?" Piper laughed. "Is that a Shakespeare word?"

Summer's nose went up, and she put on a nasal voice. "I believe it was used in *Hamlet*, dear." She grinned. "Seriously, you know what I'm talking about. And I've been thinking about it. Even if he wasn't a detective, I don't think I'd be interested at all. I mean, he is very hot."

"Very."

"And he seems to be just a guy trying to do a good job."

"But?"

"He's not—"

"Cash?"

That wasn't what Summer had been about to say. But there it was.

They rode the rest of the way in silence. They pulled into the parking lot.

"I was going to say that Liam is not interesting to me. He's handsome, a decent guy, and is quite cultured. But the thing that interests me is that I have a feeling he knew where Lana's things were before he went to Tina asking for them. What is that about?" Summer opened the car door, and Piper came around to help her with her crutches.

"I admit that's odd. I wonder if he knew about the drugs."

"Even if he did know we had her things, it seems as if he at least didn't think we had all of her things. He must've suspected or known there was something else there.." Summer was almost out of breath, as she was trying to walk and talk at the same time, which was more difficult with crutches.

Piper stopped. "You're onto something. Maybe he wasn't really watching her because of her husband's murder case. Maybe he was watching her for the drugs."

Summer considered what her cousin had just said. She stopped on the boardwalk for a moment and gazed over to the ocean. She breathed the sea air in deeply, and it seemed to fill her lungs and her body. She missed walking along the beach every day. Damned ankle.

"The view never changes," Piper said. "I sometimes think I should have moved from here. But then there are days like this. Where the oceans resemble wavy glass against the sand, and it's just . . . home. Why would I want to leave this place?"

That was a whole lot more for Summer to unpack, given that she'd been back just a little over five years. Other places, like Staunton, Virginia, had their beautiful spots as well. But Staunton didn't have the ocean. When you were born and raised on the beach, sometimes you took it for granted. Maybe Summer had at one point in her life. But she didn't any longer.

They walked toward Beach Reads, opened the door, and walked beneath the mermaid who lived atop the door. Summer was pleasantly surprised when she walked in—there were a few customers milling about. Not a lot. But it was good that people were starting to come back. *Murder bookstore indeed.*

Poppy was behind the counter, checking out someone purchasing a book. She looked up at Summer and Piper and smiled.

Mia came around the corner with another customer. "I think the historical romance is in this section."

Summer nodded.

Things were rolling right along. But they still needed to do damage control. They needed to do a charity event of some kind, but Summer wanted to tread carefully.

"How's Glads?" Poppy asked, after the customer left.

"She's doing okay. I think." Summer imagined what kind of a mess her kitchen was in.

"She's baking brownies as we speak," Piper added.

"Oh dear. She must be stressed," Poppy said.

"She is. But she doesn't really want to be bothered," Summer said. "She's at my place, but I leave her alone, you know?"

"She's an odd bird, but I love her." Poppy grinned.

"I hear you," Summer said. "How's things going?"

"Slow but going." Poppy wiped off the counter. "Mia's been such a help."

"Good to know." Piper beamed.

"So has Rocky," Poppy said.

Piper's jaw twitched.

Summer took in the bookstore. When had she started caring so much about it? When had it become the center of her life?

She supposed it had started with the death of her mom. If ever a place had held the spirit of someone, it was Beach Reads holding Hildy. Summer felt her mom here. Maybe that was why it was so hard to stay away. This was her mom's dream turned into reality. Few people realized their dream like Hildy had.

So, what was Summer's dream now? Was it this place? Was she going to live here on this island and pick up where her mom had left off? Would that be a bad thing?

Something in her uncoiled. No, she didn't think so. Not at all.

Chapter
Forty-Three

S ummer and Piper were greeted by the luscious smell of baking brownies when they walked in the front door.

Piper groaned. "I was going to go home, but now I can't. I must have a brownie."

"Or two?" Glads poked her head out of the kitchen doorway. "I made plenty. You can take some home."

"Mia would love that!"

"I'll wrap up some, then," Glads said.

Summer was drawn to the kitchen by the smell but was reluctant to check it out, because Glads was such a messy baker. To her shock, the kitchen was pristine.

"I cleaned up already," Glads said. "I didn't want you to have to worry about it."

Several plates of brownies sat on the table, and several pans still full of brownies occupied the counters, the stove, and the top of the fridge. But the kitchen was clean.

"But I used all of your chocolate syrup," she said. "I'll replace it."

"You don't have to do that. I don't really need to have it around." Summer propped her crutches against the wall and sat down. She reached for a brownie and took a bite. It was still slightly warm, and Summer believed it might be the best thing she'd ever put in her mouth. "Oh my god! So good."

Piper shoved more in her mouth, nodding.

"So what did you find out?" Glads lifted brownies from a pan to place in a swath of tinfoil.

Summer recapped what they'd discovered.

"Both the stepdaughter and the detective were looking for the drugs?" she asked.

"Not necessarily, but maybe," Summer said.

"Someone has to know about those drugs. That was a lot." Glads wrapped up the pile of brownies with the foil.

"What if they were just for her?" Piper said.

"Do you mean like a stash of her own, like that she was doing drugs?" Summer asked.

"Why not?" Piper reached for another brownie. "Maybe she turned to drugs when her husband passed away."

"Thousands of dollars of drugs?" Summer's mind swirled. Lena didn't seem the type, but you never knew about people. Was there a type who did drugs? She doubted it.

"Well, whether she was doing them or she was selling them, it was a lot. I've never seen anything like it," Glads said. Summer and Piper both looked at her. "Yes, I've seen some cocaine in my day, and thank goddess I don't see it anymore."

Later, Summer lay down on the couch and picked up the journal. She had started to read it earlier and been interrupted by Piper and her jaunt to see Tina.

I know you'd be so disappointed in me if you knew . . . but darling, I am in a huge amount of debt. When Steve approached me and told me how much money I could make, I couldn't say no.

Summer batted her eyes and squinted. She sat up. Was this talking about what she assumed it was talking about?

All I have to do is take the products with me on my tour. And some- one will pick them up. I wait for a call and I meet them with the books. It's all very simple.

"Damn!" Summer said.

Piper and Glads came running.

"What is it?" Piper asked.

"It's right there in her journal. Lena was selling drugs."

The room silenced.

"She was in debt, probably because of her husband's illness, and someone named Steven approached her about selling drugs. It was the perfect arrangement. They set it up so that it would be during her tour, and she'd deliver what resembled books to her contact."

"Does it have anything about a contact? Like who they were?" Glads asked.

Summer turned the page. Blank. The rest of the journal was blank.

"We need to turn the journal over to the police. I believed you gave them everything." Piper crossed her arms.

"Everything but this. I wanted to read it."

"Does Cash know you have it?" Glads asked.

"I don't know."

"Let's call him and tell him we found it and we read it and he needs to read it," Glads said. "I don't want him to think we've been withholding evidence."

Had Summer been withholding evidence? It hadn't felt like it at the time . . . she'd just wanted to read the journal. But she was ashamed. This could have helped Glads's case earlier, perhaps.

"Okay," Piper said. "That's the story. We found it under the couch or something and read it."

Summer frowned. Could she lie to Cash?

"You're going to have to lie, Summer, or you can be in big trouble. Cash too," Piper said.

Well, she didn't want that. No indeed.

Chapter
Forty-Four

"You found it where?" Cash asked.

"Under the couch. It must have slid under there when we were digging through her things." Piper handed him the book.

"Why were you under the couch?"

"I dropped a pen. It rolled under there, and she picked it for me because of the ankle," Summer added.

"Okay, but you read it?"

"Yes, most of it. We read it while we waited for you to get here."

"We can definitely say that she was here to move those drugs," Glads said.

"For sure," Piper said. "Check out on the last written page."

He cracked open the book and thumbed through until he found the page and read it. "Well, would you look at that?" He slammed it shut. "This is great! I need to get this into evidence right away!" He started to walk away, then stopped. "Thank you for calling me. That is going to make a difference, Glads!"

She beamed. "I hope so."

Summer tried not to think about all the lies she'd just participated in telling the man she was considering dating again. What if they ever got serious? Would this lie come between them at some point? Lies always rose to the surface.

"Have another brownie." Piper handed her one. It wasn't warm, but it was still a perfect chewy texture and a rich chocolate.

"I think I will," she said.

"You did the best thing." She picked up her bag and the tinfoil that held brownies. "I need to go. Husband is actually off tonight. I promised him dinner."

"That's nice," Summer said.

"Glads will be here if you need anything, right, Glads?"

Glads poked her head out from behind a book. "Uh-huh. I'm here."

"Oh! Before I go. Mom said to tell you she'll be over tomorrow to help you go up those stairs."

"What? She mentioned that before, but—"

"You need to try." Piper tucked her scarf around her neck. "Okay?"

Summer nodded. "Yeah."

She was pretty content on the couch. But her own bed would definitely be a step up. She peered over at the steps. She didn't think she was ready.

She sighed. If she wasn't ready by tomorrow, Aunt Agatha would make her ready.

* * *

Later, Glads brought Summer water to make sure she took her last pain pill of the day and her sleeping pill.

"Are you more optimistic?" Summer downed the pills with a gulp of water.

Glads smiled and nodded. "I am. I think the tape and now the journal would give a jury more than a shadow of doubt, so maybe the charges will be dropped."

"Let's hope so. It would be a waste of taxpayer money for them to take you to trial."

"Thank you." She sat back down on the La-Z-Boy. "I might go home tomorrow."

"I love having you here, Glads. No pressure to leave."

176

"I know that, but thanks. And thanks for everything you've done for me. I mean, now the police have other avenues to explore. They're searching for Mary Laura. Cash is researching the detective more. And we have the tape and journal. Things are looking good." Summer held up the book. "Sometimes happily-ever-afters are for real."

The last statement caught in her throat as she said it. Her eyes watered.

"Are you okay?"

"It's just that Mom used to say that—"

"And she believed it."

"When I think about that . . . and how good she was . . . and think how she died. It just seems so unfair. I get so angry."

"Oh, honey. Me too. I wish I had some comforting words, but it sucks. I feel the same way. Heck, we all do." Glads rubbed her hands through her pink hair. "But I was just thinking the other day that Hildy wouldn't have made it through the pandemic. She needed to be around people. She thrived on giving to them and being with them. She'd have hated the way we all have to be separate in our homes."

"All of us hated it," Summer said. "But Mom? You're right. It would've driven her mad."

"I had no problem with being alone. I was just worried that one of us would get sick. I fretted over it and couldn't sleep. Kept checking on people."

"Yes, I remember," Summer said, and slid down farther into the couch. Her pills were starting to take effect.

"Looks like it's bedtime." Glads stood up and took her book with her.

"Good night, Glads," Summer barely said before nodding off. In the space between asleep and awake, she was adrift in warm and fuzzy good emotions. Glads was going to be okay. She just knew it.

Chapter
Forty-Five

The next day, Glads dropped Summer off at Beach Reads and then went back to her home. Summer was going to miss their daily chats.

"Well, look who's here!" Poppy exclaimed from behind the counter.

Agatha turned around. "I was just coming to see you."

"Well, I'm here for a few hours, then if you don't mind taking me home?"

"I'll pop back around to pick you up, and we can work on getting you up those stairs," Aunt Agatha said. "Have a good day!" She exited the shop.

"How's everything going?" Summer asked Poppy.

"Things are picking up, but slowly." She paused. "There are invoices on your desk."

"Thank you," Summer said. "I suppose the one thing I can do is sit on my behind. I can also give you a break from time to time."

"No need." Mia came from around the corner, holding a coffee, which she handed to Poppy. "I'm here. We need you to get those invoices." She turned to Summer.

"How are things with Glads's case?"

"Very good. We may have had a breakthrough." In a low voice, Summer proceeded to tell them about the journal and the drugs and so on.

The shop door opened and closed. Poppy looked up, and her facial expression changed, as did Mia's. Summer turned to find Mary Laura standing before them.

She had to wait a moment of two before she said anything. She was stunned to see her. She'd assumed she was back in Pittsburgh.

"Can I help you?" Summer said. *And did you know the police are looking for you?*

"Um, actually, are you Summer?" She had a deep, throaty voice.

"Yes, yes I am."

"I'm Mary Laura, Lana's daughter. Well, stepdaughter."

Summer held out her hand to shake Mary Laura's hand. "Nice to meet you. I'm so sorry about what happened."

"Thank you."

Poppy and Mia stood close by, not saying a word.

"The thing is, Lana could be a bit of a scatterbrain. I understand she mistakenly had her things sent to your place."

Mia went into the back. Poppy wiped off the counter.

"That's right. She did."

"It's funny, because our addresses are similar, except that mine is a Pittsburgh address. See?" She pulled out her license and showed it. She was right. "So I think she meant to have her things mailed to me in case of an emergency."

"Well, I'm sorry for the mix-up," Summer said.

"Might I come and collect them?" Mary Laura's black eyes were actually a very dark brown, and Summer didn't know if they were beautiful or evil.

"I'm sorry."

One of the few customers in the store walked by.

Summer leaned in. "The police have your mother's things."

Mary Laura appeared confused and startled. "Why?"

"They're seeking clues to who killed her, I suppose." Could this young woman be so daft? Or was she just playing stupid?

"In her own things?" Mary Laura rolled her eyes. "Small-town cops, I guess."

Summer bit her tongue—a rare occasion, "Well, maybe you should head over to the station. I'm sure they'd give some of her stuff back to you. By now, they must have gotten all the fingerprints and whatnot they needed." *Go to the station. They're looking for you.*

"Oh, probably," she said. "I'll stop over later. I'm starting a new job today."

"In St. Brigid?"

"Yes, I came here to see Lana's book event and fell in love with the place." She waved her arms.

Summer couldn't help the pride swelling in her chest. "It's a lovely community," she said.

The shop door opened again. Summer turned to find Ben Singer.

"Mary Laura Roberts?" he asked.

She looked confused. "Yes?"

"We've been searching for you."

"Me?" she squealed.

"Yes. Do you mind coming to the station with me? We just have a few questions for you."

She looked at Summer and then back to the chief. "Well, I was going to stop by later to pick up Lana's things. I'm starting a new job today in like an hour."

"I'm sorry. You'll need to start that new job tomorrow," Ben said.

Her face fell. She blinked hard a few times. "Okay," she said in a weak voice.

"Come with me," Ben said. He leaned over and whispered in Summer's ear, "Tell Mia thanks."

He escorted Mary Laura out of the bookstore.

"Mia?"

"Yes?" She came out of the back.

"Good work," Summer said. "Ben said to tell you thanks."

"Do you think she did it?" Mia asked.

"I have no idea. But I do know she didn't like Lana at all. They quarreled often. And when her dad died, she blamed Lana."

"And she had a book about poison plants," Mia said. "The day before her wicked stepmom is poisoned and dies."

"It's odd the police didn't find her. She's been here all along. I wonder where she's staying," Mia said.

"Must not be in a hotel or B and B." Summer's brain raced. Where else could she be staying? Did she know someone here? "May she's be staying at an Airbnb. It would be hard for the police to find you . . . Although they could run a search for all of them on the island," Mia said.

"I think you could be a detective," Summer said.

"No thanks." Mia rolled her eyes. "I've got bigger plans."

Chapter
Forty-Six

As Summer finished paying the invoices, she could have sworn her mom was standing right there peeking over her shoulder. She turned her head—and of course, nobody was there.

Her ankle had begun to throb, and she wondered when Aunt Agatha would arrive. In the meantime, she couldn't help herself, so she Googled Mary Laura.

There was nothing particularly menacing in all of her social media. Nor was there anything else online about her. Summer did find out that she was in the culinary arts. A pastry chef. She'd mentioned getting a job here—it must be at one of the restaurants or hotels.

Summer dialed Tina. "Tina, how's it going?"

"I'm quite busy right now, so I can't talk for long."

"I understand. Have you heard about anybody hiring a new pastry chef named Mary Laura?"

"Let me think. I generally am aware of staffing situations at all the good restaurants, but I can't think of anybody hiring a pastry chef recently. Why?"

"I'm just trying to figure out where Mary Laura got a job."

"Mary Laura? Isn't she Lana's stepdaughter? She's gotten a job here?"

"That's what she said."

"I've heard nothing, which makes me think she's lying, or else she's not working at one of the good restaurants or bakeries. You know?"

Summer understood exactly what she was talking about. The network of restaurants and food places that were high-end were geared toward tourists, but there were still decent places not in the network. Places Summer quite liked.

"Okay, thanks for the information, Tina."

"Anytime," she said, and hung up.

Well, Summer could at least cross the network off her list.

Mia popped her head in. "How are you doing?"

"I've finished the invoices. Thank god."

"Well, you've got another matter to take care of. Detective Connor is here to see you."

"What? Why?"

Mia shrugged. "Want me to send him back?"

"Not really, but I suppose I should see him. Bring him in." Summer wasn't looking forward to this. Whether he was here on business or for pleasure, she was going to have to put her foot down. She had no interest in the man or in helping him with his case.

"Okay," Mia said, and left.

The next time Summer spotted her, she was showing Liam into her office. "Thanks, Mia."

Mia tried to smile, but it came across as a mean sort of snarling look.

Mia would never get an Academy Award.

"How are you, Summer?" Liam sat down. "I've not been in touch. The case has been keeping me busy."

"It's quite all right." She honestly couldn't care less.

"So we're in possession of Lana's journal now," he said.

"Good." She shrugged.

"I hear it was found under your couch."

"Yes. So?"

He leaned his elbows on his knees. "Funny. I'm sure I spotted that book on your coffee table a few days ago."

Damn. "It wasn't that book, I can assure you. I have lots of books and journals. Maybe you saw one of those." She tried to sound as flippant as possible.

"Do you know what I think?"

She didn't answer.

"I think that's your writing in that journal. I think it's a fake."

She laughed, and his face grew stone cold. "Oh. You're serious?"

"I am. And this is a serious matter. It's a forgery."

"Why would I do that?"

"To help Glads." His face contorted.

She folded her hands on her desk. "I'd do anything to help her, for sure, but not commit a crime."

He lifted his torso off his knees, squinting as if he was trying to concentrate.

"You can test my handwriting or whatever. I'm happy to oblige," she said.

"Why are you trying to destroy my case? I thought you liked me." Liam jutted out his chin.

Summer could not believe what she was hearing. But her hackles were raised. "Excuse me? I'm not trying to destroy your flimsy case. Glads is a friend of mine, and I'm just being supportive. And for the record, as for liking you? I don't. Please leave."

He harrumphed and stood, then leaned on the arms of Summer's chair. "Stay out of my way."

Fear gripped her. She reached for her crutch.

"I mean it. Glads is going to fry, and I'm going to see to it!" His face turned monstrous as his voice rose. Summer was certain they could hear him in the store.

She lifted her crutch. "I said to leave. Now."

He sneered. "What are you going to do with that thing?"

In the blink of an eye, she cracked him over the head with it, and he tumbled back.

Mia popped her head into the office just as he hit the floor. "I saw the whole thing," she said. "I had a feeling . . ."

Summer had shocked herself—she'd never struck anybody before. "Is he okay?" She struggled to get up on her crutches.

"You killed him," Mia said.

"What?" Summer's heart almost stopped.

"I'm kidding. He's still alive, unfortunately."

"Mia!" Sometimes she wanted to throttle her niece, and now would be one of those times. "What do we do with him?"

"I have no idea."

Just then, Cash came rushing around the corner into her office. "What the—"

"Don't ask." Summer's voice cracked.

"He was threatening Aunt Summer," Mia said. "Got in her face. She smackedhim right in the face with her crutch, and he went down like a freakin' sack of potatoes!"

Summer waited for Cash's reaction. He was trying not to laugh, but one bubbled out anyway. "I'm sorry. This isn't a laughing matter." He cleared his throat. "Mia, please get some water and ice."

"Will do," she said.

"Seriously, Summer?"

"It was self-defense."

"I know, but you just struck an officer of the law. There's going to be ramifications."

"I'm sorry. I had no choice. I felt like . . . he was going to hurt me."

Cash came to her then, and she fell into his arms. Before she realized it, she was sobbing.

Chapter
Forty-Seven

"She did *what*?" Summer heard a raised voice. It was Aunt Agatha, coming to take her home.

Summer was still in Cash's arms and wanted to bury herself there. But she lifted her head.

"Summer!" Agatha's voice rang through the tiny office. "I came to take you home, and Mia said that—"

"It's true," Summer managed to say. "I thought he was going to hurt me, and I hit him with my crutch."

Liam stirred in the corner.

"Well, I'm taking you home. Now."

Cash nodded. "I think that's a good idea. I'll take care of everything here."

As he helped Summer stand, she gathered her composure. "He thinks I wrote that journal. He thinks I forged it."

"Well, that's ridiculous. One simple handwriting test will prove him wrong," Agatha said. "The man is deranged. Clearly." She reached for Summer. "Let's go, dear. We need to get you home, off of the foot and away from that man."

Summer and Agatha left the bookstore through the back door. Aunt Agatha helped her niece into the car.

They drove to Summer's house quietly. There was nothing to say. Agatha had not turned on the radio.

Summer had wanted to hit several people in her life, but she'd never done it. And she was proud of that. She hated that she'd struck Liam.

"I hate that I did that," Summer said. "I should be able to control myself better."

Aunt Agatha pulled into the driveway and shut off the engine. "You listen to me, girl."

Summer hadn't been a girl in a long time, but she listened.

"You were defending yourself. You should feel empowered, not ashamed." Her blue eyes were alight with indignation. "No man has a right to get in your face like that. I don't care if he's a detective or a judge. Do you hear me?" She pointed at Summer. "Your mom would be very proud of you." Her voice shook.

"No. Mom always said there's a better way than violence. Always."

"I know what she said. But I also know she defended herself a few times. It's different when you need to do it. I'm proud. Hildy would be too." She opened the car door. "I'm hoping that your medicine allows for a drop or two of bourbon."

Bourbon. Yes, that could help her nerves right now.

As Summer and Agatha made their way to the front door, they heard Darcy squawking loudly. "Help! Help!"

Agatha pushed the door open.

"Was that not locked? I swear I locked it," Summer said. But as they walked into the house, she struggled to make sense of what was in front of her.

All of her things were scattered. Her books and magazines had been thrown on the floor. Pictures had been taken off the wall and were scattered all over.

"Help!" Darcy said.

The bird's feathers stood on end. He'd been frightened. Summer went to him.

"Who could have done this?" Agatha said with a trembling voice. Summer's focus was on Mr. Darcy. She reached into his cage and pulled him to her and cradled him. "There, there, Darcy. It's going to be okay."

"I'm calling Ben," Agatha said.

"Good idea." Summer looked up from Darcy and noticed that her couch cushions had been completely shredded. "Why would someone do that?" She gestured toward the couch.

Agatha shrugged.

"Help Darcy!" the bird said.

He had to have seen the intruder. Summer hoped nobody had harmed him. She kept stroking him. "Darcy wants Hildy!"

"I know, Darcy. Summer wants Hildy too."

"Well, Ben is coming over. He said not to touch anything." Agatha glanced around. "The place is trashed!"

"It is," Summer said. But somehow it didn't surprise her. She'd had a feeling that someone would come searching for those drugs. Well, it was a little too late. Those drugs were right where they should be—with the police.

"Why are you not more upset?" Agatha flailed her arms.

"I am, but I'm trying to calm Darcy. He's been frightened."

Agatha looked down at him. "Poor bird."

"I'm not going to be able to stand here much longer on these crutches. Can you get his traveling cage? It's in the laundry room on the shelf."

"Are you going somewhere?"

"Yes, Darcy and I are going to sit in your car and listen to music. Care to join us?"

Agatha's face softened. "I think I'd like that."

The three of them waited in Agatha's car while listening to soft jazz music, Darcy's favorite. And before she knew it, the bird was fast asleep in her arms.

When Ben arrived, Agatha took him inside while Darcy and Summer waited in the car. The next thing Summer spied was a team of uniformed officers. She took a deep breath. It had been quite a day. She'd struck a man. A detective, no less. And someone had broken into her house, searching for those drugs, certainly. And here she was with a sleeping bird in her arms.

A few things became clear to her. She loved this bird. She'd always considered him Hildy's bird, but he was hers now. Heart and soul. If she found out who had frightened him so much, she might strike a person again.

The other thing was how at peace she was in this moment—hurt ankle, bird in arms, house nearly destroyed and all. What mattered was that everyone was still okay. Mr. Darcy. Her friends and family. And dare she think it, Cash.

Chapter
Forty-Eight

"Ben is going to lock up, and you're coming home with me." Agatha set a bag in the back seat of the car along with a container of bird food. "Will he be okay in that cage for a few days?"

"I think so." Summer continued to stroke the bird. "What's going on? Why am I going to your place?"

"You can't stay here tonight. They will be at it for quite some time. And you need your rest," Agatha said, and started the engine.

"Did they find anything?" Summer asked. "I mean, leading them to know who did it?"

"Yes. I think so. And it's not good." Agatha's voice shook.

Summer's heart raced. She held Darcy tighter.

"Evidently, there's a huge drug ring here." Aunt Agatha started the car.

"Where?"

"St. Brigid."

"I don't believe it!"

"Yes. It's true, and some of those criminals were in your living room. They leave their mark on everything."

Summer's jaw dropped.

"That's why I'm taking you home. They were in your house. It needs to be fixed up before you can go back. The couch is destroyed. The mattresses have got to go, and, well, so much needs to be done."

"Thank god Glads went home this morning," Summer said. "She would've been there."

"Yes, thank god," Agatha said. "Ben told me to keep you for a few days. He feels they're close to making an arrest."

"Of the drug ring?"

"Yes. But he needs you out of the way. He doesn't want any harm to come to you."

"That doesn't sound like him," Summer said.

Agatha shot her a serious glare. "He's a cop. He knows these people and knows they are nobody to mess with. He doesn't want to see anybody get hurt, including you."

"Well, if I were him, I'd check out Bo. You can smell the weed on him from twenty-five feet away," Summer said.

"We're not talking about pot. It's legal in most states now anyway. I admit, Bo is a little strange, but he's probably harmless," Agatha said.

So open-minded. Summer knew at least a dozen people who were stoners and had gone on to become addicted to something stronger. You name it—heroin, cocaine, whatever. She also knew that wasn't always the case.

They drove along in silence. "Did he say anything about Glads's case?" Agatha asked.

"Nothing."

"I'll call Cash later."

"You know, Liam was just so aggressive with me today. I don't know what happened. He accused me of forging that journal, and then, I don't know, he got in my face. He didn't seem like the same man at all."

"Sounds bipolar." Agatha made a turn at the stop sign.

"It does, doesn't it?" Summer remembered a psychology professor she used to hang out with. One of her pet peeves was armchair shrinks.

"Or maybe he's on drugs, who knows? The whole word seems to be on something these days."

"True. Even me!"

"You have a darned good reason to be on that medicine. It's getting close to time for you to take it, isn't it?"

"Yes. I can be a little late. My ankle is feeling much better."

"We'll be home soon. You can have the guest room all to yourself."

"A real bed!" Summer said. She mulled over everything she'd learned about her hometown just now. Drugs? Well, of course; they were everywhere. But Brigid's Island had always had an air of wholesomeness about it.

She wanted to find out more. But how? Maybe Cash was aware of it. Would Piper know anything? Summer didn't think she'd read anything in the newspapers about it.

Drug ring. It sounded very serious, like a professional group of people who were selling drugs. Bad people.

When they pulled up to Agatha's house, Cash's car was there, and he was sitting on the front porch. A sight for Summer's sore eyes. When had she started to care about him again? Was it before or after Valentine's Day? She didn't need to go deeper and try to remember; she just wanted him. Wanted to try again.

As he walked over to the car, he peered down into her lap, and his face mellowed.

He opened the door and reached for the cage, put it on the ground, and then reached for Darcy, who was sleeping soundly.

"You heard," she said as he placed the sleeping bird in the cage.

He nodded. He was wearing a blue oxford shirt, which made his blue eyes stand out.

"I wanted to see how you're doing."

"I'm fine, oddly enough. Hit a man, my house was ransacked, and my bird was terrorized. But I'm fine."

Agatha handed her the crutches. She stood.

"We don't need the crutches," he said. "Agatha, open the door."

He scooped her up in his arms and carried her to the sofa in Agatha's jewel box of a living room.

"Well, thank you, kind sir."

"My pleasure," he said.

"Can I get you anything?" Agatha asked as she propped the clothes on the corner of the couch. "Cup of tea?"

"Yeah, I think that would be good."

Cash sat down next to Summer. She turned to him.

"I'm glad you're okay." He leaned in and kissed her. She should've been surprised, but she wasn't. She was ready. And while there were no fireworks like in the romance novels, there was a little tingle, and something warm and deep moved through her. A comfort. A knowing.

They disengaged from the kiss just as Agatha walked into the room with tea.

"I've got good news and bad news." He took a cup of tea from Aunt Agatha, as did Summer.

"The good news is the charges against Glads have been dropped." He sipped the tea.

Summer wasn't sure, but she thought he blinked away a tear.

"This is why I don't usually do criminal law. I get emotionally attached." He smiled and blew on his tea.

"I'm afraid to ask," Agatha said, and sighed. "What's the bad news?"

He set his tea down and rubbed his jeans with his hands. "The bad news is whoever killed Lana is out there somewhere."

Chapter
Forty-Nine

Later, as Summer was stretched out in the bed, covered in a quilt made by her grandmother, surrounded by objects that each held stories, she heard Agatha go around the small home and check all the windows and doors three times. Their family was superstitious like that. If you were going to take precautions, do it at least three times, because that was a magic number. You'd have a little extra help from the universe. And they could all use it.

Even though Summer's mind was buzzing with everything that had happened that day, she slept quickly and soundly, disturbed only by nonsensical dreams.

She awakened as sunlight shone into the room. A beam reflected off a vase that had held the flowers from Agatha and Peter's wedding long ago. It had been given to them by Peter's mom, brought over from Sweden "on the boat" with his ancestors. There was the family Bible belonging to Agatha and Hildy's great-grandparents, brought over from Germany, written in older German. And the framed baptismal gown that belonged to Summer's grandmother. Her mom, Hildy hadn't wanted any of the family things. "I want to create my own story," she'd said.

Hildy was kind of stubborn that way. Summer smiled.

Summer, conscious of being surrounded by her family in this room, observed that when she was younger, she might have perceived it as suffocation. But not now. Now she felt comforted. She drew in the air and believed she smelled patchouli. She smiled. It was her mom. She was probably in this room right now. Maybe snuggled up next to Summer, the way she always did in the morning, no matter how old Summer was. She warmed even more.

Her ankle pulsed, alerting her to the fact that her medicine was wearing off.

A light rapping at her door. "Are you awake?"

"Yes." Summer sat up in bed.

Agatha came in with a tray, holding her medicine and some stuffed French toast. "I made your mom's favorite. She loved this French toast. She's been on my mind more than usual."

"Thank you. This is so kind." Summer sat up even further, and Aunt Agatha placed the tray in front of her. Summer swallowed the pill. If she took it on an empty stomach, it would work faster. "Are you going to join me?"

"I ate hours ago. I've been up since five." Agatha sat down in the pink shell chair near the bed. "I swear I heard someone outside, but I must have been dreaming. There was nobody out there."

Aunt Agatha was frightened. Summer didn't blame her. Learning about a drug ring and seeing the damage at Summer's place was scary. "I didn't hear a thing."

"Good. Your medicine is helping with your sleep, I'm sure."

Summer took her first bite of the French toast, and her taste buds rose and saluted. So spicy and creamy at the same time. Cream cheese between eggy bread, doused with sugar and cinnamon. She hadn't had it in such a long time. She'd never made it, and yet how easy it would be to dress up her ordinary French toast.

"I am troubled by everything Cash said last night," Agatha said. "Sometimes I don't recognize this island."

"I know. This is delicious, by the way," Summer said.

Aunt Agatha smiled and nodded. "Do you believe a drug ring is here?"

"I do. He said they know someone is shipping drugs out from the harbor, but they don't know how." Summer took another bite.

"Our little harbor . . . ," Agatha said with whimsy in her voice. "I remember when there wasn't a harbor. Or at least not one that shipped anything but fish and fish products. It seems strange to even call it a harbor. Your grandfather did so well as a fisherman. But sometimes he'd be gone for days. Mom hated that."

"I've heard the stories." Summer reached for her coffee. "I'm sure they'll find the drug ring and the killer."

"Maybe the two are linked."

"That makes sense, since Lana was carrying drugs to deliver to someone here. But how?" Summer took another sip of coffee.

"Well, finding out who that person is isn't our concern, right?" Agatha said with eyebrows lifted.

"I hear you. I'm not getting involved. Now that Glads is off the hook."

"I'll believe that when I see it." Agatha crossed her arms. "In any case, I'll be here to remind you you said it."

Summer had no doubt about that.

It was hard, indeed, to keep from wondering about it all, because she couldn't even go back to her house—it was a crime scene. She tried to piece it all together while sitting at her desk at Beach Reads. But nothing added up.

Lena—dealing drugs to help pay medical bills.

Mary Laura—had accused Lana of killing her father and was now living in St. Brigid.

Liam—a detective who claimed to be keeping an eye on a murder suspect. And a man with a strange short fuse.

Summer realized Liam had probably been reeling since the charges had been dropped against Glads. It had probably angered him, and he'd taken it out on her. What a creep.

The names and characters of each person rolled around in Summer's mind. She was missing someone or something.

Aunt Agatha's stern face popped into her mind. Maybe it was better left unsolved—at least by her.

Oohing and aahing sounds came from the front of the house. She grabbed her crutches to go see what all the fuss was about. But just then Mia came in with Gina, the chocolatier, and a box of chocolate.

"Hi, Gina. How's it going?"

"Business has really slowed down after Valentine's Day. I was expecting it to, but wow, what a difference."

Summer smiled and nodded.

"We've been experimenting with some new combinations. We're not going to sell these, so we're giving them away. Just let us know what you think of them." She set the box down on Summer's desk. "Hey, I heard about your trouble. If there's anything I can do . . ."

"I'm okay. Staying with my aunt. It could've been worse."

"I suppose that's a good way to look at it. But how scary."

"Yes, a bit. But I took my bird and a few clothes and figured that's what really matters. Note that my couch and bed were destroyed. The insurance company will take care of all that. Things can be replaced, right?"

"Yeah, for sure." Gina sat in silence for a few beats. "Hey, thanks so much for the books and basket. I loved the books. I might find a few more while I'm here." She stood.

"Okay. Well, ask Mia or Poppy to show you where they are. I'm a little incapacitated." Summer pointed to her ankle.

"Yeah, I see that. How's it doing?"

"Good. Much better than I'd think."

"That's good to know."

"Have fun checking out the books," Summer said as Gina walked out.

Summer opened the box. There were six artful chocolates. Underneath each nugget was a paper labeling it. *Mexican Spice Chocolate* was the first one Summer picked up and plunked into her mouth. She spit it back out into a tissue. How awful. No. Way too much pepper. She took a gulp of water, and that didn't help at all.

She shoved the box aside. Maybe later. Maybe.

* * *

An hour later, Summer had written and posted a blog and was ready to go home. But she wanted to walk through the store. She texted Aunt Agatha and told her she was almost ready to leave.

She made her way to her crutches and out into the fray of the store. Well, *fray* wasn't the right word. There were just a few stray shoppers. And only Poppy sitting on the floor, not looking so good. "Where's Mia?" Summer asked.

"In the bathroom. She's been in there a while. I need to get in there myself," she said.

"Are you ill?"

"My stomach's been churning since I ate that chocolate."

Made sense. Summer would've reacted the same way if she'd eaten it.

"Yeah, I spit mine out. It was horrible. Way too much pepper."

"I'll say." Mia came up behind Summer, and Poppy raced in.

"I hope she doesn't ask me how it was," Summer said. "That could be awkward."

"Oh, I have a compulsion to tell her," Mia said. "It went straight through me. Most unpleasant. She doesn't want that to happen to a paying customer."

Summer grimaced. "I guess you're right." She hesitated. "It's so strange that it was so bad. Everything I've had from her so far has been so good."

"Well, I guess they're just experimenting."

"Indeed." Being a new person with a new business in St. Brigid wasn't easy. And Summer had kind of taken Gina under her wing since she arrived. There was nothing like a chocolate shop. It was unusual for a beach community mostly geared for tourists. But Summer assumed it would do well. It was a welcome change from the game shop that had been there until the owner died. COVID had taken his life, and nobody else wanted the store. Which suited Summer just fine. Now it was a beautiful, mostly quiet chocolate shop. Some days she could smell the delicious aroma.

"Excuse me, are you Summer Merriweather?" A woman approached her. "The owner?"

"Yes. Can I help you?"

"I'm Elain Gallagher of the *Island News*. Can I have a comment from you about the murder of Lana Livingston?"

Summer's heart raged. "No comment."

"Come on, you don't have any comment about a famous author's murder when her last event was at your bookstore?" Elain persisted.

Think, Summer, think. "All I can say is that we are very sorry about her death, and our deepest condolences go to her family and readers."

"Anything else? Have they figured out who killed her?"

"I can't comment on what's happening with the investigation," Summer said. "Now, if you'll excuse me, I have work to do."

"It's just so strange that this bookstore—one that celebrates love and romance—is linked to so many murders," the woman said as Summer walked away.

"Get a life," Summer heard Mia say to the reporter.

That Mia.

Chapter Fifty

It was almost time to close the shop. Summer walked through the bookstore, cleaning up the shelves as best she could. She'd tied a trash bag around her crutch and hopped along.

The bell above the entrance door went off as someone walked in. Of course. A customer would have to come in at five minutes before closing. Wouldn't you just know it?

"Summer!" It was Fatima, her half sister. "I'm just back from your house. It has yellow tape all around it. What's going on? What happened?"

"Someone broke in and trashed my house." Summer moved toward her. "I mean trashed. I'm staying with Aunt Agatha until things get sorted."

"Oh! This is terrible! You must be frightened. Did they steal anything?" Her deep-brown eyes were as wide as the moon.

"I don't think so, though I haven't been inside to take stock." Summer had wondered about that earlier. She'd have to ask Aunt Agatha if she'd noticed anything gone.

"Oh, why would someone do such a thing?" Fatima flung her arms around her, and Summer could hear jangles from her bracelets beneath her coat.

Summer shrugged. "My guess is they were searching for drugs. But I handed the drugs I found to the police."

"Maybe they think you kept some?" She shivered dramatically. "Do you want to come and stay with us?"

Summer's heart yearned to become closer to her brother and sister. But this was not the time. She wanted to stay close to Aunt Agatha and Piper. "Thank you, but I'm settled in at Agatha's."

"Okay, but you know you're always welcome."

Summer nodded. "Of course I do. But thanks for reminding me."

Fatima embraced Summer again with a huge hug. She smelled of lilac. It was her scent. She always smelled of it. Once again, Summer wished she could find a fragrance she liked, but she never could.

"Well, okay." Fatima stood back from Summer. "I'm so glad you're okay. I am concerned, because there is a killer on our island somewhere."

"I hear you," Summer said, and reached over to straighten a group of werewolf romances. "I keep hoping that the guilty party is gone."

"That's what I hope for too."

Later, Agatha came to get Summer and take her home. As they were walking out the back of the store to her car, Summer spotted Mary Laura in the parking lot. She was leaned into a car talking to someone. Heatedly.

Summer grabbed on to Agatha and pulled her back against the brick wall, putting her finger to her lips. Agatha nodded.

Mary Laura was gesturing wildly. But Summer couldn't quite hear what she was saying, because the car was running. Summer was surprised she was here—the last she'd seen her, Ben was taking her down to the station for questioning. She must have checked out okay, which was surprising to Summer. Mary Laura had motive. Of any of the people in Lena's life, she had the most reason for revenge, for she believed that Lena had killed her father.

* * *

"Killed her . . . drugs . . . damn you . . ." Summer thought she caught a few words. She glanced at Aunt Agatha, who had her phone out. She snapped a photo of the license plate.

The car sped away. Mary Laura stood in the parking lot making odd movements with her shoulders. Wait. She was sobbing.

Summer grimaced. What was going on here?

They heard the sound of footsteps and a woman's voice. Mary Laura gazed at whoever it was and walked toward her, out of Summer's and Agatha's eyesight.

They stayed where they were for a few minutes, afraid to move lest they be found out. Both sensed that they'd witnessed an important exchange. But Summer couldn't stand anymore. Even on the crutches. It was getting late. She was in pain.

She started walking, and Agatha followed behind her silently. She helped Summer into the car and surveyed the area. It seemed as if Mary Laura was gone. But where did she go? Who was she yelling at in the car? And who was the woman who'd called to her and comforted her?

"What was that?" Aunt Agatha said, once they were safely driving away.

"I'm not sure. But Mary Laura was very upset at someone."

"I took a photo of the license plate. Look at my phone and call it in to Cash or Ben or someone," Agatha said, and switched her turn signal on.

Summer found the picture and dialed Cash, explaining to him what they had just witnessed.

"Okay," he said. "I can get Dad to run those plates so we at least know who she was talking to. But this case isn't even mine now. Glads is off the hook."

Summer understood. But she also understood that this case was still unsolved and there could be a real danger to her community. "Okay. I get it. But if there's a killer in St. Brigid, wouldn't it be good to get them off the island and into jail?"

"I'm with you there," he said.

"Mary Laura was very upset. We couldn't hear everything she was saying. But it did sound like she said something about drugs and killing. Right, Aunt Agatha?"

"Yes!" Agatha yelled into the phone.

"Ow!" Cash said, and laughed. "Okay. I get it already. I better go and call Dad."

"You better," Summer said. "You don't want to get on Aunt Agatha's bad side."

"No, he doesn't." Agatha said.

They hung up, and Agatha sighed loudly. "I don't know what's happening to this island. There was a day you'd never see people arguing in public."

"Well, that wasn't exactly in public. It was behind the stores."

"Still, anybody could come along and—"

"Anybody did," Summer interrupted. "And I think it was a good thing. Don't you?"

Agatha smiled. "Well, if you put it like that. Yes, it was."

Chapter
Fifty-One

The next morning Summer had a doctor appointment. Piper stopped by to pick her up, but she had a box of sweet-smelling treats. She held it up. "I've got the last of the honey cake from the bakery!"

Brigid's Bakery had been in operation since Piper and Summer were kids. Every year for Valentine's Day, they'd offer these delicious honey cakes.

"Ohmigoodness. I almost went a year without having a honey cake!" Agatha took the box from her daughter and kept it with her as she walked into the kitchen, the other two trailing her. She set it on the table. "How about coffee, girls? Do you have time?"

"We have a few minutes," Piper said. She sat down at the table, and Summer placed her crutches against the wall and also sat down. "Have we heard anything from Cash or Ben?"

"Nothing." Summer reached into the box and pulled out a heart-shaped honey cake. She took a bite as Agatha set a cup of coffee in front of her. Just one bite brought back so many memories: her and her mom sitting on the boardwalk, Piper and Summer having a tea party featuring the cakes when they were little kids, and she'd never forget the time someone had given her a box for free. They'd never been able to find out who it was. Though she wondered if it could have been her father.

She took another bite and swore she could taste the sea and the sand of her youth. It was like biting into a sunny beach day. At least in Summer's mind.

"What gives? Cops never take this long to run a license on TV." Piper took another bite, then a sip of coffee. "I can never make coffee as good as you, Ma."

"I know. It seems to be taking a while," Summer said. "If I've not heard back by the time I'm finished at the doctor's office, I'll ping Cash."

At the mention of his name, Agatha and Piper changed knowing glances.

"You two," Summer said. "You both need to get a grip and mind your own business."

"Whatever you say, dear," Aunt Agatha replied.

"Well, I'm going to keep asking whether you like it or not," Piper said.

"That's a surprise," Summer muttered.

"You know, I think the cakes are even sweeter this year," Agatha said.

"I don't." Piper shoved the rest of her cake into her mouth.

"So ladylike." Agatha pursed her lip and rolled her eyes.

Piper belched, leaving her mom gasping, swiping at air, and Summer laughing.

* * *

In the car, Piper turned up the radio, and they danced to Stevie Nicks tunes all the way to the doctor's office, just like they had when they were teenagers. You'd never know they were both looking at forty. Not until they stopped and tried to get Summer out of the car, with much effort.

"Piper, let me go. I can do this. You're just in the way."

"Okay!" Piper placed her hands in the air so that Summer could prepare. Then she held the office door open for Summer.

After waiting a few minutes, Piper and Summer were ushered into the exam room. The doctor checked her over. "It appears as if you're healing nicely. The swelling has gone down even further. We'll need a smaller boot. I'll send the nurse in to boot you." He started to walk away, then turned back around. "I've lost track of the case. Have they found the killer yet?"

"What are you talking about?" Piper asked.

"Lana's Livingston's killer."

"Oh, no. Nothing," Summer said. *But we think it has links to a drug ring here on the island,* she thought. She kept her own counsel. She didn't want to spread rumors.

"Oh, it's too bad. I was hoping they'd gotten the killer," he said, and left the room.

"He must not know about Glads." Summer studied her exposed foot. Her ankle was still quite bruised, but the swelling was just about gone.

The nurse walked in and started booting her foot and ankle. Summer was girding her loins, waiting for the nurse to ask about the case. But she surprised Summer. Not a word was mentioned.

* * *

Later, when they were back in the car, Cash called.

"Hey, Cash, what's up?"

"Sorry it's taken so long, but there were complications."

"Really? What kind?"

Piper stopped at a stop sign and gawked at Summer.

"The car you saw belongs to Liam Connor."

"*What?* Liam? He knows Mary Laura?" Summer asked, as Piper danced frantically around in her seat while she tried to drive.

"Yes. They know each other."

"I'm confused."

Cash drew in a long breath and let it out. "So am I. We need to back off. Something big is happening, and we don't want to get in the middle of it."

"But—"

"No *buts*, Summer. That was a direct order for me. To back off. I don't know exactly what's happening. I'm not privy to that kind of information. But Glads is free. We've done well by her, and that's all that matters, right?"

Summer wanted to scream. But she used her calm voice. "Of course that's all that matters. But let's not forget, someone nearly destroyed my home. So it feels kind of personal to me."

"Summer—"

"I don't want any trouble, Cash, believe me. I'm not going to go looking for it. I promise." Even as she said those words, she wasn't quite sure they were true.

* * *

Summer clicked off the phone with Cash. "He said Liam and Mary Laura know one another."

"How?" Piper asked. "I mean, like, are they related? Went to school together?"

"Cash didn't say. But he said something big was happening and he was ordered to back off. And so he wants me to back off."

"Back off what?"

"I guess trying to find Lana's killer."

"You helped so much. What's his problem?" Piper said as they pulled into Aunt Agatha's driveway.

"I helped when we were trying to get Glads off. So I suppose that's okay. And he's right that the case isn't really any of my concern at this point." Summer hesitated. "Except that Lana sent her stuff to me. And in that stuff was a lot of drugs. I'm sure that's why my place was ransacked."

"Why would Lana's stuff get sent to you in the first place? That makes no sense." Piper got out of the car, came around, and opened the back seat door to get the crutches.

"Tina said I was her emergency contact, and she gave my address." Summer hoisted herself onto her crutches.

"Odd. I don't think I've ever been asked for an emergency contact when I've checked into a B and B." Piper opened the front door of the house.

"Well, you aren't a bestselling author," Summer said as she walked through the door.

"It's almost as if she was setting you up in case something happened to her," Piper said.

Summer mulled that over. "She may have figured I was responsible because I hired her. That's the only thing that makes sense."

"I suppose. But what did she think you were going to do with all those drugs?"

"Good question. I don't think she thought she was going to die," Summer pointed out. She leaned down as far as her crutches would let her to see Mr. Darcy coming for her.

"Summer! Summer!" Mr. Darcy ran up to her. "It's about time!"

"He's getting some exercise." Agatha trailed him.

"Hello, Mr. Darcy." Summer kept moving toward the plastic-covered couch. Agatha had had the same couch for forty years and wasn't planning on spending the money to buy a new one. As long as Summer had been coming over, this same couch had sat here, covered in plastic. "What a day."

"How did the appointment go?" Agatha wanted to know.

Summer filled her in.

"Do you want to go to Beach Reads?" Agatha scooped up Mr. Darcy and put him in his cage.

"Yes, in a little while."

Piper recapped what Cash had told Summer.

"They know each other?" Agatha appeared as if she didn't believe it. "How odd. But of course, they are both from the Pittsburgh area."

"Pittsburgh is huge," Piper said. "They might know each other professionally."

"She's a chef and he's a cop. I don't think so," Summer said.

"Maybe they've dated?" Agatha said, and then tittered. "That would be funny, since he took you out."

"Well, even if that's the case, he won't be doing that again." Summer sighed.

"Not after you hauled off and hit him!" Agatha laughed even harder.

"With her crutch!" Piper added, laughing. The next thing Summer knew, she was laughing as well. Even though she was embarrassed that she'd lost her cool like that, it was kind of funny.

"I think he might press charges," Summer said, growing serious.

"No he won't. He wouldn't want the judge to hear his story," Piper said. "In fact, I've been meaning to research Liam Connor. He seems like an un-detective."

"How would you know?" Agatha asked.

"Well, he asked Summer out and was all over her, and then he became aggressive toward her."

"Thinking back, I think that's the day he was informed that the charges had been dropped against Glads."

"That's no excuse." Piper sat down at Agatha's desktop computer. "Does this thing work, Ma?"

"Of course it does. I like the big screen."

"It's big, all right." Piper clicked it on. "Mom, you've got about a million tabs open."

"I like it that easy, because I can just click and I go there. Like magic." Agatha shrugged.

Piper's long fingers stroked the keys. She keyed in more words. "That's odd."

"What?" Summer asked.

"There's nothing about Liam Connor anywhere online."

"That can't be. There must be a million Liam Connors." Agatha said.

"Yes, but none of them are him. There are no Liam Connors living in the state of Pennsylvania," Piper said. "Humph. How weird."

"People can have their online presence scrubbed," Summer said.

"But why would you? Unless you have something to hide?"

Summer mulled it over. "Well, I supposed being a cop would make you not want to be online."

"Another possibility is that he's been using a fake name. Cops do it all the time," Piper said.

"Not legitimate cops," Agatha said.

"Maybe undercover cops?"

"But he wouldn't be an undercover cop posing as a detective, would he?" Piper said.

Summer's brains were scrambled. "I have no idea."

Chapter
Fifty-Two

There were people who just never went online, Summer told herself before she slept that night. The fact that Liam wasn't online really could be that simple—he wasn't a man to follow the crowd by living his life online. Summer realized the wisdom in that. Now that she did social media as a regular thing for Beach Reads, she realized the power in it, but she also considered the huge amount of time she put into it as almost a waste. Did people come to the events because of those clever little posts? Summer didn't know. She'd start polling people at the next event to see where they'd found out about it.

So if Liam just didn't want to bother with it, more power to him.

She's often considered doing the same thing. She despised the way people thought it was okay to be rude, critical, and obnoxious online, even if they wouldn't be in person. It was weirdly dissociative.

And Summer had definitely noticed a difference in people coming in after the pandemic. There was always an undercurrent of fear and sometimes rage. People had little patience.

She closed her eyes. All you could do was your best. Put one foot in front of the other. Take one thing at a time.

Glads popped into her mind. Summer hadn't seen or heard from her in the two days since she'd left Summer's house. She imagined she was enjoying her freedom. Enjoying the fact that everybody understood she hadn't killed Lana. Summer smiled.

* * *

The next day, Summer and Agatha sat and waited for Piper. It was Piper's turn to take Summer to Beach Reads.

The doorbell rang.

Agatha rose to answer the door. "Bo? Please come in. Is everything okay?"

"Yes, thank you," Bo said. "I heard that Summer was staying here, and I brought her a few little things."

If Summer could have run, she would have. Bo just rubbed her the wrong way.

He followed Agatha into the living room, where Summer sat on the plastic-covered couch. He glanced at Summer shyly. That was one of the things that creeped her out. He never could look straight at her.

"How are you?" He sat down next to her. "I went to your house, and there's crime scene tape everywhere."

"My home was broken into."

"Robbed?"

"We don't think so. It was vandalized."

"How strange and cruel," he said, looking past Summer's shoulder.

Summer's thoughts exactly. "What can I do for you?" She'd like to move this visit along. He didn't smell as bad as he usually did, but she detected a slight pot smell on him, which was more than a bit nauseating to her.

"I brought you something." He held up a little bag. "I know how you feel about CBD and science and all that. But I'm telling you, this salve is good. Just try it."

"It can't hurt," Agatha said.

Summer lifted the salve and twisted open the container. "It smells good."

He laughed. "Yeah. I know you can't get to your ankle yet. But I'm sure there are other places that are getting sore. So I brought you the salve and the oil. My mom swears by the salve for her arthritis."

"Your mom? Does she live locally?"

"Yes. She's living with me for the time being. She can't quite be alone. But we're seeking another place for her." His voice lowered to almost a whisper.

Summer couldn't believe what she was hearing. Bo was taking care of his mother. He'd just restored her faith in humanity.

"Do you mean assisted living?" Agatha asked. "There's nothing like that on the island."

"Yeah. There's the problem." He smiled. "Anyway, I don't want to take up too much of your time. Just wanted to give you the products, and I hope you try them."

"I believe I will." Summer had been trying creams and other concoctions for her sore arms and legs. She'd gotten little relief. She couldn't believe she was going to try this stuff. But what could it hurt at this point? "Thank you, Bo. I appreciate it."

"Sure." He stood.

"And thanks for coming to the event the other night."

"Oh, I like to support," he said. "Sorry about everything that happened after. Did they find her killer?"

"Not yet." Agatha stood as well.

"I keep asking myself if I observed anything suspicious that night. And I really didn't. I'm sorry."

"All of us who were there are doing the same thing, racking our brains trying to help." Agatha led him to the door. "Thanks for stopping by."

He muttered something as he was leaving that Summer couldn't quite hear.

Agatha walked back into the room. "Will wonders never cease?"

"Indeed, Aunt Agatha. Indeed."

"Poor young man, living with his mom and trying to help her." Agatha shook her head slowly.

"I know. Why are they here? I should've asked. He should take her to Raleigh or somewhere stateside. We have nothing like that here."

"Right? That might be a good business for someone to start." Agatha's hand went to her chin.

"Why not you?"

Agatha laughed. "I'll be needing a place like that myself in a few years."

"Bite your tongue, Aunt Agatha."

* * *

When Piper arrived, she seemed a bit confused. "I thought I saw Bo. Pulling out of the driveway. In fact, I'm almost one hundred percent sure I did. What is Bo doing here?"

"He brought me some CBD salves. I think I'm going to give it a try." Summer stood and grabbed her crutches. "I'm ready to go."

"Wait. Did I just hear you say you were going to try CBD? You've been ranting about it. You said there's no good science about it. What happened?" Piper asked.

Summer sighed. "Sometimes science doesn't know everything; it can't hurt to try this. God knows I'm sore everywhere. I've tried a lot of the other over-the-counter stuff, and really, there's just not much relief."

Mr. Darcy whistled. "I love Piper, she's a good girl, good girl."

"Thank you, Mr. Darcy. I love you too. You're a good bird." Piper helped Summer get her coat on, and they said their goodbyes to Aunt Agatha.

Summer was really beginning to miss being able to drive herself where she needed to go, but she didn't think she'd be able to drive anytime soon. And she knew that her aunt and Piper would not allow her to take a cab.

When Summer and Piper got to the bookstore, they were happy to see Glads in all her glory, wearing a pink jogging suit that matched her hair. Marilyn was with her, bundled up with scarves and a hat along with a winter coat. She was not happy about the lower temperatures, though the cold didn't seem to faze Glads at all.

"Well, look who's here," said Poppy as Piper and Summer walked up to the group, who were hanging out near the coffee station.

"Any news?" Glads asked.

Summer understood what she was seeking. She didn't have to ask what news. "I'm sorry, there's no news."

Glads followed Summer into her office. "I just wanted to say that I'm very sorry to hear about your place. I guess you'll be staying with Agatha for quite some time."

Summer sat down at her desk chair. "The house doesn't have to be perfect for me to move back in it, for sure. As soon as my ankle is better, I'm going to start searching for new furniture, and I'm hoping insurance will cover a lot of the damage. I hope I don't have to stay with her too long. And I'm really getting sick of having people have to take me where I need to go. It's just an extra thing to worry about."

Glads shifted her weight back and forth. "You could come stay with me. If you get sick of staying with Agatha. I have plenty of room. Just figured I'd put that out there."

Summer was touched that Glads had offered a place for her to stay, but she realized Aunt Agatha would have a heart attack if she went to stay someplace else. "Thanks so much, Glads. I'll keep that in mind. So, how are you doing?"

"I'm doing fine. I think people are still talking about me, even though the charges have been dropped. But I don't care. Let them talk. All I care about is what the law says, and the law says I'm a free woman." She was all smiles and beaming. It was as if the dropped charges had given Glads a new light and a new lease on life. Then she became serious. "But I would rest better if the real killer was found."

"Wouldn't we all?" Summer flipped on the computer screen. "I don't think they're even close to solving the murder."

"It can't be that hard. She was selling drugs, and something went wrong. There's not too many people on this island who would be buying drugs from her. Come on."

"Cash says there's a drug ring. That's probably who was in my house. They were probably searching for the drugs that I'd already given to the cops."

Glads gasped. "That's hard to believe."

"This island has become a drug-trafficking island." Summer turned to her computer and hit the browser button. Her screen went to her home page, which was the local news. *Beach Reads Owes My Mother* was printed in large caps across the screen. A picture of Mary Laura appeared beneath the headline. "Oh my god."

"What?" Glads came around to see the screen.

Mary Laura Roberts, stepdaughter of Lana Livingston, says Beach Reads Bookstore has not officially apologized to Livingston's family and has not been cooperative with the investigation into her murder.

"I mean, she was poisoned at the store. Didn't anybody notice?"

Summer couldn't read anymore. Her stomach tightened. She snapped her computer shut and banged her fist on the desk.

"Summer! Calm down. Let's think. What are we going to do?" Glads asked.

"I'm going to call my friend Macy, who knows about crisis communications. And we are going to fight back."

"That's my girl. What I don't understand is how Gina hired her. She's such a lovely person. How could she hire Mary Laura?" Glads asked.

"What? I knew Mary Laura was a pastry chef and that she'd gotten a job here, but I didn't know it was right next door. We'll have to warn Gina about her." Summer didn't want to put anybody out of a job, nor did she want to tell someone else who to hire. And she needed to be careful about how she accomplished this. But since it now was public knowledge how Mary Laura felt and she had launched a campaign against Beach Reads, maybe Gina would see it for herself.

"How much do we know about Mary Laura?". Glads asked.

"I know the police questioned her, but I don't think they got far." Summer's heart was still pounding. She took a deep breath. "As you know, she believed that Lana killed her father."

"Maybe she did."

"Glads!"

"No, listen. You said he was ill and suffering. Maybe she helped him to die. There's a big difference between committing murder and helping someone to die because they're suffering." Her face reddened. Her eyes shifted to the corner.

An intuitive bite snapped at Summer. This was a raw and emotional subject for Glads.

"You're absolutely right, Glads." Summer paused. "In her journal, she wrote that she was struggling with that. He wanted her help. She couldn't do it. She was hoping for a cure."

The room silenced for a few beats.

"That poor woman." Glads's voice cracked.

Chapter
Fifty-Three

Summer dialed Macy.

"Hello, Summer. Has it gotten worse?"

"Sort of. Lana's stepdaughter was interviewed by a local reporter. She said Beach Reads never reached out to the family and we never issued a statement. But I did talk with a local reporter and say how sorry I am. And I was certainly going to send flowers to her funeral when they have it."

"Maybe you should issue another statement. Put it on your blog and give it to the local paper," she said. "I wouldn't engage with Mary Laura directly. If a reporter comes to see you, be careful with what you say. Don't talk about the ongoing investigation. Only talk about how sorry you are."

"I'm thinking about holding a charity event."

"What kind of charity?"

"Maybe the women's center. Something to do with violence against women. We do this kind of thing every so often. It wouldn't look like we're just trying to score good PR points."

"Has your business been affected by all this?"

"Yes. It's slowed down a lot. But it did start to pick back up. Now this."

"Keep track of everything in the papers. If you have to, you can press charges."

"That would do no good for my reputation." Summer tapped her fingers on the desk. There was no way Macy could realize what a small community St. Brigid's was.

"Wouldn't it? Someone is spreading lies about the business. Maybe you should fight back—legally."

"I don't know about doing that." Still tapping her fingers.

"It's funny, most of my clients are like that. They don't want to ruffle any feathers. They tend to hyperfocus on the one thing—PR—and not see what's right under their noses. But there's only so much you can do with PR. If you slap someone with a cease-and-desist order, they often will shut right up."

Summer mulled that over—she'd not considered that. Maybe she should talk with Cash about it. "Well, you've given me a lot to think about."

"Have they found the killer yet?" Macy asked.

"No. But my friend Glads is off the hook." Summer's fingers stopped tapping.

"That's good news. But you'd think they'd have nabbed the person by now. Such a small town."

"You've be surprised how difficult it is, even in a small town." Summer paused. "I think the police are making headway."

But she was beginning to feel like they weren't. They wanted Cash off the case, but why had there not been an arrest? What was going on? She'd certainly feel safer if they nabbed this killer.

* * *

Later, Summer mulled over what Macy had said about people not seeing things that were right under their noses. What were the police missing? What was she missing?

Her mind kept turning to Mary Laura. And why wouldn't it? The woman had said some mean and untrue things to the newspaper. But Summer had the impression she'd ranked high as a suspect. She had not gotten along with Lana. She'd been at the event, and the day before, Summer had seen her with a book on poison.

But now she was acting like Lana had been her best friend. Like she considered her stepmom a part of her family. And Summer knew from the journal that wasn't true.

Then she stopped herself. That journal was Lana's perception of the matter. Maybe that wasn't how Mary Laura felt at all.

What a sticky situation. Mary Laura was now working with Gina, one of Summer's favorite people. Summer wondered if she had jumped to the wrong conclusion. Maybe Mary Laura was reacting out of a genuine hurt.

She picked up a pencil and rolled it back and forth between her hands. She didn't like this at all. She wasn't quite sure what to do. At times like this, she really missed her mom, who was always full of good, if not unusual, advice.

What would you do, Mom?

What would Hildy do? What would she do if someone had just publicly trashed the bookstore and was working right next door at the chocolate shop?

Summer closed her eyes. "What would you do, Ma?"

Her eyes popped open, and she knew what Hildy would do. She'd bake some delicious vegan treats, take them next door, and talk things through. But could Summer really offer vegan brownies to a chocolatier and a pastry chef?

It's not the gift that counts; it's the thought behind it. Hildy's words rang in her head.

"Indeed, Mom, indeed."

"Aunt Summer, are you okay?" Mia poked her head in the office. "Because it seems like you're having a conversation with yourself."

"I was talking to Mom."

"Really? Did she answer you?" Mia teased.

Summer hesitated before answering. "Believe it or not, Mia, I think she did."

220

"Okay, weirdo." Mia grinned.

Summer ignored that. "Would you like to help me bake brownies tonight at your grandmother's?"

"You bet," she said. "As long as your mom doesn't make an appearance."

Summer rolled her eyes. "Go do some work or something."

Mia left the room.

Summer had a plan. She'd make the brownies and try to make amends with Mary Laura—even though she sensed it should be the other way around. She'd write and release a statement tomorrow. And while she was playing nice, she'd find out more about the mysterious Mary Laura. And maybe the dark-eyed woman would tell her how she knew the detective.

Chapter
Fifty-Four

When Summer and Piper got back to Agatha's that evening, Cash was in the kitchen with Agatha.

"Hello." Summer entered the kitchen. "What's going on?"

Agatha was wearing an apron and looked as if she was on a mission. "I had a hankering for your mom's veggie meat loaf. I mentioned it to Cash, and he said he remembered how to do it. So here we are. Veggie meat loaf in the oven."

"The mashed potatoes are ready," Cash said.

"Well, isn't this a lovely little domestic scene." Piper walked in and rolled up her sleeves.

Aunt Agatha's kitchen was probably close to the version that house had come with. Yes, she'd upgraded some of the appliances, but only because she'd had to. The counters and decor were in the olive green and gold of the 1970s.

"Indeed," Summer said.

The front door opened and closed. Mia bounded in. "I thought we were going to make Hildy's brownies."

"We can make them after supper."

"What? Why are you making brownies? We just had brownies. In fact, there's a ton still back at your place," Agatha said.

"Yes, but we can't go there." Summer pictured the brownies petrifying in the meantime. Gosh, she was going to have a mess to clean up. "I plan to take the brownies to Mary Laura and Gina."

Aunt Agatha spun around.

"Oh boy," Cash said. "You've done it now."

"Why would you do that?" Agatha's voice shook. "That Mary Laura has done nothing but cause trouble. What she said about the bookstore . . ."

"Calm down. I hear you. I was livid when I read the article. But she was right: at this point, we haven't reached out to the family."

The room quieted.

"We were concentrating on Glads." Summer hesitated. "I did give a statement, which wasn't used in the article, evidently. So I plan to write a blog post and call the paper myself. In fact, I might run an ad just to get our point of view out there. I might add there have been no funeral arrangements made—and when they are made, we will be there."

"That sounds like a measured approach," Cash said. "But I don't get the brownies."

"Mom used to take them to people to make amends or talk through some issue. It often worked."

"She should be making amends to you," Agatha said, waving a spoon, then pointing it at Summer.

"I have to agree." Piper sat down at the kitchen table. "I don't think Mary Laura is the friendly sort."

"No, she's not, but she's working at the chocolate shop. I respect and like Gina, and they are right next door." Summer moved toward the table and placed her crutches against the wall, next to the orange-and-brown mushroom plaque. It had been there forever.

"Besides, Mary Laura is not the killer," Cash said, and thwacked the potato masher on the pan.

"How do you know?" Agatha said.

"The police questioned her, and she had a solid alibi. That's what Dad said."

Summer plunked herself in a chair. "Did he say how she knew Liam?"

"I didn't ask. It doesn't matter. He's back in Pittsburgh. They released Lana's body. He'll be there waiting for it, I suppose." He paused. "How's your ankle?"

"It hurts. It's almost time for a pill. Are you sure Liam went back to Pittsburgh?"

"Yes."

"We researched him online, and there was nothing. I mean nothing." Piper drummed her fingers on the table. "We found people with his name, but none of those people were him."

"There's not much about me either," Cash said. "I don't have any social media. I have a professional website and an email and that's it."

Mia sat down and pulled out her laptop. "What police force is he linked to?"

"Aliquippa. It's just outside Pittsburgh," Cash said. "What do you want me to do with these potatoes?"

"Just leave them there. The loaf is almost done," Agatha said.

Mia's finger clicked over the keyboard, and in just a few minutes, she had an answer. "There he is. There is a picture of him, but Liam is not his name."

"What?" Cash spun around and went over to the computer. "Detective Andrew Lokomski."

Summer's head was spinning. Why was he using a fake name?

"I knew it!" Piper said. "He was using another name while he was here."

"Why would a detective do that?" Agatha asked.

"He must have been here undercover. Not doing what he said he was doing," Summer said.

"You're right," Cash replied. "But if that's the case, what was he doing here?"

"Said he was here to watch Lana because she was a suspect in a murder case." Summer's face heated. *So foolish for buying everything he said.*

Mia took her computer back and typed. "When I key in his real name, I can see him on LinkedIn and Facebook." She paused. "On Facebook, he doesn't post often. But this is very interesting."

"What?" Piper leaned over to view the screen. "Oh my god."

"Close your mouth, Ma." Mia looked at Summer. "He's in a relationship." She used air quotes.

"With whom?"

"Guess."

"Mia, now is not the time to play games," Agatha said.

Summer searched her mind. There was only one possibility, judging from Piper's face. "Must be Mary Laura."

Agatha plunked down the meat loaf on to the counter. "Maybe what they were arguing about that night was that she moved here. Maybe he's not wanting a long-distance relationship."

Summer grunted. "And that explains why he came on so strong. He was just feeling me out to see what I was aware of. He had no real interest in me."

"I told you it was overkill," Piper said. She had never been one to not point out when she was right.

"But it doesn't explain how aggressive he became with me. It was almost as if he was a different person."

"Like he could have killed you?" Mia said.

"I have no doubt." Chills ran through Summer. Had he killed Lana? If so, why? And had she been next on his list?

"Thank god he's gone. Out with the trash!" Agatha placed the loaf on the table.

As Summer drew in the scent of it, memories flooded her mind. Her mom spinning around in the kitchen as she waited for the fake meat loaf to bake. Her mom slicing it onto her plate. And the hours she'd sat and chatted with Summer while they ate it.

Summer considered Cash, who sat next to her. He'd remembered how to make it. Summer did not. When had he learned how to do it? She searched her mind and couldn't remember him ever being in her mom's kitchen except to eat in it. But, evidently, more had happened than what she remembered. It wasn't lost on her that Cash loved her mom. It also wasn't lost on her how dear it was that he knew how to make the loaf. Her hard heart softened just a bit.

Chapter
Fifty-Five

Later, Summer and Cash sat on the plastic-covered couch while everybody else helped Mia make the brownies and made themselves scarce.

"We need to find out why Liam or whoever he was was really here," Summer said.

"Why? Why do we care?" Cash asked.

She shrugged. Why indeed? "I guess it's moot. It's just curiosity, I suppose." She hesitated. "Maybe he's our killer."

"A detective?" One of his eyebrows went up. "Well, it's not like there aren't bad cops out there. But most of them are good sorts."

He was thinking of his dad.

"How is Ben?"

"Very busy. Just the way he likes it. I've not seen much of him." He leaned in. "Which is okay with me."

Summer laughed.

"You know what else is okay with me?" He slipped his arm across the back of the couch, and she settled in the crook of his arm against his chest. "This. Sitting here on the couch with you."

Summer had taken her medicine and was getting woozy, but she liked it too. Warm fuzzies spun into sparks.

Cash's phone rang. He glanced at the screen. "Speaking of the devil. Hey, Dad."

Pause. Pause. Pause.

"Well, she's right here. I can ask. Hang on." He lifted his chin toward Summer. "How many times was the detective at your house?"

Summer tried to recall. "I think five times."

Cash told his father. Pause. "Oh, that's strange. I don't think he was upstairs."

"No," Summer said.

"Interesting," Cash said. "I can call tomorrow, Dad." He held the phone out from his ear as Ben told him, emphatically, that he needed to call tonight. "Okay, I'll call him right now."

Summer had no idea who or what he was talking about.

"Shoot. Dad wants me to call this guy I know in Aliquippa." He set down the phone. "But first, you need to know that Liam's DNA is all over your place. Even in the beds."

"What? He's never been up there!"

"He would've been up there if he was the one who ransacked your house."

"I thought it was a drug gang coming to look for those drugs, and it was Liam? What for?"

Cash shrugged. "Who knows? At this point, all they have is DNA evidence."

"What's going on?" Agatha, Piper, and Mia entered the living room.

Cash recapped the whole thing.

"Liam or whoever he is is appearing more and more suspicious," Piper said.

"Yeah." Cash stood. "I need to make a call."

"You can go in the guest room." Agatha showed him the way.

"What do you think is going on?" Piper said.

"I'm confused."

"That's exactly how whoever's been doing all this wants it. We need to simplify things. Stay focused if we want to find Lana's killer," Mia said.

"That's easier said than done. What do we know, really?" Piper said. "We know that Lana drank poisoned tea at Beach Reads and went back to the B and B and died."

"We know Glads was not the person who did that," Summer added. "We also know that Mary Laura came to the event and the day before had a book about poisons."

"We also know that Liam—let's just call him that for the sake of clarity—was here to keep an eye on Lana."

"That's what he *said*. But now that we know he was here under-cover, I suspect there was another reason."

"And he behaved in some inappropriate ways," Mia said.

Agatha, quiet until that point, cleared her throat. "We're missing something. It feels like we're quite close, like it's right under our noses. But what is it?"

"I've been feeling like that too." Summer went back through all the things she'd done to try to figure out who the killer was when Glads was a suspect. She'd worked on the sales records, She'd viewed the tape—and spotted the shadow there of someone else who must've been the poisoner. She'd read Lana's journal, which had led the investigation in another direction.

Aunt Agatha was right. They were missing something.

"I think I should go with you to the chocolate shop tomorrow," Agatha told Summer. "I don't want you going alone. I have a bad feel-ing about this."

"Gram, what are you going to do if they attack her?" Mia said. "I should go. I'm the youngest and the strongest."

"Ha! You will not go, young lady. I will go." Piper stood. "I'm every bit as strong as you, and I have kicked some ass in my day."

Mia *pshaw*ed.

"It's true," Summer said. "She used to beat up boys frequently."

"What?" Agatha said. "Why did I not know about that?"

"Because you are her mother and we kept it from you," Summer said.

All eyes went to Piper, who shrugged. "It's true."

The room went silent—which was when Cash walked back in. "I'm going to tell you all this in confidence." He pointed at Mia. "I mean it. Keep this right here."

"Okay," Mia said, and her mother nodded.

"Our man Liam is still on the force, but barely. He's on extended leave."

"What does that mean?" Piper asked the same thing Summer was thinking.

"It could mean a lot of things. Cops, even detectives, need to take a break from time to time. The work is extremely stressful," Cash said.

"Maybe he had a breakdown," Summer said.

"Well, he did, of a sort. He was addicted to cocaine, and they forced him into rehab." He rubbed his hand over his mouth.

"But he was here, so he's not in rehab," Mia said.

"He may have been at one point," Cash said.

Summer's head was spinning. Things were starting to make a certain amount of sense. "I wonder if he was on drugs when he came to Beach Reads. That would explain his behavior."

"It would also explain him trashing your place. He knew the drugs were with the police, but maybe he figured you had some tucked away," Piper said.

"There's a whole lot of conjecture going on," Cash interrupted. "He may just have been angry because Summer rejected him. Or angry because the charges were dropped against Glads." He paused. "This does not mean he killed Lana."

Summer shivered. Maybe not. But she wasn't so sure.

Chapter
Fifty-Six

The next day, Piper drove Summer and her brownies to the board-walk, where Beach Reads sat right next to the chocolate shop. They pulled in behind the store, as they usually did.

"Maybe I should check on Beach Reads first," Summer said.

"Why?" Piper asked.

"Well, it is my store, and I feel obligated. I'll poke my head in there and see that everything is okay." Summer stood, using her crutches, and swung herself around to face the store. A pile of boxes sat outside Beach Reads, which was not too uncommon, but they needed to be broken down and taken to the local recycling place. Maybe nobody had had a chance to do that, but Summer hated to see the boxes.

Hers wasn't the only store with stuff outside on the stoop. She noticed that the chocolate shop had a couple of barrels and the CBD shop also had some empty boxes, and that made her feel just a little bit better.

* * *

Piper opened the back door for her, and she swung through the door-way. She walked through the stacks of books and boxes into the book-store, where Poppy and Glads were chatting with a customer. Poppy looked up and waved.

And appropriately enough, Gina walked in with Mary Laura, their arms full of boxes of chocolate. Gina peered over at Summer. "Hello, neighbor."

Mary Laura tried to smile. "We brought you some goodies."

"Thank you so much." Summer took the boxes, puzzled.

"Actually, I wondered if we could chat. Is there a place where we could talk?" Gina said.

"Sure. Let's go back to my office." Summer led the way, Piper next to her. Gina was behind her, and Mary Laura trailed behind Gina. Summer hobbled into her office and said, "I'm sorry; there may not be enough chairs for everybody."

"No worries. We won't be here long." Gina put her arm out, and Mary Laura took her place next to Gina.

What was this? Summer wondered. They were turning the tables on her. She had been planning to take them goodies and attempt to make amends.

Mary Laura's face grew pink. "I just wanted to say I'm sorry about the newspaper article. I didn't mean it the way the newspaper made it sound. They asked me questions, and I answered, but I didn't know what context they were putting it in. I'm so sorry."

Summer glanced at Piper, then at Gina, who was beaming. "I want to keep our relationship good, and Mary Laura is the best pastry chef I've found, but I told her I won't have her putting down other businesses in public. It was really a mistake."

"I can see how that would happen. The newspapers around here are not known for their accuracy." Summer gestured for Gina to sit down, and Mary Laura stood right behind her, her shoulders stooped, her head hung low. Summer read that she was embarrassed, but as she studied her cousin, it didn't seem that Piper was buying any of it.

"I completely understand, Gina. It's been a trying few days, and I have to say I'm sorry that it seems like I was not supportive to your family, Mary Laura." Summer regarded the young woman. "It was just that we were busy with our own trauma. Our friend Glads was being accused of a murder she didn't commit, and we were trying to support her. I'm so sorry that in that moment, none of us considered reaching out to the family."

Mary Laura lifted her head and smiled.

"I did issue a statement through that same paper, which I don't think they ever published," Summer continued. "So what I'm going to do is issue a statement on our blog and buy ad space in the paper so they know exactly what our stance is on the loss of Lana Livingston, your beloved stepmother."

"Thank you so much," Mary Laura said.

Piper looked as if she wanted to throw up. But Piper had no idea what it was like to run a business and how important a solid reputation was—or how important it was to have the support of your neighboring businesses.

"So, Mary Laura, we have Gina's story. We know she was trained in France, that she was born in Brooklyn, and it's always been her dream to have a chocolate shop. What brings you here?" Summer leaned forward to show her interest.

"I just needed to start fresh. I am a pastry chef with a lot of experience in working with chocolate. When I came here, I fell in love with the place, and I asked Gina if she needed help," Mary Laura said.

"It must be hard just to pick up and move away from your family and friends," Piper said.

Mary Laura shrugged. "Not really. There's not many people left back where I came from. My dad died and now my stepmom, and I've been trying to get away from my boyfriend for quite some time. This provided the perfect opportunity."

Interesting. So Mary Laura had been trying to get away from Liam, or whoever the hell he was. At least, that's what her story was right now as she stood here in Summer's office. Who understood the real story? In truth, most relationships couldn't be described in a sentence or two. They were more nuanced than that.

"So, I think we're squared away then," Gina said, smiling. She stood. "Thanks, Summer, for being so understanding."

"Certainly. I'd walk you out, but walking is a little bit difficult for me these days."

"I'll walk them out," Piper said.

"That's not necessary," Gina said. "We know our way out, but thank you."

After they left, Piper took a seat. "What do you think of that?"

"It was ironic that they came just when we got here, and they came bearing gifts. Which is exactly what we were going to do. And it looks like Mary Laura was trying to get away from you-know-who."

Piper crossed her arms. "It felt a little fake to me, I have to say."

Summer sighed. "I agree."

"But I did find it interesting that she said she was getting away from her boyfriend. She didn't say who her boyfriend is or was. We're assuming it was you-know-who."

* * *

Later, Summer sat in front of the laptop and prayed to the muses to bless her. How many times had her writing saved her? How many times had she had to reach down deep within herself and pull out some words for the page? Most people surmised that you just put some words on the page; maybe they considered it more an act of typing than of creating. When Summer was writing her second book on Shakespeare, her editors had acted like it was nothing for her to write an eighty-thousand-word manuscript. That had been her last book—not that she hadn't considered writing another, a different kind of book, but her life had taken quite a turn. The life of a Shakespearean scholar was not really hers any longer. But she did love a good story, and she loved thinking about the roots of story, and how Shakespeare had contributed to the mechanics and the roots of telling stories, even now.

So her fingers flew to the keyboard. But her heart was what propelled her forward.

To our customers, readers and loyal fans of Lana Livingston: We are deeply sorry and saddened that Lana has died. We are heartbroken that her last event was at our beloved bookstore, Beach Reads. Knowing how much she loved it here and had a history here makes it even more sad. We know the circumstances of her death were not pleasant. We, like you, her loyal readers, are seeking answers. All of us here at Beach Reads, and our reader community, are thinking of her family and her readers at this sad time. This was not the death befitting a woman who gave so much to her readers and her family. We will put our thoughts and hearts together to come up with a way to honor her as she honored us by giving us beautiful stories of the heart.

Summer then called the newspaper. "I'd like to run an ad. I have written it and I want to see it printed, every word. I do not want to see one word changed. I am paying for this ad to be run as is. If you want to charge me double to do so, fine."

The person on the other end of the phone seemed to consider it a good idea. "Your ad will run tomorrow first thing."

Summer wasn't quite pleased with herself, but she felt a little better. The weight of obligation hung heavy on her. She hadn't known the woman, and she probably wouldn't have liked Lana, as her mother had not, but she had died from drinking poisoned tea at Summer's establishment.

In that moment, Summer's insides were filled with something like revenge. Who had dared to kill this woman, whether at Beach Reads or anywhere else? Who had perceived they had the right to take this woman's life? It was truly maddening. Summer trembled with anger. She remembered her mother and the way her life had been taken from her. She somehow felt the weight of many of the murders she'd read about before her mother was killed. There was too much murder and violence in the world for her to give it even more of a place in her heart by reading fiction or watching movies about it. She didn't want to be in that mind space again, and yet here she was, thinking about murder, thinking about the tragedy of somebody taking another person's life on purpose in spite or anger. Summer wasn't one for fire and brimstone, but she hoped their souls would burn in hell.

She closed her laptop. The stirring of customers and the buzz of transactions came from the front of the building. People were visiting, but not at the rate they usually did. Her mother's legacy would continue, even though people like Mary Laura and whoever the murderer was would probably like to see it disappear.

Summer would not have it. She would fight to keep her mother's legacy alive. It was more important than writing another book or teaching another class or almost anything she could think of.

Her phone rang. When she saw the 412 area code, she knew it was Mary Laura calling, and her heart sped. What could it be? Why would she be calling? Was everything okay, or was Piper's intuitive distrust of this person on target?

"Hello, Mary Laura."

"Summer?"

"Yes." Summer considered it odd that she was the one calling and yet wanted to make sure it was indeed Summer on the phone.

"It's Mary Laura. I just wanted to touch base with you."

"Everything here is okay. I just wrote the blog post online, and I have submitted the ad to the newspaper. I'm sorry. I should've done it earlier." Summer assumed that's what she was calling about.

"That's great, but it's too little, too late."

"Come again?" Summer's mind reeled. She wondered if she'd heard correctly.

"Yes, I think it's best if you and I are honest about our feelings here. My new boss made me apologize to you." She took a deep breath. "And I think it's best if you never come to this chocolate shop again." She sounded serious, threatening even.

Summer's hackles rose. "Excuse me?"

"You heard me right. I mean it. I really don't want to see you ever again, especially not in this chocolate shop." And she hung up.

Summer's ears stung from Mary Laura's words. Piper was right: Mary Laura was fake. Now Summer had glimpsed the real Mary Laura, and she shivered with the cold reality of knowing she would be right next door for the foreseeable future.

Chapter
Fifty-Seven

Piper walked into her office. "You look just like you've seen a ghost. Are you talking to your mother again?"

"No. I just received a phone call."

Piper sat down. "Is it bad news? What's going on?"

"Well, it turns out you were right about Mary Laura. It was all fake. She came over here because Gina insisted. But her apology was a complete fake." Summer's eyes met Piper's. "She just called and threatened me."

Piper's mouth dropped open. "What?"

"Yeah, she told me to never come to the chocolate shop again."

"The utter audacity," Piper said.

"I've been thinking about how to handle this. I don't know if Gina would believe me. She really seems to like Mary Laura and need her. I think Mary Laura has her fooled," Summer said.

"I think you're right, but Gina is no dummy. I think you should tell her and let her make up her own mind."

Summer wasn't so sure. "I think I need more evidence before I talk to Gina."

"What kind of evidence? I mean, she called and threatened you. It's your word against hers, and Gina knows you're a pillar of this community." Piper set up straighter. "I mean, god, who is this Mary Laura? How dare she launch an attack against this bookstore and you? That is exactly what she's doing, whether Gina knows it or believes it or not!"

Summer caught Piper's indignation, and a fire brewed in her belly. "I hear you. I am angry, and I have to admit I'm a little frightened. What kind of woman comes in here and apologizes and then a few hours later calls and warns me? To say she is imbalanced is an understatement. We need to be careful here."

A few beats later, Piper cleared her throat. "I think you're right. There's a part of me that wants to go over there and beat the shit out of her. But there's another part of me that's like, what is up her sleeve? Does she have a gun? Does she have more poison? Does she want to kill more people? I swear she must be the person who killed Lana!"

"It would seem there's more to Mary Laura than we even imagined. Right from the start, I figured she was involved in killing Lana, and I wonder if we can ever prove it." Summer had sensed something off about her all along. Reading about her and Lana's relationship had given her what she figured was a clearer picture, though she'd been willing to give Mary Laura the benefit of the doubt, because the journal was from Lana's point of view. Summer had given this woman a chance, but now she had demonstrated exactly who she was. In Summer's book, that gave her a leg up.

"I think we need to find out more about her," Piper said. "Where do we start?"

"Well, the police have questioned her already, and she had a solid alibi. That's what Cash said. But maybe we can find out what that alibi was and see how solid it really is."

"Okay, how do we find that out? I mean, do you think Ben would tell you? Does Cash even know?" Piper folded her arms. "Maybe we can work around Ben and Cash. It seems unfair to put them in the position of telling us what must be secret information."

Summer agreed. "Do you know anybody else at the courthouse or with the police force?"

Piper thought. "I don't, but Tina's daughter works as a receptionist for the police force part-time."

Summer felt a little awkward about asking Tina about this. But Tina was as affected by this death as anybody in the community, given that she was the person who'd found Lana dead. Maybe if they spoke with her about everything going on, she would help. They would have to be honest. And Summer was sure that Tina would see how important it was to find out who Mary Laura really was. They really needed to know what that alibi was, the alibi that cleared her of this crime that Summer was beginning to think without doubt she had perpetrated. "Fancy a trip to see Tina?"

"Absolutely. And if my calculations are correct, we still have brownies in the car." Piper smiled. "They are coming in handy after all."

Summer grabbed her crutches and stood, placing the crutches under each arm. Her underarms were still sore, but not quite as sore as before. She'd been using the CBD salve, and it turned out Bo was right: it was more helpful than anything she had tried. She was trying to place more and more weight on that foot so it would heal, but she had to be careful. She didn't want to hurt herself further. The doctor had said a little at a time.

"Are you ready, or do you want to say goodbye to everybody?" Piper asked.

"I think I should say my goodbyes, and then we'll go and see Tina."

* * *

Forty-five minutes later, Tina, Piper, and Summer sat at Tina's kitchen table. The woman's kitchen was always pristine, as she always had guests. It was one of three B and Bs on the island, and it was the oldest and probably the most charming.

Piper and Summer had filled Tina in, and she was in shock.

"So, we've come to ask you a favor. We know it's a lot, but we understand your daughter Emma works for the police department part-time." Summer stirred her tea.

Tina took a deep breath. "Listen, you two. I would do anything to help the daughter of Hildy Merriweather. Believe me, I will ask Emma how she feels about this, and if she agrees, I'm all for it."

Summer was grateful for Tina's response. She didn't want Tina to think she was taking advantage of their friendship, but she realized if the shoe were on the other foot, she'd be glad to help too. She'd known Tina a long time.

"I want to see justice." Tina filled Piper's teacup up again. "To tell you the truth, I have another item in my back pocket toward that end." She lowered her voice. Piper and Summer leaned in. "Mary Laura is staying here." Piper's eyes widened, and Summer's mouth dropped. She put her hand in front of her mouth. "She wasn't here until she'd been hired by Gina. She had evidence of a job, and she is staying on the top floor. She will be there until she can find an apartment."

Summer envisioned a way forward, a way to maybe learn more about this woman, but she trod lightly, as once again, she didn't want to take advantage of her friendship with Tina. "Have you noticed anything odd about her behavior?"

"Not really." Tina shrugged. "She gets up very early, and I don't have breakfast prepared at that time. But she is a baker, and bakers and chocolatiers, they get up and do their work early, so that's not really unusual. I make sure she has a bagel, sometimes a biscuit or two. I lay it out here in the kitchen for her. She's really not here most of the time, and when she's here, she's sleeping."

Piper set her tea back in its saucer. Summer admired the china. Blue willow had always been her favorite pattern. "Just keep an eye on her, please. I don't trust her. I never have bought this whole thing, even through her apology. I knew she was faking."

Tina waved her hand. "I think I can handle her. But I will take your warning to heart."

Summer was glad that Piper had said that, because she was thinking the same thing. Tina had no idea how dangerous Mary Laura might be if she was indeed Lana's killer. And Summer was beginning to think she was—in fact, she was almost a hundred percent certain. Who knew who she would kill next? Or if she would kill next? "Do you ever go into her room?"

Tina stiffened a bit. "Not me, but Emma does, because she cleans. I could go in there anytime I want, but I do respect the privacy of my boarders."

Privacy? Summer understood, but in this case, she didn't believe Mary Laura was entitled to much of anything, let alone privacy. "Well, I understand that. But the next time you're in there or the next time Emma is, if you see anything out of the ordinary, make note of it."

"I hear you," Tina said. "I think it's more likely for Emma to find something at the police station than it is for us to find something in her room. But you never know."

Summer supposed it was out of the question for Tina to allow her to search Mary Laura's room, and she guessed she couldn't blame her. Tina took her role as an innkeeper seriously, and that was a good thing.

"I'd like to examine her room myself," Piper said. "I know it's out of the question, but still, you never know what you might find in there. If she indeed did kill Lana, there might be poison up there. There might be any manner of items that could help the police." Piper hesitated. "I admire your integrity. I'm not sure I could resist." She held the teacup to her mouth and blew on it. "This is good stuff."

"I agree," Summer said. "It's really good tea."

"I think what makes a difference is that it's made from loose tea and it's much fresher. It doesn't take much more to make it with loose-leaf than it does from the teabag." Tina appeared glad for the change of subject. She had been as supportive as she could be, and Summer understood that as the three of them finished the tea.

Summer and Piper soon left, thanking Tina profusely for the tea and for her willingness to ask her daughter to check into Mary Laura's alibi.

"This has been wild," Piper said. "I guess now we wait."

"Unless we can figure out another way to approach this, I guess we will. There may be other information out there for us, but who knows where to find it. We've searched on the internet, and I've read Lana's journals. I just don't know what else we can do."

Summer was a bit frustrated, and she sensed Piper's frustration as well. She was grateful for Tina's attitude and support, but she would be even more grateful if she could snoop around in that room. She wondered if there was a way she could manage that. At the same time, she respected Tina and didn't want to use their friendship that way.

It was a no-win situation. The best they could hope for was that Emma could find a little something out about that alibi. For the time being, Summer would endeavor not to go into the chocolate shop, as she didn't want to agitate Mary Laura, and the fact that she was on crutches made that easier. Gina wouldn't suspect anything was up.

Summer felt her frustration mount when she considered Gina, who had such a kind and loving heart. Mary Laura was taking advantage of her.

Well, everything would work out once they gathered the information against Mary Laura. They would go to the police, and Summer would tell them how the woman had threatened her. Maybe Mary Laura would be brought in for questioning, and this time something would stick and they could get her off the streets.

"I hope Emma doesn't get in any trouble if she does this for us," Piper said.

"Well, she won't get into trouble if she doesn't get caught. And if I remember correctly, Emma is brighter than your average bear," Summer said.

"So is Tina." Piper pulled into her mother's driveway. "I bet Tina isn't going to be able to resist going up to Mary Laura's room and investigating. What do you think?" The car came to a stop, and Piper turned off the engine.

"I hope you're right." Summer didn't want to think what would happen if Mary Laura took a dislike to their friend Tina. "It could mean the difference between life and death, and I hope she realizes that."

Chapter
Fifty-Eight

When Summer and Piper pulled into the driveway, they caught sight of Cash's car, and Summer felt a little lighter knowing he would be inside.

Piper helped her to the door. She was pretty tired. She'd been on her feet way too much and was anticipating propping up that foot and taking her pain pills.

When she walked into the house, she was surprised to see Cash and Aunt Agatha building a bird gym. Darcy appeared to be thrilled. He was hopping from one perch to another and whistling.

"Hey there." Cash stood. "We're just about done here. Agatha ordered a pizza, so you're going to have a new guest for dinner two nights in a row."

"That's great, and it looks like Darcy is one happy bird." Summer plopped down on the couch. Piper put a pillow on the ottoman in front of her and helped Summer lift her foot onto it.

"Rough day?" Aunt Agatha asked.

Summer sighed. "Yeah, I guess you could say that."

She and Piper hadn't discussed whether they should tell anyone about what they were up to. Summer decided not to say a word.

But Piper had other thoughts and told Cash and Agatha everything except the part where Emma was going to examine records to find Mary

Laura's alibi, which Summer was content with, because it would have put Cash in an awkward position.

"The police questioned her and found she had a solid alibi," Cash said, as if reading her thoughts. He took the hammer and finished pounding in what looked like a swing for the bird.

"Well, it wouldn't be the first time somebody lied about an alibi," Piper persisted.

"We have checks and balances in our system, and that's the way it's built. For the most part, it works. I'm sure the police thoroughly checked that alibi." Cash stood. "As for her threatening you, that's grounds for worry. We also have a system in place to deal with that kind of stuff."

"But Cash, I have no proof. It's my word against hers, and I wouldn't want to drag Gina into something like that. She's a new business owner and good for this community. And part of this has played out too much in the public eye. I don't want that." Summer's ankle vibrated with pain.

"I get that, but just keep it in mind if she does it again." He walked over and sat down next to her. "Are you okay?"

"It's about time for my medication. I can tell, because I'm in a little bit more pain. But I'm fine. In fact, I think it's starting to itch. I know it sounds strange, but it's like an itchy pain."

Agatha went to get her medication, and the doorbell rang. It was the pizza man, and the scent was overwhelming and pleasant and in some strange way, soothing. It was so very ordinary compared to where Summer's mind had been most of the day. It was exhausting to think about murder. It was exhausting to have to talk about these unpleasant things with neighbors and friends. Yes, she wanted a slice of pizza. Ordinary pizza was always a good thing. You couldn't mess up pizza. No matter how good or how bad it was, it was still pizza.

Cash brought her a plate with two slices, and they settled in on the couch together. Piper and Agatha sat in chairs across from them.

"Where's Mia?" asked Summer.

Agatha gazed sheepishly at Piper. "She's out on a date with Rocky."

"Great," Piper muttered between bites.

Piper's attitude was also normal. And normalcy was what Summer craved more than anything right now. Just to go back to before Valentine's Day, before all this talk of poison and murder and detectives with false names. That would be a good thing.

"Well, what are you going to do, Summer?" Agatha asked. "I mean, are you never going to go into the chocolate shop again? Are you not going to have a relationship with Gina because of this Mary Laura person?"

Summer finished the bite of pizza she was working on. "Yes, I'll stay away from the chocolate shop for now until this all blows over. Until we see what's really going on. I see no cause for me to agitate the situation."

"I think that's a great idea," Cash said.

"I'm not sure I do." Agatha flung her crust onto her plate. "I don't think you should negotiate with terrorists. Well, not a terrorist, but you know what I mean. If you want to go into that damn chocolate shop, you should go in. If you want a relationship with Gina, you should have one."

"I can see your point, Agatha," Cash said. "But I think in this case, a more measured approach is called for."

"I think it will work out. I think the police will find the killer. Whether or not Mary Laura did it remains to be seen." Summer took another bite of pizza, and it was so good, so ordinary. She loved it. She wanted to concentrate on each cheesy bite.

"I think Summer is right on this one. I think Summer's done everything she could do," Piper said. "She wrote a beautiful blog post, which will also go into the newspaper tomorrow. She's covered all her bases as a business owner and as a person."

"In the meantime, who knows what Mary Laura will get up to?" Agatha said. "Is she going to hurt somebody again, kill somebody? I mean, what is wrong with you people? Why aren't you doing more about this? I don't understand. I feel like I want to go into that shop and give Mary Laura a piece of my mind."

Summer eyed Piper.

"Please don't do that, Mom," Piper said. "We have no idea what we're dealing with, and until we figure it out, it would be best if you didn't go into the shop either."

Chapter
Fifty-Nine

Despite the emotional day Summer had just had, she found a way to sleep that night. She didn't know if it was the medicine or just plain exhaustion, but she slept well and dreamed deeply. She dreamed of her mother and of receiving an embrace from her. It was warm and golden and as comforting as Summer remembered her mother's embraces to be. Hildy mentioned something in her ear. It was a whisper, but Summer couldn't quite hear it, and she lost it before she woke up. Whatever those words were, Summer was sure they had answers for her.

She lay in bed for several minutes after waking up, trying to recall the words, trying to conjure the warmth of that embrace. Instead, all she had was the quilt on the bed that her grandmother had made and the objects surrounding her in the room.

She sat up reluctantly. She smelled bacon frying and something sweet, maybe pancakes. Aunt Agatha loved pancakes.

Despite a little nausea from her medicine, which Summer was familiar with by now, her mouth watered. She reached for her crutch and used it to lift herself from the snug bed.

"Good morning, Aunt Agatha." Summer hobbled into the kitchen and sat at the table. "Something smells really good."

"Pancakes and bacon." Agatha set a plate of buttered pancakes with bacon on the side in front of Summer.

Just as she began eating, her phone buzzed. She didn't have it with her; it was charging in the living room. Agatha brought it to her. She had a text message from Tina.

Good morning, Summer. I have to tell you that I was shocked last night rather late when someone knocked at my door. It was about 11 o'clock and I answered it. When I opened the door, guess who was standing there? Liam Connor. He needed a place to stay. He said the police called him in on some new investigation. I told him I had no room, and that I rarely would, in any case, rent to someone at this hour. I was very sorry, but he would need to go to a hotel. I suggested that he stay at the Seaside Inn, and as far as I know that's where he is. What kind of investigation do you think he is called in on? I imagine he just got back to Pittsburgh, stayed a night or two, and had to turn around and come back. He is odd, and I really didn't mind turning him away. I figured you might want to know because maybe he was brought in to investigate the murder and maybe to investigate Mary Laura.

What Tina didn't know, of course, was that Liam's name was not Liam and that he wasn't really a detective anymore. The other thing she didn't know was that he probably had been called back into town not because of an investigation but because he was the prime suspect for trashing Summer's house. In any case, Tina had done the right thing. She certainly didn't need that man staying at her house, especially with Mary Laura there.

"Well, it looks like our favorite detective is back in town." Summer poured maple syrup over her pancakes and cut them.

"What's he doing here?" Agatha poured a cup of coffee for Summer.

"It seems he's telling people he was called back for the investigation, but I think he's been called in to be questioned about my house. Cash said his DNA was all over everything, even my bed. That grosses me out." She took a bite of the pancakes and relished the flavors and textures in her mouth.

Agatha's face squeezed in displeasure. "What possessed him to do such a thing? This whole thing is just crazy. Crazy town. We're living in crazy town. Everything used to make so much sense, and now I can't find a thread in any of this that adds up."

Summer mulled that over. She agreed that most of what was happening appeared to be illogical, but she figured that once they had all the pieces of the puzzle, some kind of logic could be applied. But what were they missing? She asked herself that over and over again. She had to hope that Tina would find something to link Mary Laura to the murder or that Emma would find something in the files about her alibi. Something that Summer could debunk.

In the meantime, she planned to go to Beach Reads to walk the floors and clean up a bit if she could and to try to keep her mind off Lana Livingston, Mary Laura Roberts, and their favorite detective. She would also try to keep her mind off the possibility of Tina and Emma being in danger. In fact, she might pop in to see Tina later today just to check on her. She texted back:

Hey Tina, thanks so much for the information. Very curious indeed. I might have Piper run me by your place later on just to check in on you to make sure everything is OK. I hope you don't mind. I'll touch base later. Cheers.

She then texted Cash to let him know the news. And heard back right away. He said he'd figured Liam Connor would be back in town because of the DNA evidence the police had against him. Cash said there was no way Liam hadn't been present during the trashing of her place and the scaring of Mr. Darcy. The scaring part angered Summer more than anything—more than Liam lying to her about his interest in her, more than his whole fake name and fake business and his lies. That bird had done nothing to deserve the fright he'd received. Summer hoped Liam got busted. In the meantime, she received a text from Glads.

Hey, Summer, just wanted to let you know I'll be picking you up tonight from the store. I have a little surprise for you.

"Well, Glads has a surprise for me. I can't wait. I need a good surprise," Summer said, and shoveled in more pancakes.

"Don't we all?" Agatha said flatly, and took a sip of coffee.

Chapter Sixty

Agatha and Summer walked through the front door of Beach Reads. There were few customers. Poppy was wiping the counter and looked up when the bell sounded to greet a customer, then saw who it was. Her face brightened. "Hello, boss."

"How's it going?" Summer asked.

"We're getting a few customers here and there." Poppy paused. "Lovely ad in the paper this morning."

"Thanks," Summer said.

"A few customers have already mentioned it to me," Poppy went on.

"Good to know," Summer said. "I'm here until about six, I think."

"There's more invoices on your desk. I've got it covered in the front of the store." Poppy smiled.

"How many days have you been working? You're going to need a day off," Summer said.

"I'm okay." Poppy shrugged. "It's not been that busy."

Summer nodded and made her way to the office to deal with the invoices.

She decided not to tell Poppy that the detective was back in town, as it would just make her nervous. He wouldn't dare show his face at the bookstore anyway, since they were about to arrest him for vandalizing her house. What an asshat. What had prompted him to do such a thing? And why make it appear as if it had been done by a local drug ring? Aunt Agatha was right. It was crazy town. Summer wanted her old life back.

"I'll see you at six." Agatha stopped in the doorway of Summer's office. "But if you feel like you need to leave earlier, call me. I'm running a few errands this afternoon. Other than that, I'm free."

"Thanks for everything, Aunt Agatha," Summer said, and opened her laptop.

"You're welcome," Agatha said, and left out the back of the store.

Summer had meant to tell her to be careful, but she knew Agatha would be extra cautious, knowing the crazy detective was back in town.

Summer was surprised to find her inbox filled with email from readers, who were supportive of the statement she had made in her blog and the ad she'd run in the paper today. She breathed a sigh of relief. It was a good thing, what she had done. And she was still considering how she would honor Lana.

In the meantime, those invoices needed to be taken care of. She kept trying to go paperless with the invoices, but publishers weren't quite ready for that. At least, not for an independent bookstore on Brigid's Island.

Her personal phone rang. It was Cash, and she smiled. "Hello. How are you?"

"I'm fine. I would like to tell you this in person, but the circumstances don't allow it. Maybe I'll see you tonight?"

"What is it?" Summer asked. What could it be now? How much more craziness could they take?

"Liam—Andrew, or whatever his name was—is dead."

Summer didn't think she'd quite heard him right. "Come again? I thought you said Liam is dead."

"That is what I said. They found him this morning. He'd been shot out on Mermaid Point."

Maggie Blackburn

The breath almost left Summer. Mermaid Point, the same place where another murder had taken place over twenty-five years ago. Was there some kind of message here?

"I know what you're thinking, but I believe it's just happenstance. He was involved in something unsavory, and who knows what he was up to when he was out walking along the shore. Maybe he was meeting somebody there; maybe there was a disgruntled criminal that he ran into. I just don't know, but Dad was called out early this morning, and he called me to tell me. That's all I know."

"Do you think this has anything to do with Lana?" It was the first thing Summer thought after wondering if it might have been a sign.

"It could. But I have no idea. Everything is still under a fresh investigation, but I wanted you to know, because I know him being back put you on eggshells. Now you don't have to worry about him."

She flashed in her mind's eye to the night Liam had taken her out and all the things he'd told her about himself. How much he loved ballet. How he appreciated Shakespeare. And all the roses he'd bought for her. Of course, none of it had any meaning, because he'd been faking the whole thing. But she'd like to think that at least some of it was true and that he'd had a full and rich life before something happened to screw things up. He was a mystery.

"Thank you, Cash. I appreciate you telling me."

"Are you okay?"

"I'm fine. It's a terrible thing to say, but I feel a little bit better knowing he's not going to be bothering anybody or causing any more trouble. But I'm sorry that he met his end this way."

"I'm probably going to be working late tonight, so I won't see you for dinner. But maybe we can go out tomorrow night. How does that sound?"

"It sounds fabulous," Summer said.

After they hung up the phone, Summer considered Liam's death further. She wondered if the same person who'd killed Lana had killed him. Could it be? Could there be a single person on the island who was

252

killing people, or was it a separate incident altogether? If so, that would mean there were two people on the island who were killers. That is, if they were both still in St. Brigid. She didn't quite know what to hope for. It seemed that either way, there was a killer among them, and if that person had left the island, they might never receive justice.

Chapter
Sixty-One

Even though Summer was generally happy to see Cash, she was a little relieved that he wouldn't be stopping by tonight. She just needed a night to relax, but she and Piper would stop off and see Tina first. Glads had canceled, saying the surprise would wait until tomorrow night.

Tina met them at the door and rushed them inside. "I'm so happy to see you two. Have you heard that the detective has been shot? How terrible!" Her eyes were alight, and her face was flushed with excitement. Or was it anxiety?

Piper and Summer followed her into the kitchen.

"I have some new tea I thought you might like to try. It's all ready for you," she said.

Piper and Summer sat at the table, and Tina poured tea. After they'd each had a cup of elderberry tea, Tina leaned across the table and whispered, "I have news."

Piper sat back. "This tea is delicious." She said it a little too loudly, and Summer realized what she was up to. If anybody was listening, they would hear Piper and not realize there was another conversation happening. Summer and Piper used to do this when they were young. Sleight of hand. Misdirection. Magicians used it often to divert the audience's attention in one direction because they didn't want them to see what was really happening. Piper was quite good at it.

Summer leaned in farther so she could hear what Tina said.

"Emma searched everywhere today looking for you-know-what," Tina whispered. "She couldn't find a thing."

"What was the name of this tea again?" Piper asked loudly. They didn't know if anybody was listening, but the bed-and-breakfast was one of those big old houses that sometimes made it easy for people to sneak up on you. There were so many dark corners and hallways and interesting nooks and crannies that you never knew who might be standing in the shadows.

"It's elderberry, dear," Tina said in a somewhat normal voice, which Summer was grateful for.

"Who knew the elderberry was so delicious. I think this is the first time I've ever had anything that was elderberry," Piper went on.

Summer sliced her finger across her neck, signaling for her to stop. "What exactly do you mean, she couldn't find anything?" Summer asked.

"She said there was nothing in the records at all about Mary Laura." Tina waved her hand as if to say, *That's it. I have no more.*

"How can that be?" Summer asked. "She was brought in and questioned. There should be a record."

"What else is in this tea besides elderberry?" Piper said loudly again, ignoring Summer's gesture.

"I'm not sure," Tina said. "Maybe some stevia." She leaned in and whispered, "That's what Emma said, and she was a bit flummoxed. She said she searched everywhere. It was a slow day, and she didn't need to do much. She has no idea where those records are, and now she doesn't know whether or not she should report it, because she shouldn't have been looking for them."

Summer sipped her tea. This was curious, very curious indeed. Had someone taken the records? Who would have access to those records that could possibly have taken them? Only the police, or maybe a lawyer or judge. Summer would think somebody off the street couldn't go in and get police records, so that left those who worked in the police force or at the courthouse. Unfortunately, that was a lot of people.

"Emma should keep it to herself," Piper whispered. "We don't want her to get into trouble."

"But I see her dilemma," Summer said.

"Well, since we know Mary Laura's boyfriend was our favorite detective, it stands to reason he may have destroyed her records," Piper whispered.

Tina's face fell. "I suppose it does."

"Have you been able to check her room?" Summer whispered.

"Not yet. But now I feel I must. Stay tuned." Tina sipped her tea.

Now that there was no record of Mary Laura's alibi, they certainly couldn't check on it. What else could they do to find out more about her?

* * *

Later, when Summer was in bed trying to sleep, she wondered if Liam and Mary Laura had been working together to kill Lana. It made sense—nobody in St. Brigid would suspect a detective who was here to keep an eye on a murder suspect. But nobody had recognized he was Mary Laura's boyfriend either. The two of them had kept that a secret, which added to the injury and suspicion. If they weren't hiding something, why would they have kept quiet about their relationship?

Summer sorted through two emotions at once. On the one hand, she felt like they might be closing in on Mary Laura at any moment. Her intuition plucked at her chest. But on the other hand, a person couldn't get arrested for murder based on intuition. So Summer was a tangled mess of frustration.

Sleep on it. Her mom's voice came to her. It was what she would always say when Summer was wrangling with a problem. So many times, it had worked.

Sleep on it, darling. Things will be better in the morning. You may not have the answer right away, but you will soon.

Summer closed her eyes and drifted off to sleep.

Chapter Sixty-Two

As Summer ate a breakfast of French toast and sausage, she formed a plan in her mind. What she needed to do was go back over all the other evidence. She couldn't go back over the journal, because the police now had it, but she could review the video and the sales receipts to see if there was something she'd missed.

"How's the ankle this morning?" Aunt Agatha asked.

"I'm starting to develop a pattern when it comes to my ankle. It feels pretty good in the morning, but as the day wears on, it gets a little swollen and painful and sometimes itchy." Summer took a bite of the French toast.

"So you said Glads switched to tonight? She's going to pick you up tonight?" Agatha drank her coffee and set down the cup. "I'm eager to see what the surprise is."

"I am too. With Glads, it could be anything," Summer said, just as Piper walked into the kitchen.

"Good morning, ladies. Are you almost ready to go?" Piper asked. "Are you sure you want to put in a whole day?"

"I'm going to try. Agatha is on deck in case I need to come home." Summer hoped she was able to put in a full day. It had been a while, and Poppy must be exhausted.

"I'll be at the school for a big part of the day, so I'll be unavailable." Piper sat at the table and poured herself a cup of coffee. "I'm assuming I have time for a cup of coffee."

"Of course you do." Summer smiled and toasted her cousin with her cup of coffee.

"So I was thinking about our favorite detective and wondering when his body is going to go back to Pennsylvania." Piper sipped her coffee. "I wonder if they have to keep it here a little longer. I mean, he's a person, so I feel a little bad that he died like that. But at the same time, it's so obvious that he wasn't quite right and was causing trouble everywhere he went, right?"

"It is a terrible way to die," Summer said. "I'm sure detectives probably die by gunshot more than your average bear. The thing that worries me is wondering if his death had anything to do with Lana's death. We know she was selling drugs. We know he was a drug user. And we also pretty much know he's the one who trashed my house."

Agatha harrumphed. "I'm sure it's all linked, and I'm sure that Mary Laura has something to do with it."

"Well, we need to find out more about her for sure, but it's difficult," Piper said. "We don't have the tools the police have. Plus she's not from around here, so we can't even ask people about her."

Summer finished her breakfast and poured another cup of coffee. Tonight when Glads brought her home, she planned to watch the video again and then maybe check the receipts. Depending on how her day went, she might be able to examine the sales of the day.

Summer recognized it was best to loosely plan her day. Owning a bookstore, or probably any kind of business dealing with the public, you just never knew when you'd have to drop everything and deal with a customer.

Beach Reads was quiet. Poppy was able to sit behind the counter most of the day, which was what Summer wanted her to do. She'd been on her feet a lot.

After Summer finished with the invoices and orders for new books, she went through the sales records again for the day Lana had died. She found nothing and grew even more frustrated.

Glads walked into her office to collect her. Whatever the surprise was, Summer had to admit she was more tired than she'd predicted. But she went along, because it was Glads and because she was curious.

She and Poppy locked up the shop, and Poppy left, walking toward her house. Glads helped Summer into her car.

"I want you to know how much I appreciate your help when they suspected me of killing Lana." Glads turned the engine on, and the radio blared the B-52's. She turned it down.

"It was no problem at all, Glads. We all know you aren't a killer. It was absolutely ridiculous. I'm happy you stayed with me. I got to know you a little bit better, and I enjoyed it," Summer said.

"Well, thank you anyway." Glads continued to drive, bobbing her head to "Love Shack." Summer, of course, recognized where they were: they were in her neighborhood. The next thing she knew, they were pulling into her driveway. There were quite a few cars.

"Oh my goodness, the crime scene tape is gone! Is that the surprise?"

"Kind of." Glads shut off the car, got out, and helped Summer exit. "Your surprise is in the house."

"In the house?" Summer hobbled forward and made her way to the front porch. "Well, there are people in here."

Glads opened the door, walked through, and stepped off to the side so Summer could enter. Summer couldn't believe what she was seeing as she took in the scene. Tears burned her eyes.

"Surprise!" Glads said. The others standing around were Piper, Mia, Poppy, Marilyn, Aunt Agatha, and Cash. "We all pulled together and fixed your place."

Summer was at a loss for words. She had a new couch, a new La-Z-Boy chair, and an end table. She poked her head into the kitchen and saw her new dining room set. Darcy had a new cage, and he was a happy boy swinging back and forth.

"There's even a new bed upstairs for you," Aunt Agatha said. "But you're going to have to climb the stairs to see it."

Everybody laughed.

Summer beamed. "I think I can do it."

"Of course you can, and we'll help you," Cash said.

So with Cash on one arm and Agatha on the other, Summer took one step at a time. Once she reached the landing to take a break, she turned around and took in the folks looking up at her. Tears welled in her eyes.

"Are you okay?" Cash said quickly. "Is it too much? I'll carry you up the rest of the stairs."

"No, I'm just so moved that you all did this for me. I just don't know what to say."

"Well, don't say anything and just keep moving," Aunt Agatha said. "You've got a brand-new bed waiting for you."

Chapter Sixty-Three

Summer slept better than she had since she'd sprained her ankle. In fact, she even slept in a little. She slept so deeply and soundly that when she first opened her eyes, it surprised her a bit that she was in her own bed. She lay there for a few minutes, and then somebody rapped at her door.

"Aunt Summer, it's Mia. I have your breakfast for you." Mia opened the door, and she held a tray of bagels and fruit and coffee. Summer almost cried again. "As soon as you get up, let me know, and I'll help you. But take your time and enjoy your new bed. The store is covered today. Glads and Marilyn are running the show. Poppy took the day off because we knew you wanted her to."

"Has there been any news? Like an arrest of the person who killed Liam? I feel like I've been sleeping for two days." Summer popped a strawberry in her mouth.

"Nothing." Mia sat down on the chair next to the bed. "It's never this hard to find the killer on TV shows."

"Well, we know TV shows are nothing like reality." Summer put cream cheese on one of her slices of bagel.

Summer's phone buzzed, alerting her to a text message. It was Tina.

Call me please.

Summer took a sip of coffee and pressed Tina's number.

"Do you need privacy?" Mia asked.

Summer shook her head.

"Summer, thank god. You'll never believe what I found." Tina breathed heavily into the phone.

"Okay, okay, Tina. Catch your breath," Summer said.

A few beats later, Tina cleared her throat. "Okay, I think I can breathe now."

"What is it, Tina?" Summer asked.

"I was upstairs cleaning Mary Laura's room, and I found a gun." She said it quickly, as if removing a painful bandage.

Summer spilled her coffee all over her tray, and Mia went running to find a towel to clean it up. Summer pushed the tray away and tried to sit up more in bed, swinging her legs around to the side and hitting her ankle, which sent shards of pain circling her foot. "Have you called the police?"

"No, I wasn't sure what to do. I mean, I was in her room," Tina stuttered.

"Tina, you had every right to be in her room. You were cleaning. There's nothing wrong with that."

"Yes, yes, you're right. I'm just not thinking clearly. I don't like the idea of there being a gun in this house. It shakes me up."

"I understand." Summer helped Mia sop up the spilled coffee. "But please call the police and let them know you found a gun in her room when you were cleaning it. There's nothing suspicious about that."

Mia's eyes widened. *A gun?* she mouthed.

Summer nodded. "Listen, Tina, just call the police. It will be fine. Do you need me to come over there to help you?"

Tina paused. "I don't think so. I think it would be suspicious if you came over here. We don't want them to know we've been discussing any of this, right?"

"Exactly," Summer said. " You can just give them a call. You'll be fine."

After they hung up, Mia wanted answers. "Who has a gun, and why does Tina know about it?"

"Well, you must promise not to say anything to anybody. Tina really should've just called the police first. But she found a gun in Mary Laura's room. She was just in there cleaning and ran across the gun."

Mia took the sopping towel out of the room but returned quickly. "I wonder if it's the gun that shot Liam."

"Well, we'll find out. She's going to call the police, and they'll come and check it out, I'm sure." The wheels in Summer's brain were spinning. If Mary Laura had a gun and it was indeed the gun that had shot Liam, then she would be arrested, probably within the next few hours. But would a woman who would use a gun poison someone? It seemed as if those two modes of murder were different and would be employed by completely different kinds of people.

Then again, what did Summer know about murder, really? And how much more did she really want to know? She didn't want to go into that dark tunnel—thinking about murder, thinking about her mother's past. But she would like to see justice for Lana and even for Liam. Even though she hadn't cared for the man, he was a human being, and nobody deserved to die like that.

Summer hurried and ate a bagel and a few more strawberries. She really didn't have much of an appetite any longer. There was just too much commotion today. The morning had started off so peacefully here in her new bed, in her own house, up the stairs she'd climbed last night for the first time in weeks. And now things were spinning out of control again. Mary Laura had a gun. What purpose would that serve if not to kill somebody? Summer was glad that Mary Laura hadn't used it on anybody else, especially Tina, who was a nervous wreck.

"Mom will be here any minute to take me to school, and Gram will be over shortly to help you out and to take you to work if you want to go." Mia gathered the plates and cups. "Are you going to be able to dress yourself?"

"I can manage."

"I hope we know something by the end of the day about that gun and what it was used for. It would be something good—anything, just anything, that we could cling to," Mia said.

"I hear you, Mia. I feel the same way. I can't imagine any good reason Mary Laura would have a gun tucked in her room."

Chapter
Sixty-Four

Two hours later, Summer was dressed and Aunt Agatha was trying to talk her into staying home and not going to work.

"Everybody is taking care of everything for you today. We just want you to stay in your house and enjoy your new things with Mr. Darcy," Aunt Agatha said.

"Darcy loves Agatha. Darcy loves Agatha. Darcy loves Agatha," the bird said.

"I love you too, Mr. Darcy. Are you a good bird?"

"I am a good bird. I am a good bird, good bird." He rocked back and forth.

Summer opened her laptop. "I'll just check the local news to see if any arrests have been made."

Her phone rang, and she picked it up. "Hello?"

"It's me, Tina. You are not going to believe what happened." She breathed heavily into the phone again.

"At this point, I'll believe just about anything," Summer said.

"Well, Ben came over here, and you know how he is," Tina said. "Why does he have to be so nasty sometimes? Well, not nasty, but like brusque or something. You know what I mean?" Summer could hear Tina doing dishes in the background.

"I know exactly what you mean." Summer closed her computer.

"Well, Mary Laura has a permit, and there's nothing illegal about her having a gun in her room. How about that?"

Summer hadn't counted on that. Evidently, neither had Tina. "Well, I suppose you could make it a policy that you don't want people bringing firearms into your B and B. Did Ben say if it was the kind of gun used to shoot Liam?"

"He said it was a different kind of gun completely and that I should just mind my own business. That man! I was just trying to help. I was trying to be a good citizen. I mean, we just had two murders, and one was a police officer who was shot. You would think he'd be more interested."

Ben Singer was a complicated man. It was difficult to tell how he truly felt about anything. He was reserved and an experienced police officer. "I'm sure he appreciated it. He probably just has a lot going on with two murder investigations."

"Well, I suppose you're right, but I feel better now, knowing it wasn't the same gun used to kill Liam or whatever his name was. And I do believe from now on I will make it a policy that people are not to bring guns into my establishment. Lordy, I didn't think I needed to make that a policy. I mean, it's just common sense. You don't go around carrying guns and bringing them into a bed-and-breakfast. What is wrong with people?"

"Did she say why she had a gun?" Summer asked.

"She says as a young woman, she feels like she needs it to protect herself."

"That's a shame she feels that way. I guess it's good that she has a permit. That means she probably knows how to use it, and hopefully it also means she's a responsible gun owner."

"Lordy, I hope so." Tina paused. "Have you heard anything else?"

"Nothing at all. I'll let you know if I do," Summer said.

They hung up, and Summer reopened her laptop to scan the local news. There was nothing new on the murders. The same stories were running that had run yesterday.

Summer clicked on the store's website and found a lot of responses to the statement she'd written.

"I'm getting some thoughtful responses to my statement. I'm really glad I did that," she told Agatha. She clicked on the event page to watch the video again and see if there was anything she or the police had missed.

She tapped the little arrow so the event film would start. Then she watched it all over again and observed the same people, saw the same shadow.

She rolled the film back and decided to focus somewhere else—not on the shadow but on Lana to see what she was doing.

She was drinking tea.

But what about before that?

Summer backed the video up even further. Lana had shoved something in her mouth.

Summer went back a couple more moments. What was Lana eating? It was small, whatever it was. Summer rewound a few more seconds and spied her taking a chocolate from a box.

Her heart stopped.

Maybe it wasn't the tea that had the poison in it.

Maybe it was the chocolate.

Just how long had Mary Laura been working for Gina?

Chapter
Sixty-Five

First, Summer called Glads. "Yes?"

"Glads, can you think back to when you gave Lana her tea?"

She groaned. "Do I have to?"

"Bear with me. Was she eating anything?"

Agatha was about to burst and was hopping around trying not to squeal.

"Yeah, I think she was eating some chocolate."

"Could she have gotten the poison in the chocolate instead of the tea?" Summer bit her thumb.

"I don't think so," said Glads. "The police said the poison was in the cup."

"But if she had been eating chocolate and drinking tea, it stands to reason that the poison could have gone into the tea and onto the cup."

"I suppose so, but it really doesn't have any meaning right now, because what does it matter if she got that poison in the chocolate or the tea?" Glads asked.

"It matters because we've been looking at the wrong thing if she got poison in the chocolate, and it's chocolate that came from Gina's. I have to wonder how long Mary Laura has been working for Gina," Summer explained.

"She's only been working for Gina for a few days. She wasn't working for Gina during the event, so if the chocolate was poisoned and it came from Gina . . ." Glads paused. "Then it stands to reason it was . . . Gina who poisoned Lana."

"Can that be? Gina? It doesn't seem like she would harm a fly." Had Summer been blinded by Gina's warm personality? What reason would Gina have to poison Lana? "I just can't see it. What would her motive be? Why would she poison Lana? Whereas Mary Laura knew her and didn't like her."

"I agree," Glads said. "We all like Gina. But she's new in town, and we really don't know that much about her. She could have easily poisoned Lana as much as Mary Laura could have. I think you should call Ben and let him know what you found. I've got to go, but thank you for calling."

"She thinks I should call Ben," Summer said to Agatha after she'd hung up. "She thinks it could be Gina who poisoned Lana, but it makes no sense to me."

Agatha stood with her hands on her hips. "What do you know about Gina?"

Summer shrugged. "I know about her training, where she grew up, and I know that she's been a very supportive business owner and neighbor."

Agatha frowned. "That doesn't sound like much at all. I have to say I agree with Glads. Maybe she's in cahoots with Mary Laura. Maybe they've known each other longer than we think."

"Maybe. I guess I should call Ben and see what he has to say."

"Yes, you should call Ben and tell him what you found out. He could turn the investigation around. We could find out who killed Lana. It may be the exact thing he needs to hear."

Summer dialed Ben and explained the situation to him. He said he was going to call forensics to see if her theory that the poison could've come from the chocolate was possible, and he also told Summer to stay away from the chocolate shop.

"Of course I will. I have a sprained ankle and I'm barely going in to work, let alone going to the chocolate shop. Besides, Mary Laura warned me not to go there, and I'm not in the mood or the shape to have a fistfight with Mary Laura."

"I think that's the smartest thing I've ever heard you say," Ben said, and hung up.

Summer's mouth dropped open. Ben had just complimented her. Kind of. She couldn't remember a time that had ever happened.

"What did he say?" Agatha made an impatient rolling motion with her arm.

"He's going to check into it, but he also gave me a compliment."

"What? What? Will miracles never cease?" Agatha laughed.

Chapter
Sixty-Six

Summer prevailed upon her aunt Agatha to take her in to the bookstore for just a few hours. She needed to show her face and to help out if she could. She was under no illusions that she was going to be that big of a help, but at least she could try.

Agatha agreed, and added that she would stay with Summer instead of leaving and coming back to get her. "I'd much rather help out too."

They both came in through the back door, since that was the easiest thing for Summer, but Agatha went out front to let the staff know they were both there and to ask what they could do to help.

Summer made her way to the front of the store as well.

"You should've just stayed home," Marilyn said. "We've got everything."

"Well, I'm here now, and I just wanna have a glimpse around to see how things are going." Summer started to walk back through the vampire romance section, toward the overstuffed chair with Anne Rice's signature painted above it. Rice's vampire series continued to outsell all other vampire series.

Summer rounded the corner on her crutches. She straightened up some books in the werewolf section.

The bell to the front door rang, alerting everybody that somebody was walking through the door. Summer walked to the end of the row to see who it was.

271

"Hey, ladies, I have some chocolate for you. Some of these are a mess, and I do apologize for that, but we haven't been able to get the temperature quite right for these," Gina said as she walked toward the counter, bearing a box of chocolates.

Summer made a beeline for the chocolates and grabbed the box. "Thank you, Gina. We'll have a feast after work tonight. How are you?"

"I'm doing well. I guess I should get back to it. Thanks, ladies, for being my test subjects," Gina said. She turned and waved as she walked out the front door. Then she walked back in. "By the way, have you seen Mary Laura? She took a break, and it's been quite some time. I'm hoping she's okay. I tried her cell phone, and there's just no answer."

Glads, Agatha, and Marilyn looked at each other, and Summer shrugged. "I don't know what to tell you. I haven't seen her." The other women nodded in agreement.

"Oh well, I'm sure she'll be back soon." Gina left the bookstore.

That was about the time they heard something fall down in the storeroom. "Who's back there?" Summer asked.

"I'll go find out," Aunt Agatha said.

There were only a few customers hanging around. One was in the historical romance section, and the other was in romantic suspense. Summer wasn't sure if there was anybody upstairs or not, but at least there were two customers. Two customers was better than none.

Agatha came out, holding Mary Laura by the collar. "Look who I found hiding in our storeroom."

The others gasped as Mary Laura pulled away from Agatha.

"Summer, I need you to listen to me. Tell me how many customers are in here right now." Mary Laura glanced from person to person to person.

"And why would I tell you that?" What was going on here?

"Listen, I need to gather everybody up and get you all into the storeroom, pronto," Mary Laura said in a take-charge voice.

"You're not answering my question. Why would we do that? Why would we let you take us into a storeroom?" Summer demanded.

"Summer, listen to me. I'm a cop, and there's something really bad about to go down next door at the chocolate shop. For your own protection, and for the protection of every customer in this shop, I suggest we gather together and go in one room. In fact, I suggest you lock the door."

The room silenced.

"A cop?" Glads said. "Let's see your badge."

Mary Laura yanked a badge out of her inside coat pocket and held it up.

"Summer, Glads, please listen to me."

The badge seemed legitimate, and Summer motioned for everybody to follow her. Tried not to look as stupid as she felt. Her heart was racing. Glads went upstairs to make sure there was nobody on the second floor, and the two customers on the floor happily went with the booksellers. Summer locked the door and put the CLOSED sign on, then joined the others in the storeroom. She pointed at Mary Laura. "I think you owe us an explanation."

Mary Laura held her sleeve up to her mouth. "All safe here." She held up her finger as if to say *Just a minute* to Summer. It was then that Summer noticed that she had an earpiece and was carrying on a conversation with somebody else. "She was just here with a box of chocolates. Looking for me." She dropped her arm. "Thank goodness you're all safe."

"What on earth is going on?" Aunt Agatha asked. "What is going on with Gina? Why was she over here with chocolate? And why are you here?"

"I'm sorry to involve you all, but I can't really talk specifics right now. I just need to keep you safe."

"How will we know we're safe? When can we go?" Glads asked.

Mary Laura gazed upward and put a finger on her earpiece once again. Her other finger shot up to silence everyone. "Got it." She turned to the women. "It should just be a few more minutes. The SWAT team should be here any second, and you don't want to get in their way."

The women huddled together. Eyes meeting, eyes rolling. But they were quiet. Tension filled the room. A SWAT team was heading next door to the chocolate shop. They could all only imagine why. Summer was putting the pieces together as she stood there. It wasn't Mary Laura who'd poisoned Lana; it was Gina. Marie Laura was here undercover, and having her stepmother here to do the event at Beach Reads had been the perfect setup. But what were the police seeking? And why had Lana been killed?

Summer didn't think this was the time or place to ask, but after this was over, she was certainly going to find out the answers to her questions. Here they were in her mother's bookstore with friends and customers waiting for a SWAT team to take down Gina. It was surreal.

Suddenly, a loud scuffling next door erupted, along with a man's voice yelling. A few long minutes later, Mary Laura told them it was safe. They could go back to doing whatever it was they had been doing before.

"I've got to go and assist, but I'll be back to explain later," she said. "I'm sorry, Summer, for all that we've put you through. Just know that it was very worth it, and I hope you'll soon agree with me." It was like Mary Laura was a completely different person from the sarcastic, sullen person she'd been before. She was professional and upbeat.

Summer was floored. Her mind was reeling, and her whole foot and ankle ached.

She made her way to her office and sat down, and Agatha came in behind her.

"Well, what do you make of that?" Agatha asked.

"I'm going to need some time to unpack all that."

"You and me both," Agatha said. "Well, so now we know it was Gina all along. It was Gina who killed Lana, and I wonder if she killed Liam."

"It doesn't seem like her style, but I've been wrong about almost everything, so who knows?"

Summer looked at the clock and realized that store hours would be over in two hours. She decided to go ahead and close now to give everybody a couple of hours of their lives back. She couldn't imagine that anybody could concentrate on work right now. The air was buzzing with confusion and excitement.

* * *

On the way home, Summer called Tina to fill her in.

"What a relief," Tina said. "She's a cop. No wonder she has a gun."

"So now we know that Gina killed Lana. We're not sure about Liam. But we don't know the reason behind any of this," Summer said.

"We'll find out soon enough," Tina said.

"Indeed," Summer said. It embarrassed her to think just how wrong she'd been about Gina. It had been so easy to fall for her charm.

When Summer and Agatha pulled up in the driveway, they were surprised to see Ben sitting in his police car. He exited when he spotted Summer and Agatha.

Summer rolled down her window. "Chief. What's going on?"

He leaned over into the window. "I figured you might need to talk. I'm here to answer any questions."

"Let's go in and get some tea," Agatha said. She got out of the car and brought Summer's crutches to her.

"Mary Laura said she was going to explain." Summer hobbled onto the porch.

"You won't be seeing her again." Ben opened the door for them.

"What? Why?" Agatha said. "I have a million questions for her."

"Don't we all?" Summer said as she walked toward the couch and sat down.

"Summer! Summer! Darcy loves Summer!"

"Summer loves Darcy!" Summer said back. "Please sit down, Ben. Agatha will get the tea."

"Just don't say anything until I'm back," Agatha said.

"Nothing?" Summer said. "That's going to be hard."

"You know what I mean, smarty-pants." Agatha rushed off to the kitchen.

"How are you, Ben?" Summer asked.

"I'm doing better now. Thanks for asking." His eyes were puffy, and dark circles rimmed them. "I hear you're dating Cash."

She drew in air. This thing between her and Ben would have to end soon. "Yes, we're dating."

"Things are different now. He has a daughter."

"I know," Summer said. "She's a great kid."

"Damn straight she is."

"I never meant to hurt him . . . before . . . you know . . . I was confused, and I think wrong in a lot of my notions. I'm ready to try again with him. Slowly." Summer met Ben's eyes. "I hope you don't mind. But it won't matter if you do."

His eyebrows shot up, and he laughed. "Well, okay then."

Agatha brought in a tray of tea and brownies and laid it on the coffee table. She sat down. "Spill, Ben."

"Okay. We've been watching Gina for a long time."

"Why?" Summer asked.

"Would you let the man talk?" Agatha said. Summer nodded.

"She has connections to a well-known crime family in Brooklyn," he went on. "Anyway, to make a long story short, she was running drugs through her candy. Shipping drugs through candy."

"Shipping?" Summer said.

"Well, not just shipping, but yes. She was sending drugs all over the US and parts of the world through her candy."

"What does any of this have to do with Lana?" Summer asked.

"Lana was selling drugs for her. When Mary Laura found out, she took it personally. She also saw her stepmother's conundrum. She was in debt. Broke. So Mary Laura told Lana she'd help her out of debt if she helped her nab Gina. Bad idea."

"And somehow Gina found out that Lana was going to turn her in," Summer concluded. "That's why she killed her."

"What about Liam?" Agatha asked.

Ben lowered his head, then gazed back up at Agatha and Summer. "This is a dangerous business, especially for a junkie. He was a cop on leave to deal with his drug problem. He started using again. And he got involved with Gina's unsavory crowd."

"How did he know Mary Laura?" Summer asked.

"They worked together. As far as we know, Liam was shot by one of Gina's men who found out he was a cop." He looked off to the side. "Poor guy."

"Why won't we see Mary Laura?"

"Well, she's a special agent. She was trained in culinary arts before she became a police officer. She gets sent to establishments that are most likely running drugs. She can't be seen around an investigation once it's gone public."

"I can't imagine," Agatha said.

"Restaurants, bakeries, and so on are some of the biggest spots for drugs. And internationally, it's worse," Ben said. "So her skill set is in very high demand."

"What about Glads?" Agatha asked, and sipped her tea.

"She was a decoy, unfortunately. We knew she didn't commit murder, but we had to make it look like she was a suspect."

"That was not cool, considering how sweet Glads is," Summer said.

"She was the one giving her tea. There was no way around it." Ben slurped his own tea and reached for a brownie. He took a bite.

Agatha and Summer sipped their tea.

"Oh my god. I've not had brownies this good since Hildy baked me some," he said.

"It's her recipe." Summer beamed. "Mia made a new batch the other night."

It seemed only fitting that her mother's sister and Summer's once-nemesis Ben sat there with Hildy's daughter, enjoying vegan brownies, after such a trying few weeks. A person had been poisoned in Summer's beloved bookstore. Another man had been killed on Mermaid Point.

A woman would face justice—a woman whose hand had dealt them all such treachery. With each bite of brownie, warmth spread through Summer.

Nobody knew what the future held. But Summer hoped it held more evenings like this. Maybe the cast would change, as there were several people missing from the tableau: Piper, Marilyn, Glads, Poppy, and Cash. But the feelings of warmth, of knowing, of healing remained.

Summer held up her cup of tea and said a silent thank-you to her mom. And despite having been called a weirdo by her niece, she knew Hildy was right there is this room with them all tonight.

Epilogue

One year later

Summer had always loved the beach in the winter. She stood in front of the mirror and wrapped her shawl around her. Her aunt Agatha had handmade it from thick warm wool, weaving in bits and pieces of Summer's grandmother's wedding dress along with her mother's christening blankets. She'd also decorated it with seed pearls from Cash's mother's wedding dress. Summer wore it over a sea-blue silk-and-wool pantsuit.

Summer rubbed her stomach, which was high and tight. She rested her hands there. Her baby. Nothing mattered more.

She knew her mom's story, had inherited the trauma and the love, meshed together like some kind of strange alchemy. But Summer Merriweather was creating her own story now. Her one regret was that her mom wouldn't be there to welcome her grandson. Or to see her take vows with the man she loved. Had always loved. Her fear had gripped her back then. But now? Fear of love was in the past. Each step she took toward Cash would be a step toward a future they would create together.

Getting married on Valentine's Day was ironic; it was a holiday she'd always despised. Until last year, when Cash had given her the Shakespeare folio and made his intentions clear. Of course, last year Lana Livingston had passed away after being poisoned by Gina, the drug lord/chocolatier. Since then, Summer had established a scholarship through the university she used to teach at, geared for women who wanted to become writers. Fifteen enterprising young women had applied to the Lana Livingston Scholarship.

So much had changed since last Valentine's Day.

"Are you ready?" Agatha poked her head into Summer's room.

Summer took one last glance at herself in the mirror. Physically, she was the same short, round person, except for the baby bump, which made her even more round. But she was so different from the woman she'd been when she came back to the island six years ago for her mother's funeral. She'd found a kind of happiness in managing Beach Reads that her younger self could never have imagined. She'd found contentment living in her childhood home—still pink with turquoise-blue shutters. She'd found a community, one she'd always had but had never appreciated. And she'd found love, love she'd been running from for silly, immature reasons.

Was she ready?

"Yes, I am." She took her aunt Agatha's hand. Agatha was the next best thing to her mother. She looked so different from Hildy, but it was only a matter of grooming. Hildy had barely worn any makeup, and her hair was always free-flowing and wild. She dressed as any self-respecting hippie would. And Agatha? Neat as a pin.

Piper and Mia stood at the bottom of the stairs.

"We better hurry." Piper held out her arm. "We don't want to be late. Cash will have a heart attack."

Summer took the offered arm and fell into an embrace with a woman she'd known her whole life. She hoped to know her the rest of it.

Mia, her eyes soft, hugged her neck. "You are so beautiful," she whispered.

Summer turned to find her half sister, Fatima, and half brother, Sam, who ushered her into the limo. All of them rode together to Mermaid Point, the place she and Cash had chosen to hold their brief ceremony.

She glanced at the clock on the dash.

"We have plenty of time to get there before sunset," Fatima said. She was decked out in a sea-green suit and speckled with emeralds around her neck and on her wrists. Her long black hair was wrapped into an updo.

Agatha and Piper both wore different shades of sea blue. Given that it was February, nobody wore dresses. Mia was dressed in a sand-colored tunic with blue wool leggings.

Piper popped a champagne bottle open, and each of them held up plastic champagne glasses as she poured. Summer had one as well, but she didn't take a sip. No, sir. But she did hold her cup up for the toast.

"It's about damned time!" Piper said.

The crowd in the car echoed the sentiment.

As the rest drank, the limo sputtered. "What is that?" Summer asked the driver.

"I need to pull over," he said.

He barely made it off the road before the engine quit. Stone dead. He tried to start it, but the vehicle didn't make a sound. "I'm sorry. I'll call the office and see if they can send someone."

Summer's heart raced. What if she was late to this wedding? Would Cash think . . . ? No—he couldn't think she would stand him up again.

"Stay calm," Piper said. She glanced at Sam. "Do you know anything about cars?"

Sam shrugged. His sister laughed. The driver exited the car and popped the hood, allowing smoke to escape from the engine.

Suddenly, Summer had to pee, as only a pregnant woman could. She examined the area and spotted a restaurant. Would they take pity on a pregnant bride? She swung open the car door and hoofed it into the restaurant.

"Where are you going?" Piper asked.

"Bathroom."

Summer opened the restaurant door, and a waitress approached her. "Can I help you?"

"I'm on the way to my wedding, and I really need to use the ladies' room." She looked around in a panic. She might not be able to hold it much longer.

"Right over there, honey." The waitress pointed.

Summer raced to the restroom. She wanted to hurry. But there was no way to hurry underpants down when you were pregnant. Or to hurry them back up again when you were done.

She washed her hands and caught a glimpse of herself in the mirror. For a split second, Summer saw her mother in her own face. She'd never believed she resembled her mom, always thinking she took after her mysterious father.

She touched the mirror. "Mom?"

She blinked, and the resemblance was gone.

Summer was a mess. *This is what you get for not marrying him all those years ago*, she told herself. *Or when he found out you were pregnant.*

* * *

"Please," he had said. "Let's just go and do it."

"Because I'm pregnant?" Summer asked.

"Well, I can't think of a better reason."

"Cash!"

"I've wanted to marry you for a long time, and a baby will just hurry it along. That's all I mean. Don't get indignant with me."

"It so presumptive of you."

"Yes, it is," he said, and kissed her. "What do you say?"

"No. I won't marry you at the courthouse. But yes, I will marry you before the baby comes." She kissed him back. "I want to do this right."

"I want to do this however you want."

* * *

So here she was, splashing water on her face in a dive of a restaurant. Taking deep breaths to calm her racing heart. It would be okay. Even if she was a little late. Cash knew by now everything they'd had to go through to get to this point together. He knew she'd be there. Didn't he?

Her legs trembled as she opened the door and stepped out, turned the corner, and viewed Piper out front talking to a police officer. Lights flashed in the background. What was going on?

Summer stepped outside into the cold, pulled her wrap tighter around her. "What's going on? What's the problem?" As she said it, she realized there were two police cars. Mia, Fatima, and Sam were in the back seats. "What—"

One of the officers approached her. "Summer Merriweather?"

"Yes?"

"I'm here at the request of Chief Ben Singer."

"What? I'm confused."

"Just get in the car," Piper said. "I texted Ben and told him what happened with the limo."

Summer slid into the front seat and pulled the seat belt around her.

"Chief Singer wants to make sure you get to the wedding." The officer grinned.

And so this was how Summer and her entourage arrived at Mermaid Point. Lights flashing and sirens blaring. The police cars drove out onto the beach to deposit the bride and her family.

There was no music, no fanfare, just a circle of friends and family coming together to witness the day.

As the sun set, crimson and pink splayed across sky and sea. Summer and Cash joined hands and said quick vows in this place where so much had happened. The place where Liam had met a cruel end. But he wasn't the first to have been murdered here. A woman had been murdered here many years ago, a woman whose death had changed the trajectory of Hildy Merriweather's life, and therefore Summer's. It seemed the perfect place to hold a life-affirming ceremony, with nothing but the sound of the ocean as music, holding Cash's hand, and feeling the stirrings of life within in her.

A perfect place to start again.

Recipes

Brigid's Bakery Honey Cakes

Ingredients
- 1 egg, well beaten
- ¾ cup sugar
- 1 tablespoon unsalted butter, melted
- 1 cup sour cream
- 1 teaspoon vanilla extract
- 1½ cups all-purpose flour*
- 2 teaspoons baking powder
- ¼ teaspoon baking soda
- ¾ teaspoon salt

Honey Coating
- ½ cup honey
- 2 tablespoons light brown sugar
- ½ teaspoon cinnamon
- 2 tablespoons unsalted butter, melted

Directions

1. Preheat oven to 350°F. Grease a twelve-cavity muffin tin. Set aside.

2. In a large bowl, beat egg until frothy. Beat in sugar and butter and mix together on a moderately high speed until well blended, fluffy, and pale yellow.

3. Add sour cream and vanilla. Blend well.

4. Sift flour, baking powder, baking soda, and salt together; add to the sour cream mixture. Mix by hand and blend well.

5. Pour into greased muffin tins.

6. Bake 15 minutes. Remove from oven and spread honey topping over the cakes. Return to oven for 15–20 minutes or until topping is bubbling. Serve warm.

Aunt Agatha's Stuffed French Toast

Ingredients

- 8 ounces cream cheese, softened
- ⅓ cup powdered sugar or more to taste
- 1 tablespoon vanilla extract
- 12 slices Texas toast (one loaf)
- 2 eggs
- ¾ cup milk
- 1 teaspoon ground cinnamon
- 1 teaspoon granulated sugar

Directions

1. Beat together cream cheese, powdered sugar, and vanilla until you have a spreadable consistency.

2. Spread a thick layer of cream cheese filling on one side of half the slices of Texas toast. Top with a second piece of Texas toast, forming a sandwich with cream cheese filling in the middle.

3. In a small bowl, whisk eggs, milk, cinnamon, and sugar together. Dip the sandwiches in the egg mixture to coat completely.

4. Melt butter on a griddle or skillet over medium heat. Cook sandwiches until golden brown on both sides.

5. Top with strawberries, syrup, and whipped cream.

Glads's Blueberry Muffins

Ingredients

- cooking spray
- 1¼ cups all-purpose flour
- ¾ teaspoon baking powder
- ¾ teaspoon baking soda
- ½ teaspoon salt
- ¾ cup white sugar
- ⅔ cup whipped cream cheese
- ½ cup table cream
- 2 eggs
- ¼ cup plus 1 teaspoon vegetable oil
- 8 ounces fresh blueberries

Directions

1. Preheat oven to 350°F. Grease muffin cups with cooking spray or line with paper muffin liners.

2. Sift flour, baking powder, baking soda, and salt together into a bowl. Combine sugar, cream cheese, table cream, eggs, and vegetable oil in a large bowl.

3. Fold flour mixture into sugar mixture until batter is smooth. Stir in blueberries. Scoop batter into prepared muffin cups.

4. Bake in a preheated oven until golden brown, 10 to 15 minutes.

Glads's Brownies With Chocolate Syrup

Ingredients

- 1½ cup butter
- 1 cup sugar
- 4 eggs
- 1½ cup chocolate-flavored syrup
- 1¼ cup all-purpose flour
- 1 cup walnuts, chopped (optional)

Directions

1. Preheat oven to 350°F and grease a 9 × 13–inch pan.

2. Beat butter for 30 seconds; add sugar and eggs and beat until fluffy.

3. Stir in syrup, then flour.

4. If using walnuts, stir them in.

5. Pour into the pan and bake for 30–35 minutes.

Acknowledgements

Thank you to the dedicated Crooked Lane team. Special thanks to my agent Jill Marsal, editor Terri Bischoff, and copy editor Rachel Keith. A heartfelt thank you to my readers, who have stuck with me for many years. It brings me joy to know you love these characters as much as I do. Keep reading!

Thank you,

Mollie